FALSE
HOPE

ALSO BY LYNNE LEE

Can You See Me?

FALSE
HOPE

LYNNE LEE

THOMAS & MERCER

Text copyright © 2021 by Lynne Lee
All rights reserved.

Published by Thomas & Mercer, Seattle

www.apub.com

Amazon, the Amazon logo, and Thomas & Mercer are trademarks of Amazon.com, Inc., or its affiliates.

ISBN-13: 9781542017534
ISBN-10: 154201753X

Cover design by Tom Sanderson

Printed in the United States of America

For Felix

But I will wear my heart upon my sleeve
For daws to peck at. I am not what I am.

From *Othello* by William Shakespeare

Chapter 1

Brighton, Sunday 15th December 2019
5.12 a.m.

I have a well-developed sixth sense when it comes to calls in the small hours. So when my phone screen lit up that night, a fraction of a second before it rang, I automatically reached for it, even though I was still only half awake. It was Sid. Which was a relief. Not my mum again, thank goodness. Though it could have been, because she'd been making small-hours calls to me too. Two a.m. Four a.m. Would the next come at 6 a.m.? I knew I needed to do something about this new development, but what? I didn't even have a clue what it was about yet.

Our special nocturnal relationship meant I knew Sid would wait for me, so I peeled the duvet off and padded out on to the landing, then pulled the bedroom door shut again before answering. Not that Matt had stirred. Or was likely to, either. My husband, out of necessity, slept with earplugs.

'So sorry to call again so early, Mrs Hamilton.' Sid, short for Siddhant, was my surgical registrar. As ever, he was politeness personified. He was also conscientious, hard-working, and capable beyond his training grade, and barely a day (or night) passed when I didn't count those blessings. I made another mental note, to remind him to stop apologising all the time. To understand that calling me, if he needed to, was exactly what he *should* do. 'I just wanted to fill you in,' he went on, 'on a new trauma case, just come in. It's a male. No ID yet. Late thirties, early forties. RTC overnight. Driving under the influence. Lost control – on the ice, they think – and hit a parked lorry at speed. Crush injury. Right forearm and hand. Significant soft-tissue loss. Open fractures. I couldn't feel a radial pulse, and there's mottling of the hand and fingers.'

All of which was longhand for *Serious. Please come in.*

'Extensive damage, then.'

'Yes.'

'And how is he systemically?'

'He's in shock. Low GCS. But we suspect that's to be expected. Alcohol, as I say, and they found drugs in the car too.'

'Okay. Half an hour,' I said. 'I'll meet you in resusc.'

Having showered before bed, it was only the work of moments to get my clothes on, plus a minute or two more to scour my face and tie my hair back. I then checked on the boys, who were still sharing a bedroom, and not just because Daniel's needed decorating. It had been four months since we moved in, but there were lots of big adjustments – new home, two new schools, brand-new friendships to make and navigate. It was taking its toll on them both – especially Dillon. Where his older brother, like his dad, seemed to adapt to change with equanimity, Dillon was a fretter, a chronically anxious little soul. I understood. It was a lot to deal with. A lot for us *all* to deal with. The Christmas holidays really couldn't come soon enough.

Both were soundly, sweetly sleeping, though, in their own idiosyncratic ways – Daniel face down and starfished, Dillon coiled into a little comma. I touched the warm shapes beneath the duvets only fleetingly and lightly, so as not to wake them, before heading downstairs.

I continued on autopilot in the kitchen, assembling phone, bag and car keys. And while the machine spat strong coffee into my travel mug for the journey, I chatted, as had become something of a habit, to Mr Weasley, the toffee-coloured hamster who'd become part of the family when we'd moved here. Along with the magnificent tree house Matt had promised to build for the boys come the spring, he'd been a sweetener, a bribe, and, seeming to know that, he regularly nipped the boys to remind them. But the two of us had struck up an unlikely small-hours friendship.

But perhaps it wasn't so unlikely, I thought, as I watched him clean his whiskers. Though his hours were from choice, and mine professional necessity, we were both creatures of the night.

Out into the garage, then, where my car was parked, so I'd be spared having to scrape a frozen windscreen. At this time of year, when on call, I took precedence. Or rather – another flashpoint among several at the moment – my patients did.

I reversed out on to the drive, into the lane, into the inky winter night. Despite the cold and dark, I was more than happy to get going. Most of the stress of being on call was in the anticipation, after all.

A bit like Christmas, which was now just ten days away. And the journey into work, at least the first part, the wooded part (the reason we'd 'agreed' to move out here to 'the bloody sticks' part), was as Christmas-biscuit-tin perfect as I'd hoped it would be. Were Daniel and Dillon in the car with me, I'd be seeing it that way too. Beautiful. Ethereal. Breathtaking. Narnian. As it was, I saw one thing only. Ice.

Ice as bone breaker. Life-changer. Maker of all kinds of trouble. If there's one thing I've learned in my years as an orthopaedic surgeon, it's that where there is ice there will always be trouble. Which in my line of work equals Trauma.

The capital 'T' Trauma that dictates much of my work life is the 'T' to the 'O' of Orthopaedics. Though they coexist in the job spec, it's an unequal pairing. Trauma, my sub-speciality, is the upstart who holds the power. It trumps routine orthopaedics every time, because it has to. It also has its own hierarchy, which is strict and unchanging, because not all medical traumas are created equal.

So I couldn't help but feel sorry for the two elderly patients, both of whom had suffered hip fractures, who were already on my morning list. Starved overnight, having waited patiently since their own mishaps yesterday, they might, given this new casualty, now be waiting even longer. If I could save his arm, that was. I hoped I could.

I was in luck. When I arrived, there was still one on-call parking space free, which would save me having to find a space in the staff car park and, of course, time. *You mean you don't even get your own parking space by now?* Matt was incredulous about that. I wasn't. As our careers had progressed – his in private-sector engineering, mine in public-sector medicine – so the gulf in our respective professional expectations had widened.

Time was of the essence, too, because I didn't need my patient's low GCS score to tell me that he was in serious trouble. The moment I saw him, it was all too obvious.

Bloodied and barely conscious, he was already being intubated, and his face, blackened and bruised, was a bloated, angry mess, all but obscured by the mask and paraphernalia attached to him and the dressing that covered much of his forehead. Whoever he was, one thing I did know, even before I properly examined him, was that it wasn't just his Sunday morning that had been derailed.

Or even just his Christmas. Every aspect of his life would now be dramatically changed too.

It was the sort of thing I saw all the time at work, this colossal change in patients' fortunes; a constant reminder that no one's future was guaranteed. It was something I'd understood, almost intuitively, since I was fourteen, when I'd stumbled upon a book of short stories by Ray Bradbury. One, *A Sound of Thunder*, involved a time-travelling safari, in which a frightened hunter (there to shoot a T-rex that the guides knew was already going to die shortly afterwards) left the designated path. In doing so, he accidentally stepped on a butterfly, and when he returned to 2055 – his own time – everything had changed. In science, it's called the butterfly effect.

It was something I now reflected on as I approached my battered patient. Another night, a different route, less treacherous weather – and things might have turned out very differently.

Both photographs and bloods had already been taken, and there was the usual gaggle of medical professionals clustered around his bed. Sid, plus the senior house officer, the emergency duty registrar, and two nurses. Plus two policemen, whose continuing presence told its own story. First on the scene, they wouldn't leave till they'd got what they needed, to be sure they were in possession of what were probably damning facts. That the patient was intoxicated, incapacitated, and in possession of illegal drugs.

That – at least from the point of view of the law, their department – he was as culpable as the ice that had caught him out.

I wondered what had happened, beyond the obvious fact that he had pulverised his right arm. I wondered what chain of events (the injury was several hours old now) had taken him from one place – travelling home, travelling to work, travelling *some*where, still able-bodied – to the forced quit and reboot that was happening to him now.

5

'Busy night, then?' I asked Sid, as I approached to inspect the limb.

'Just a bit,' he agreed, stepping aside to let me examine it. Despite the adrenaline rush I knew he'd have had, knowing what was coming, he still looked exhausted; the default status for junior doctors everywhere. 'The police doctor has already taken bloods,' he went on. 'He's just left. And I've spoken to theatres; the team in two is prepped and waiting, and the consultant anaesthetist is on his way in.'

I nodded approval – I was also pleased to see they'd left the tourniquet in place – and he watched silently as I made my assessment. Which didn't take long. Bad as it was, the man was lucky to be alive. Had it not been for the sub-zero temperatures, and the fact that his upper arm was apparently pinioned between the two vehicles, he would almost certainly have bled to death before they found him. Because what I was examining was no longer recognisable as an arm. Just a collection of shattered bone shards, clots of blood, a muddle of snapped nerves and tendons, shreds of flayed skin, and strands of muscle fibre – all of it pulverised into a mash of stringy pink pulp. Had I any hope of reconstructing such a mess? Any realistic hope?

The more I saw, the more I doubted. Sid had been conservative, even optimistic, staying on the hopeful side of stating the obvious – that the fixed mottling of what was left of the skin on the pulps of his fingers meant the damage was almost certainly irreversible. Which wasn't surprising; he had all but amputated his own arm already. My only contribution now, surely, could be to finish the job.

While Sid prepared the patient – currently known only, and perhaps appropriately, as Mr Hotel Trauma – I headed off to scrub up at the sink, already second-guessing the amended timeline of my day. This wouldn't take long. Perhaps an hour. Much less than a reconstruction. The two scheduled hip fractures might yet be done by lunchtime, this man's terrible loss their unlikely gain. Though if I saw the day out without at least one other ice-related injury, it would be a Christmas miracle.

It was just approaching six by the time I was gowned up and ready, and while Justin the anaesthetist put lines into the patient, I thought about Matt, almost certainly asleep still, though by now on my side of the bed, and whether the latest arguments about Mum (as most arguments were about these days) would be more or less complicated by her new nocturnal habit. Glancing over at my phone – which I obviously couldn't touch now – I saw another missed call from her, bang on cue.

It could be worse, I told myself. Because that was always the best thing to do. After all, seeing worse, day in, day out, was what I did. Always a great way to maintain a sense of perspective. Especially when other lives were in your hands.

And this life, at least for now, was no longer at risk, thankfully, and the amputation looked pretty straightforward. Almost textbook, in fact, and I soon lost myself within it; tinkering with the workings of a human body was a daily, compelling wonder, and one of the main reasons I'd made the stressful mid-career change from A and E to trauma orthopaedics: it meant I could spend more time in theatre.

I loved surgery. While ostensibly dehumanising – a sentient being reduced to architecture, wiring, and plumbing – it was at the same time a powerfully human thing to be engaged in. I was never happier at work than when wielding a scalpel. Never tired. Never distracted. Under stress, but never stressed.

Once I was done, I left Sid to finish closing. And despite the tragedy of the hand and wrist I'd been powerless to save, I automatically began thinking the positive thoughts I hoped, and intended, to convey to the patient over the coming days. He was alive. He could have lost so much more than he did. I'd at least saved his elbow, and retaining that would mean a lot to him. Modern prosthetics were a world away from old ones. Yes, he'd suffer shock, disbelief, even a form of bereavement. He would almost certainly experience phantom limb pain, which would be distressing for him, but he was *alive*. Whatever happened now, it could all have been so much worse for him.

So I *was* optimistic. Professionally detached and relentlessly optimistic. Because I'd yet to find out that his butterfly effect was destined to ripple out to include someone else as well.

And that that someone else would be me.

While Sid prepared the patient to be moved to ICU, I stripped off my gloves and headed to the writing-up room to do my op note. Then grabbed a coffee break, not least to make sure all was well with Mum, before scrubbing up again, in a different theatre, to operate on the first of the next two patients on the list. Neither turned out to be as straightforward as we'd expected, so it was mid-afternoon by the time I made my way up to the ward to start my round, as yet unaware that my life was about to be turned upside down and hurled into a time and place I thought I'd long left.

Sid was already there, waiting to accompany me. Just behind where he was standing there was a wall-mounted whiteboard, detailing the names and whereabouts of all the current inpatients. As I'd already spotted mine, however, I had no need to check it. I'd find out soon enough who Mr Hotel Trauma had been ID'd as; there were already visitors beside the bed.

I wish I *had* checked it. Looking back, perhaps it wouldn't have made any difference, but it would at least have given me a moment to mentally reorient. Because when it happened, it was without warning. As I approached, and saw him properly for the first time, I noticed something about the man whose forearm and hand I'd taken off. Something familiar about the jawline. The Grecian nose. The full mouth. The thatch of unkempt, almost shoulder-length black hair. *Pirate's hair*. Not my description, but definitely an apt one, and part of a package (apparently irresistible, at least to one person) whose appeal I'd had cause to consider often over the years. Though, happily, not in a long time. Not until now.

I scanned the wider picture. The slight blonde woman sitting beside his bed, her hair – thick and wavy – gathered into a tortoise-shell claw grip. Gathered chaotically, and almost certainly in haste. The two little girls on her lap, one dark-haired, one blonde, who were encircled, one per knee, by her slender arms. All three were pale and puffy-eyed from lack of sleep. So presumably his wife, or his partner, and their children. Almost definitely – we'd retrieved a ring from the third finger of his left hand. But as I revisited the man's profile – he had yet to notice I was approaching – I was sure. I was looking at someone I knew.

Someone I *used* to know. Someone I wished I'd never *had* to know. That's when I glanced behind me, finally, towards the board, and confirmed it. The name, scrawled in marker pen, immediately jumped out at me. It couldn't fail to.

It was Aidan Kennedy, my late sister's nemesis.

Nemesis is a strong word, but it was also the only word. No, he didn't kill her – but he wielded considerable power over her: he controlled her, abused her, was unfaithful to her and then abandoned her, callously leaving both her and their baby son without a backward glance when she found out she was dying from a brain tumour.

I had not seen him since, and I was shocked how much he'd aged. What must he be now – thirty-eight? Thirty-nine? Even given the circumstances, he looked as if the years hadn't been kind to him, and I recalled the drugs that were found in his system and his car. No change there, then. I thought of Hope, and I wondered if she was turning in her grave. I suspected she might be. So she could high-five the fates.

I imagined her doing it. Saw her face – forever young – swimming back into focus. Heard her voice. Felt the almost feral quality of her rage. Because this was the man of whom she'd once said no revenge would be good enough. Said she'd cut off her right arm before letting him near their son again. Those words. Those very words. That she *would cut off her right arm*.

And I had just amputated his.

Chapter 2

Things I inherited from my little sister when she died: her Italian leather jacket, the emerald earrings our paternal grandmother left her (I'd been given the matching necklace), and her collection of Thomas Hardy novels, several thoughtfully annotated, and in an unexpectedly neat version of her idiosyncratic, spiky writing. Reading her notes in the margins still had the power to make me cry, because it reminded me that there was so much I never knew about my little sister. Things just like this, hidden away behind the avatars our parents chose for us. Who or what was she analysing them for?

Hope left me something else, too. Her most cherished possession.

Her son, Dillon. Her and *Aidan Kennedy's* son, Dillon.

And, consequently, a horrible, ugly, protracted mess. The last in a long chain of interlinked messes that spiralled through Hope's life like a strand of DNA. A mess she knew for a fact would outlive her.

There was no time for a mental regroup, much less any kind of impact assessment. Though the impact this man had already had on my and Matt's life was whispering darkly at the edges of my attention. I quickly adjusted my stunned expression – how could I have failed to recognise him earlier? – because the nurse by his bed was two steps ahead of me.

'Mr Kennedy,' she was saying, 'here's your consultant, Mrs Hamilton.' And up I swept, because I had no choice but to do so.

He was on a PCA, groggy, no doubt stupefied by his situation. As seemed to be his wife and the two little girls, one of which was such a mini Aidan that she was unmistakeably his daughter.

The woman's gaze flicked up towards me, anxious, uncomprehending, and I smiled to reassure her as I walked round to the far side of the bed. She looked even more sleep-deprived than Siddhant. I wondered how much of the circumstances around the accident she knew.

Finally, having seemingly been fixed on the middle distance, Aidan Kennedy's unfocused gaze rested on me. Buried deep beneath the swelling, which was extensive, particularly on his right cheek and brow, those dark-lashed eyes, stuff of way too many idealistic romantic novels, were the same glacial blue I remembered. *I could literally drown in them*, Hope – seventeen then – once gushed at me. And I remembered finding just enough forbearance to resist explaining the meaning of the word 'literal' to her. She, on the other hand (we always dutifully inhabited our respective family boxes), naturally failed to resist explaining to me that I would *never* understand. *Never*. About true love. About anything. Any*one*. Her *or* him.

There was a good deal of door-slamming at home back then. Months of it. Hope was a good bit younger than me, and I'd long since left for medical school, but my mother was on the phone to me, often – *Grace, for pity's sake, can't you try and knock some sense into her?*

It meant nothing now. It meant nothing then, either. All those rows, all those entreaties, both mine and my mother's, had served no purpose. She would move in with him – and she did – she would follow her heart's desire, and I would *never* understand.

12

I met those eyes now, and despite Aidan Kennedy's rather different-from-his-usual brand of drug-induced confusion, realised the penny had dropped for him too. That he knew who he was looking at, and, given the way he stared at me before he looked away again, that he was equally astonished to find me standing there.

Which was perhaps understandable; there are still very few female surgeons around, after all. Disbelief that I should be let loose with a scalpel is commonplace. As is the belief that any male registrar with me must be my boss.

But this was personal. He looked traumatised now. Scared, even. Like the bad boy in school – the one who never seems to get into trouble – finding himself finally in the head teacher's office, with no choice but to brace for the reckoning. The fingers of his left hand were clenched white against the bed rail, and it occurred to me that he was probably as anxious to pretend ignorance of our common history as I was. Though for different reasons, I suspected. Three of them, on the other side of the bed.

'Do you know where you are, Mr Kennedy?' I asked. 'Do you understand why you're in hospital?'

He blinked at me, squeezed his eyes shut, as if trying to clear his vision. Mumbled something in which I could make out the words 'skidded' and 'car'.

I nodded. Said, 'I'm afraid you were in a serious car accident, and your right hand and forearm were so badly damaged that we weren't able to save them.'

The eyelids flickered open. Shut again. Reopened. The little girls' heads turned in unison towards the bandaged stump.

'We've had to amputate, Mr Kennedy,' I finished. 'I'm so sorry.'

Already aware, as she couldn't fail to be, and meek-looking as she was, the woman's cry of anguish was loud enough to make Siddhant jump.

I left Aidan, I think, as stunned by the encounter as I was. Though, in my case, it wasn't just about him. It wasn't even primarily about him. It never had been. Because once he'd walked out on my sister, he had ceased to be a problem. No, my first worry, as I joined the ribbon of Sunday afternoon traffic out of Brighton, a couple of hours later, was that wherever Aidan Kennedy was, his mother might be too. And she was someone I wanted to bump into even less.

She hadn't been there, though. And if she could be, she surely would be. So was she dead? Or in a home? Perhaps suffering from dementia, like my own mum? I knew she was older than Mum – Aidan, the product of a second marriage, had had a much older half-brother, I remembered – so it was definitely possible. It was a pretty low thing to wish for, but it crossed my mind even so. At least, the wish that she would be somewhere far, far away from where I was, because I really didn't want to cross swords with her again.

It had been one of the reasons we'd not moved to the city itself, but a village to the east, up on the South Downs, twenty minutes' drive away. And it seemed Aidan Kennedy was back here as well. Just visiting? I could only hope so. The last I'd heard, via Facebook, from one of Hope's old friends, Daisy, was that he'd run out on the last girl he'd cheated on my sister with – even before Hope had died – and got himself a new job, and a new life, up in Hull. But that news was almost a decade old in itself. Suppose he'd returned to Brighton to be closer to his mother, like I had? After all, we didn't just have my sister in common. With his half-brother long dead, he was in the same place as I was; we were both our mothers' only remaining children.

My second thought was that I must have a word with one of my colleagues asap, and ask that he be put under their care. Explain the circumstances, the connection, the potential difficulties of my overseeing Aidan's recovery and rehabilitation. But just rehearsing what I might say made me feel uncomfortable – it felt too much like hanging out dirty laundry, much too personal, particularly since I'd only been in post for a matter of months.

But perhaps I wouldn't need to elaborate too much, I reasoned. This kind of thing happened. 'For personal reasons' would be enough, wouldn't it? Perhaps the less said, the better.

I wondered if he'd said anything about knowing me. I had no idea what his wife knew of events before he met her but, based on his past form, it was conceivable that she didn't even know Dillon existed. And even if she did, was it likely she'd know the whole story? A romantic CV that included 'I abandoned my dying partner and our son' wasn't one you'd want to shout about, after all. I wondered how the facts might have been altered. What backstory he'd created to make his actions sound less questionable.

But I didn't wonder for long because as I visualised him lying there in his hospital bed, newly helpless, my principal emotion about Aidan Kennedy was pity. Pity about his accident, but also because, by any yardstick, pitiable was exactly what he had always seemed. A weak man who, when faced with a hard choice, had behaved badly – which hardly made him an endangered species.

I don't believe in karma; in my line of work, you tend not to. Bad things happen to good people all the time, just as good things often happen to bad people. And though he'd clearly contributed to his current crisis, I took no pleasure in what had happened to him, because I wouldn't wish his misfortune on anyone. Certainly not on his wife, who, as a consequence of his accident, now had so much on her plate. Judging by her tears, which had begun to flow unchecked as I'd left them (her little girls had been scrabbling to hug and comfort her), even more, perhaps, than I knew.

I forced my head away from work. I had to. I had plenty on my own plate. Mum, for example, whose deterioration up to now had been slow and mostly manageable, suddenly seemed to have reached a tipping point and hurtled over it. It was almost as if her dementia, previously hesitant to unleash its many demons, was saying, 'Ah, Grace, you're here, finally. Bring it on.' Perhaps our moving here had even contributed to her confusion, just as her deterioration, seen close up, had been such a shock for the boys.

I reached the roundabout where I'd usually turn right, and turned left. Going to see her, and hopefully getting to the bottom of her repeated small-hours phone calls, would be more productive than going straight home and having dinner, interrupted by yet more nonsense calls, before Matt headed back to London. I needed to return with some sense of having taken control.

As with Hope, Mum was my blood, and my problem. Had been so, it had sometimes felt, since my father walked out. They'd both been teachers in the same school – her maths, him geography. And he'd left her for the French teacher he'd been having an affair with. Her name was Aurélie, which meant 'the golden one'. I'd looked it up in the library. I was sixteen, turning seventeen. Hope just eleven. My mother fell apart. Completely.

With so many Sunday shoppers on the road – presumably buying last-minute presents – my detour took longer than I'd expected. I texted Matt – *Just checking in on Mum, won't be long* – before heading into the development that housed her flat, an assisted-living place called The Beeches (though no beech trees had been planted there) that she had moved into five years previously. And where it was becoming clearer by the day that the level of assistance she required would soon be more than they could provide for her.

It was a bridge I'd cross when I got to it, which is why I felt guiltily relieved that, being a Sunday, their new house manager, Holly, wasn't there, so couldn't collar me with tales of Mum's latest misdemeanours. Though once up on her floor, I was presented with one anyway – the TV (always hers) was turned up so loud that I could hear it from the corridor.

I knocked and waited before putting my key in the lock, so she was already in the hallway by the time I entered.

Mum was a good bit shorter than me (Hope and I both got our height from our father) and seemed shorter still every time I saw her, which only heightened the sense of who was mothering who. She was in her stockinged feet, in beige trousers and her favourite stone- and sand-coloured top. The only splash of colour in her usual muted palette was a shocking-pink fascinator, which was perched on her head, spewing feathers. The one she'd worn, as per the style sheet, to Hope's funeral. Hope, who, since the dementia, was coming alive again in all sorts of ways; every time I came here, Mum seemed to have unearthed a new photo of her. Some were framed, some were not, some just scraps torn from bigger photos, which she'd tuck between her many ornaments, or Blu-Tack to the walls, or arrange in overlapping lines (a muddled timeline of mini Hopes) over photographs of Dillon, which unnerved me. Wherever you looked, basically, there was my sister. It was as if my moving here had, in itself, inspired the endless trawling. Was she hoping she could magic Hope back to her as well?

Mum seemed oblivious to her unlikely headgear. Had probably forgotten she even had it on, much less why. She was clearly more interested in my own head.

'I don't know why you insist on scraping your hair back like that,' she said, as I picked up the TV remote and turned the volume down. 'It really doesn't do anything for you.'

Along with the nocturnal phone calls, the casual barbs were a new thing. As if her thoughts (I had always been 'the brainy one', and Hope 'the pretty one', she'd told me recently) had found a shortcut, a rat run, direct from brain to mouth.

I understood that this happened. I tried not to mind. 'I've come from work,' I reminded her, even though I knew it was pointless. I kept forgetting that the concept of my going to work had no meaning for her now. I was either there, or I was not.

I glanced around me, pleased to see her tea things were washed up and on the drainer – it meant her carer had been – but dismayed by the chaos on the living-room floor. 'Have you been having another sort-out?'

Sorting things out was something else that was suddenly burgeoning on my mother's daily, always treble-underlined, to-do lists. Though I understood the reasoning – it must be a comforting illusion that constantly reacquainting yourself with familiar treasures will help shore up failing short-term memory – it came with a side order of anxiety as well. For everything found, another recollection would bubble up, prompting an ever more frantic search for some other previously forgotten thing.

Mum shook her head as she returned to where she had been kneeling on the carpet. 'I'm trying to find something,' she snapped. 'For Mary.'

'Mary?'

'Yes. *Mary*.'

'Mary who?'

'You know. *Mary*.'

Another resident from The Beeches, no doubt. Since the dementia, it seemed everyone else had slipped too far away. Or she had.

'What thing?'

Mum scowled at me. 'The thing she *phoned* about. And that other thing.'

'What other thing?'

'You *know*. That postcard.'

'Postcard?'

'You *know*.' Her tone was irritable. 'That postcard from Hope. The one she sent me when she went to Cambodia. I've been right through everything and I can't find it anywhere.'

Though she had managed Amsterdam – for the tulips, allegedly – just before her terminal diagnosis, my sister never made it to Cambodia. Mum had probably just seen something on the television and fashioned another of her Frankenstein memories. 'Ah,' I said, because it worked, 'I know the one you mean. It's at mine. You left it there last week, remember?'

'Of course,' she said. 'I thought so.' The anxious lines on her face softened. 'That's alright then. I'll get it next time.'

'Where is your phone, Mum?' I asked, stepping over the muddle of stuff all over the floor. It fanned out from her in a circle, like a Georgian lady's skirts.

'Flipping thing,' she muttered. It was her only comment on the matter.

It was in her bag, as I'd expected. Along with the alarm necklace she was supposed to put on every morning, it spent most of the daylight hours there. Most of the time she professed not to even own one. Yet at night, for the last four or five, all those phone calls. I suspected, and hoped, there'd be a pragmatic reason. Another twist in the tale of the array of smart technology that I was persuaded, via an online article about 'useful aids for seniors', might be a good way to support her short-term memory. *Hey Siri, what's the date today? Alexa, turn on the radio.* Despite the instructions I'd put up, in a variety of places, I had no idea if she'd ever said either of those things.

What she had done, it turned out, when I inspected the pristine iPhone, was create a series of alarms, to be repeated every night – at two-hour intervals, from midnight till 6 a.m. This in conjunction with a note sellotaped to the back of the phone cover, which said *Remember to call Grace,* triple underlined, as per.

Et voila. Notes and buttons. It was that complicated and that simple. There was no point asking why or how. Just notes and buttons. And, apart from mine, there were no calls in her recent calls log, either. It was just what it was, I supposed.

I knocked the alarms off and dispatched the note to my pocket, while Mum, back on her knees, started returning paperwork to boxes. It was wholly random, but conducted with the same sense of purpose I used to see in the boys' faces when they were clearing their toys away as toddlers and a bribe was involved.

Except, in Mum's case, the purpose had been mislaid. I kneeled down to help her. I wondered what she'd have to say about Aidan Kennedy if I told her. How much delight she might derive from his misery. What painful memories might surface. What furies might be disinterred.

I wouldn't. Couldn't, in any case – I wasn't legally permitted to. And what she didn't know, and didn't need to know, couldn't hurt her. 'I'm off, Mum,' I said instead, touching her shoulder. And I wished, I wished, *I wished*, that I could feel a genuine rush of love for her. Something more, something deeper, than just knee-jerk compassion. It felt only right. But at the same time, I couldn't.

When I got back down to the car, the air was bitter again, full of ice spicules. I jumped in quickly, pressed the ignition button, turned up the heater. Then, infuriatingly, because I knew I really shouldn't let her get to me, I reached behind my head and pulled out my scrunchie.

I saw the house – our new, old house – earlier than I expected to, because its roof was loosely outlined in tiny points of light, shimmering on and off as I passed through the trees. It was a substantial house, double-fronted, much bigger than the one we'd left in

London, but I'd yet to make friends with it; to feel anything like at home here. More worryingly, it was a feeling that seemed to be growing, rather than dissipating. Back in June, when we'd viewed it, it had sold itself to us utterly, partly because from upstairs we had a chunk of sea in view between two copses, but mostly because the outside was dripping with wisteria in full bloom. You will be happy here, it seemed to say. Stop worrying.

But the promise hadn't yet quite materialised. Where I'd imagined I'd feel liberated from the stress of caring for Mum remotely, my new reality – my new proximity – seemed to match the steady march of the seasons; as the house lost its gloss, buried under mounds of fallen leaves, so I felt the weight of what was coming grow increasingly heavy. Even the wisteria seemed to echo the same journey. Now skeletal against the brickwork, it was lifeless and grey. Spring felt a long way away, and I felt cheated.

The artificial lights at least lifted my mood. Matt had obviously been busy while I was at work, coming good on the promise he'd made the boys yesterday, finally bringing us into line with the scattering of new neighbours, whose houses had been festively bedecked since the beginning of December. Strange, now that neighbours were both less close and fewer, that I felt their presence, their silent scrutiny, so much more.

A memory mushroomed up as I turned into the lane, and our home, dressed for the season, fully revealed itself. Of that last Christmas before Hope died, Aidan by then long gone, and Matt being co-opted to help me embellish hers. Dillon too young to care, Hope too drugged to take it in, but one moment of lucidity – *G, this is going to be our last* Christmas! – held too much power, too much pathos, for us not to do it for her.

I pulled into the drive, to see the living-room curtains were, unusually, already closed, and a shard of light, hastily extinguished, told me why. The boys were already in the garage doorway by the time I opened it, jumping from foot to foot in their excitement. So they'd obviously done the tree as well.

'Come on, come *on*!' Daniel sang.

Dillon tugged me by the sleeve. 'Close your eyes! Dad, Da–*ad*! Mum's home!' And I was duly bustled through to the living room, Daniel – older and taller – reaching up to cover my eyes before I was allowed to see again (if only darkness), just before Matt pressed the switch for them.

'*Wow*,' I said, meaning it. 'It looks *amazing*.'

'We aced it, didn't we, Dad?' Dillon said. 'Proper aced it.'

Matt stuck a thumb up. 'We did, son.'

And in my younger son's eyes, I saw something I'd never seen before. Because sometimes you just forget and other times you make a point to. I'd had no photo reference (God forbid), no ongoing comparison, definitely no wish to seek one. Yet there it was anyway, as if newly minted. I saw his biological father. An unwelcome intrusion into a present he had no part in.

'You did,' I agreed, hugging him, chasing it away. 'It's magnificent.'

'Anyway, it's dinnertime,' Matt said. 'Thought I'd head off around ten,' he added, to me, looking sad. I felt suddenly emotional, about the unwelcome intrusion I'd foisted on him too.

'I know,' I said, touching his arm. 'Sorry. Mum and everything.'

'It's fine,' he said. Even though it wasn't.

'But I think I've sorted it,' I told him, as we trooped back into the kitchen. It smelled of the waiting roast dinner, which I was almost too tired to eat. 'She's been playing with her tech again.'

'I knew that was going to create more problems than it would solve,' he said.

But we *didn't* know, I wanted to say. How could we have known? It's like having a baby – you can't know. You're in unknown territory. You can only guess.

I didn't. I said, to the room in general, 'Wow, this looks delicious. I could eat, let me see, a whole hairy hippopotamus.'

'Hippopotamuses don't have hair,' Daniel said, with conviction. 'Hey, but, Mum, guess what? You know Fortnite?'

I did. Way more than I ever imagined I would. And so, as he told me more about his latest battle royale (he was obsessed with the game), we recalibrated. Ate. Performed all the soothing Sunday-night rituals. Then it was ten, the boys in bed, and Matt's case was in the hall. As it had been at the end of every weekend since September, while he finished an engineering project he was heading up in London. As it would be till March, maybe April. When he'd hopefully find a new job – he was putting out feelers already – that would slot into a life that, for the entirety of our marriage, had been dominated by the demands of my career in the NHS. He used to joke, often (especially when we were out somewhere socially), that he was married to the health service as much as he was married to me. He didn't make that joke any more.

'Are you okay?' he asked. 'I can stay if you like. Leave in the morning.' I knew he'd picked up on my mood, my preoccupation with Aidan Kennedy, the image of whom I couldn't seem to shift. Who kept popping up in my mind's eye now, baleful, angry, accusing, despite there being no grounds for him feeling any of those things. But Matt didn't – couldn't – know about that. Patient confidentiality is sacrosanct over all. Certainly above domestic tensions, which, right now, it could only add to, because Matt naturally thought it was something to do with him.

I shook my head. 'I'm fine. I'm just weary. Difficult day.'

'Want to talk about it?'

And somehow, my treacherous, sleep-deprived brain called it wrong. I shook my head again. Added, 'To be honest, I just need my bed.'

Not him. That's how he read it. Not wanted. Not needed.

'Noted,' he said, picking up his case. 'I'll get off then.'

I went to kiss him. Got a cheek. A chilly one, and I cursed myself.

I kept on cursing myself as I watched him climb into his car and drive off, blowing kisses at him and waving madly till his tail lights rounded the corner, knowing I wouldn't go to sleep till he was back in London anyway. Then closed the door with an increasingly familiar sense of things not being quite right. As if our compass had got confused in a storm.

I padded around then, turning lights off, and double-checking window locks and doors, in a way I never used to when we were still in London. There was little sense in this new vigilance, given that our city lives had put us in harm's way almost daily, yet here, where it would be an event if a potted bay tree went missing, my responsibility for the boys' safety, especially when I was alone with them, which I was through the week, weighed on my mind so much more heavily.

The dark was truly dark here. Medieval in its blackness. And, apart from the occasional thrill of a tawny owl screeching (Daniel loved owls), the night silence was also absolute at this time of year, in a way that city nights never are. It was dark down on the ground here. It was silent in the undergrowth. All the light and noise, the stars and birds, were up above. Were I to have to run with them, escape with them, that darkness would be terrifying.

I heard my phone ringing in the kitchen just as I was heading up to bed. It wouldn't be work – another team had now picked up the on-call baton. It might be Mum. I hoped not. I hoped it was Matt, who had already texted (*Home safe. No worries.* Smile emoji. *One kiss*) in response to my rather longer one: *Sorry to be such a grouch. Nasty RTC this morning, had to perform an amputation. Bit of a grim day all round really. Sorry to take it out on you. I didn't mean to.*

It wasn't Matt. It was from an unfamiliar mobile phone number.

I said hello. Heard a breath. Not a heavy one. Just a breath.

I said hello a second time. Strained to hear through the soupy silence. Added, 'Who is this?'

Another breath. Another second. Then, 'Grace?'

It was a voice I thought I recognised. But could it really be? '*Aidan?*'

There was a beep then. A brief rustling. And the phone disconnected.

I called back. It rang once. Then went dead.

Chapter 3

Just as trauma trumps orthopaedics every time, so, for me, physical exhaustion almost always wins the battle over emotional. So, despite the unsettling phone call, which should have kept me awake – *was* it Aidan? – I realised I must have fallen asleep in a matter of minutes, because when I woke up – suddenly, anxiously – my cheek was stuck to my Kindle, as if to prove it.

It was Dillon who'd woken me. A hot little hand on my exposed shoulder.

'Can I come into bed with you, Mummy?' he whispered. 'I'm frightened. I keep hearing noises.'

It was the house. The new-old house, which wheezed and groaned and grumbled. I heard Matt's voice. *Bad habits. Take him straight back to bed.*

But it was almost five. My alarm would be going off soon anyway. So I ignored it, sliding across enough so he could slip in beside me. Dillon was asleep again in seconds, but now I was wide awake, brain whirring, picking up the stitch I must have dropped when sleep won the battle, and now tugging on it once again, forcefully.

Was it Aidan Kennedy who phoned me last night? Every instinct told me yes.

And if it was, why? To try and extract a promise that I wouldn't spill the beans about his past? I imagined his metaphorical arms – of

which he would still have two, obviously – already windmilling fran-
tically around his head, trying to bat away the inrush of terrifying
thoughts. He would be panicking by now, I knew. Might even be
hysterical. An arm was a big thing to lose, after all. Arguably, more
profoundly disabling than a leg. As a surgeon, I understood that.
And as an able-bodied human. Arms, hands and fingers, versus legs,
feet and toes.

As if to illustrate, when Dillon whimpered, I automatically
folded both arms tighter around him. I was worried about him.
Fearful that he was anxious about making friends, even though
every time I'd gently probed, he was adamant he was fine. I buried
my nose in his shampoo-soft mop of hair.

Which put me uncomfortably in mind of Aidan again. It had
to be him, didn't it? But would he even have access to a phone? Let
alone the wherewithal to make a one-handed call. He must have
only just been transferred out of ICU, surely? And have been dosed
up with opiates, physically drained and exhausted. How would he
still have my number, for that matter? *No*, I chided myself, that
was ridiculous. Why would he *not* still have my number? I hadn't
changed it since I had my first mobile.

Though that *he* would have, and probably more than once,
wouldn't have surprised me. Hard to run away with your past
weighing you down. So much easier to just jettison it. Let it go.

In contrast to the day before, Monday's dawn arrived damp, dull
and sulky, the frost on the lawn gone and the woods at the end of
the garden obscured by shifting skeins of mist. It must have been
ten degrees warmer than it had been this time yesterday, and the
white Narnian landscape had lost its dangerous beauty; it was now
the dull green of overcooked kale.

On weekdays, I dropped Daniel to his high school just outside Brighton on my way into work, and Isabel, the girl who helped us out with the boys, walked Dillon to the village primary school an hour later. Only *to* school, however. A big part of becoming accepted, I knew, was becoming 'one of the gang', by being allowed to walk home – at least to the end of our lane, where Isabel was permitted to wait for him. After all, he was in year six. He was ten now. Not *seven*. And the tug on my maternal apron strings was too strong to ignore. *And this isn't London*, I reminded myself, endlessly.

When I came downstairs after getting dressed and helping him hunt down his pencil case, Isabel was heading in through the front door bearing bin bags as big as gym balls, moving gingerly, crabbing in, keeping them away from her legs.

'Present from Mum,' she explained, in response to my raised eyebrows. 'Foliage. She thought you might like to make use of it. Mostly holly.' Her strange gait began to make sense now. 'But there's a bunch of eucalyptus and some mistletoe as well. Oh, and an Oasis ring. I thought we might make a wreath for the front door after school.'

Isabel was the granddaughter of one of the residents where Mum lived. I'd already met her a couple of times, on my increasingly frequent visits down from London, and it was during one of those, when we started looking in earnest for a new home near Brighton, that her gran told us she was keen to find some temporary work. She'd just finished her A levels, and, prior to spending six months travelling round South-East Asia with her boyfriend, she was hoping to find some part-time childcare-related employment to add to her CV, as her longer-term goal was to become a paediatric nurse.

It was as if it had been meant, childcare being our most pressing problem. Back in London, with both the boys at the same local primary, Matt would drop them to school before work every morning and I'd pick them up from after-school club. Without Matt, and among strangers, the whole edifice crumbled, as those kinds of constructions so often tend to. An Isabel in our lives would be a lifesaver.

Well, in theory, because if not quite a leap in the dark, it was still a step in the near-dark – one of many we'd had to make more using instinct than planning. Our instinct in this case being that as her gran was lovely, and she was so lovely to her gran (the evidence was widely accepted as incontrovertible), why not Isabel, over anyone we could find via an agency, to ride to our childcare-gap rescue?

We'd bonded immediately, not least because her family situation had so closely mirrored my own. Her dad, a police detective, had left her mum and since remarried, and though she'd adapted and still got on well with her father, I knew we bore similar scars. She too had been sixteen when he'd walked out.

'Guilt money,' she'd laughed when she first visited and I admired her brand-new car – a surprise eighteenth birthday gift from him. 'And I'm cool with that!' she'd added firmly.

I knew then that we were going to get on.

Isabel's mum was a florist. She had a shop down in the lanes. In the four months we'd been living here, there had been many such presents. She was grateful to us in a way I completely related to, but at the same time completely underestimated, I think, the depth of gratitude flowing back in the other direction. I wanted to hug Isabel daily. I often did. But not today. Instead, I stepped back up on to the stairs so she and her vicious bin bags could pass by without snagging my tights.

Before the brain tumour pitched up, Hope, too, had been a florist. Not in a shop, though. She was never one for normal working hours, because she didn't 'do' normal. Hope liked her lifestyle like she'd always liked her boyfriends. She liked edgy. She liked fringes. Extremely late nights and ridiculously early mornings. Sometimes within the same twenty-four-hour period. She was never happier than when awake while the rest of the world slept. When she was nineteen she had the word 'hedonist' tattooed, in tiny writing, on the nape of her neck.

Hope worked – hard and well; she had been good at the job in which she had finally found a passion, for a firm who specialised in floral creations for events. High-end weddings, corporate gatherings, award ceremonies, banquets. She'd text me. *Wahhhh! I'm on* BBC Breakfast! Or *Check out these roses!* Or, on one occasion, *G, find a television RIGHT NOW! They're interviewing Joanna Lumley by my bower!*

And if I could I always would, because it mattered to her that I cared. Because Mum, who Hope had long realised could never see beyond her disappointment (in life, in love, and especially in her second daughter), seemed not to care much at all.

I followed Isabel through to the kitchen, where Daniel was finishing his breakfast. 'Yo, DI Dan,' Isabel said. 'How's it hanging?'

Isabel already had pet names for them both. My older son – Detective Inspector Dan, to Dillon's Detective Sergeant Dill – was, in real life, usually the cheerful Sergeant Lewis to Dillon's more introverted Inspector Morse. But he was currently desperate to be selected for one of the year seven football teams, which happy circumstance was by no means assured. He was settling in okay, but I knew getting picked would mean the world to him. I kept telling myself that it would have been just the same in London; that settling into a new high school would still be the same scary step. That getting on a team wouldn't have been a given there, either. But coupled with the move, it couldn't help but matter more. Because if he didn't, he wouldn't have his mates to console him, just as I no longer had my little coterie of girlfriends.

We're doing the right thing, I told myself. *This is the right thing for all of us.* Was it, though? After the last twenty-four hours, I was having a major rethink.

'Yo, Iz,' he said, through a mouthful of Weetabix.

He looked visibly brighter at the sight of her. Though I suspected he had a crush on her, which only added to my gnawing, increasing anxiety that this state of affairs was just temporary. Come the middle of March, Matt would hopefully be down properly, which would make everything easier, but Isabel would be gone after Easter. Which meant the boys would have to adjust to yet another change. I knew they would do so in their own characteristic ways. Daniel head down and plough through it. Dillon more *Sturm und Drang*. Whatever else was true about them, one thing seemed inescapable. That nature usually holds sway over nurture.

I went across to him, wanting nothing more than to gather him up and give him a bear hug, but, reading the rules (ever shifting as he approached adolescence), I restricted myself to planting a kiss on his head instead, before doing my usual turn around the kitchen, ticking off items on my Monday-morning checklist. Packed lunches. PE kits. Money for a school trip. Cruising round the kitchen island like a tracking drone.

Finally, I unplugged my phone from where it spent the not-on-call nights. And noticed, by the 'calls' button, the number three.

More missed calls in the night, then. On any other morning recently, my first thought would have been Mum, but this morning it wasn't. It was Aidan.

I clicked through to the detail, already anticipating what I might find, even as I railed against how preposterous it was that our paths should have crossed again in such an unlikely way. But was it really that unlikely? I was a trauma surgeon, after all. And Aidan's life had always been a car crash in waiting.

Waiting for our fates to collide? Because that's what it felt like.

I was right. Same mobile. Four twenty, four twenty-one, four twenty-four, no voicemail.

But there was something else. A text message. Sent just a minute later. One word. In capitals. BITCH.

Two things occurred to me as I stared at my phone, the first being to wonder if it was the calls that had disturbed Dillon? Highly likely. And the second, that there was a certain kind of person who, sleepless, stressed, and anxious, would think nothing of sending a text in the middle of the night, calling someone a bitch. I knew because I'd seen a few texts like that before. And worse. Ones sent to my sister.

By Aidan Kennedy.

I spent the morning in theatre, working through my usual Monday list with Siddhant, during which time, after an apparently uneventful night in recovery, Aidan Kennedy had been transferred to a general trauma ward. By the time I got up there, he was already the subject of much nurse-station gossip, as patients who are attended by police officers tend to be, even ones not as famously charismatic as my late sister's errant ex.

Siddhant, who'd arrived on the ward before me to meet the juniors, updated me. Aidan had been interviewed by two of the officers, and had made a formal statement, and it seemed no one else was involved in the collision. Just him, and the ice, and an unyielding parked lorry, and the fourth component – the one that would impact all the others: the cocktail of intoxicants in his blood.

So despite the wife, and the two little ones, it seemed nothing much had changed. Aidan, who, like Hope, had come of age during the latter part of the nineties' rave culture, had always done drugs, and unashamedly so. To get him high, to bring him down, and, when he wasn't hefting pots and pans in whatever kitchen he was cheffing in, to enhance his ability to heft weights in the local gym. She'd confided in me once (they were both still in their teens then) that his then-blooming acne was almost certainly due to his steroid obsession; she had told me, strangely proudly, that she'd looked it up on Wikipedia. And then again, a few years later, I'd confided in *her* that perhaps his explosive temper was, too. That, and perhaps cannabis-induced psychosis. But if there was any telling her, which by that time I'd accepted there wasn't, it wouldn't, perhaps *couldn't* come from me. Anything I advised her was too freighted with the baggage that came with being her big sister, our mother's henchwoman, and a know-all.

Water under the bridge now. Just a ripple of disturbed memory. Though last night's calls and text now felt like a finger taken out of a dam. Particularly the text, which had shaken me. I had never wanted the Kennedys in my life in the first place. I certainly didn't want them back in it now. Not in any shape or form. Ever.

Yet in a city of almost a quarter of a million people, here he was anyway. And it seemed he was already making waves. 'Poor man,' remarked the ward sister. 'He was telling me earlier, he's a chef at one of those country-house hotels over Lewes way.' So, I thought grimly, not just visiting. He lived here. 'Which means on top of everything else,' she continued, 'he's likely to lose his job too. Not exactly the sort of thing you can do one-handed, is it?' She looked fondly across at him. He was in a corner bay, his eyes closed, his hair a sooty halo. He would be the darling of the ward, I knew, in no time. 'Still, he's left-handed. So at least he can hang on to that positive, bless him. Anyway, you want a quick brew, Mrs Hamilton?'

Normally I would, because I was keen to get to know my colleagues better, but today I was more anxious to put the past back in its box, so, after asking Siddhant to take the others and make a start with the first patient, I headed over to the far end of the ward.

There was always an atmosphere around Aidan. Hope professed not to see it, but his moods used to leach from him like the artificial fragrance in a cheap fabric conditioner. He was either on a charm offensive, or spoiling for a row, never neutral. He could hold a room rapt, or poison an atmosphere in moments. In the latter years, those two states bent almost everything out of shape, as those around him – Hope, particularly, his mother, even my *own* mother – toiled, seemingly tirelessly, at the complicated, stressful business of trying desperately not to invoke the latter.

I wondered if he'd changed, or if his wife did the same. I wondered if he hit her as well. Wondered if he called *her* a bitch.

The atmosphere around him now was thick with poignancy and sadness, his bandaged stump front and centre, always drawing the eye in – like the grisly focal point in a painting by Caravaggio. There was also, I noted, a mobile phone on his bedside cupboard, complete with a charging lead, which snaked around to one of the sockets behind the bed. So the phone must have been retrieved when they found him, and brought in with him, and perhaps the charger was brought in by his wife yesterday.

He cut a tragic figure, as any new amputee cannot fail to, and I tried my hardest to see him only as a patient. But just looking at him again made the past come rushing in. I was taken straight back to the last time I ever spoke to him, three weeks before he finally walked out on my dying sister.

I hadn't meant to. By that time, I was timing my visits carefully. But Hope had called in such a state – after a row about yet another discovery of his serial infidelity – that I'd had no choice but to drive down to Brighton. I was dog-tired from having just finished a night shift in A and E and, having driven down in the rush hour and dropped a fractious Daniel round at a reliably disgruntled Mum's, I was anxious not to even see Aidan, let alone have to speak to him, because I wasn't sure I wouldn't lose it altogether. Because by that time, reality was staring me in the face. Because by that time, I already knew too much.

He knew it too. That much was obvious from the way he scowled at me – me, heading up the path, counting to ten, trying to rearrange my expression to something neutral, him heading down it, in a too-tight muscle T-shirt, his chef's whites bundled up in one meaty fist.

Butt out, he'd growled, as we sidestepped one another on the path. *Just butt the fuck out. This is none of your business, okay?*

Which struck me now, as it did then, as a bitter pill to swallow. As if my sister had given me any bloody choice.

I had a choice now, however, to take control. And I aimed to.

There were already three cards arranged on Aidan's bedside cabinet – two of them hand-drawn in felt tips, presumably by his daughters – but we were alone, so to address him as Mr Kennedy felt nonsensical.

'Aidan?' I said. His eyes flickered open. He blinked to clear them. 'Did you phone me last night?'

His gaze darted behind me then, as if in a silent plea for help. And, once again, strangely at odds with his overnight antics, I had the sense that he was afraid of me.

'Look, I'm sorry, right?' he said, shifting his leg beneath the blanket. 'I just . . . I just thought I ought to—' He exhaled heavily. 'Thought I ought to speak to you. I really don't need any more shit in my life right now, okay?'

So it had been him. Of *course* it had been him. And now he'd obligingly confirmed it. 'So you thought a good way to achieve that would be to then send a text calling me a bitch?'

His eyes pinged wide open, then he squeezed them tight shut. Then he groaned, put his hand to his forehead. 'Fuck,' he said. '*Fuck*. Shit, I actually *sent* that?'

I nodded. In other circumstances I wouldn't have left it at that – far from it – but we were on a ward, people milling about, so this was no place for a confrontation.

'Oh, *Christ* . . . Look, I'm sorry. I mean, I'm *really, really* sorry. I must have – *God* . . .' He groaned a second time. Screwed his palm into his eye sockets, first his left, then, more awkwardly, his right. 'I'm *sorry*, right? Look, I really don't want trouble, okay . . . I can't – *shit*—' He glanced behind me again, looking anxious. 'You know. Mum.' I noted that, miserably. So she *was* still of this earth. 'And like, with Jess and that . . .'

'Jess, as in your wife?'

He nodded. 'Look, *seriously*.' His voice was low now. 'I genuinely didn't realise. I never meant . . . It was probably just, you know, all the morphine I'd been given. I was—'

'Upset,' I supplied, keeping my voice calm and level. 'Not quite thinking straight. I understand that.' I understood that all too well. With Aidan, this was familiar territory.

He grabbed at that as if I'd thrown him a life raft. 'Exactly. *Exactly.* Look, I know how it looks, and I'm not making excuses, but I *genuinely* did not realise I'd sent that.'

'Just thought it.'

'*No.* Okay, yes. I mean *no!*' He exhaled heavily. 'Oh, Christ. I don't *know*. What can I say? I'm just a fuck-up, okay?' He rolled his eyes theatrically. 'You, of *all* people, should know that.'

The corners of his mouth twitched as he spoke, as if ghosts rising to a familiar challenge. Old habits, I thought. Turn the charm on. The winning smile. But it wasn't quite a smile. Just an echo of an expression. I didn't respond – I doubted Christ would either – and it was immediately replaced by a grimace. His eyes were growing filmy and I guessed that he was trying not to cry. I suspected he'd cried a lot in the last twenty-four hours.

He's like a child, G. A man-child. A baby. You know, when I found out about that waitress and confronted him, he cried like one. Like, for hours.

Like, 'M'lud, I now present the case for the defence.' Which was how it always went with Hope. Had done since the beginning. No matter what he did to her, she always had his back. Made excuses for him. No matter how hard I tried, there was no getting through to her.

At least, till there was. Which had happened far, far too late. When the stakes had become far, far too high. I knew exactly how Hope would react to this if she were standing here now: extremely coldly. *Well, the bastard's certainly got something to cry about now.*

'It doesn't matter either way,' I pointed out. 'I want exactly the same as you do. For the past to remain in the past, where it belongs. So I'm going to have you transferred into the care of another doctor. Then you won't need to see me.' More importantly, I wouldn't need to see him. Or his mother. 'So you don't need to worry. Not on my account, anyway. Just, please, Aidan, no more calls. No more texts. No more contact.'

I watched a single tear form at the corner of his right eye, and then track down his cheek to his earlobe. Though he didn't acknowledge it – did he hope I hadn't noticed? – his right shoulder shifted very slightly, as if he was trying to move the hand that wasn't there. 'No more phone calls,' he said finally. 'No more texts. I promise. Look, I was just in a state, okay?' He lifted his left hand instead. Nodded again, towards the cannula. '*High* . . . I just—' He cleared his throat, as if genuinely struggling to speak now. 'I'm sorry. It just . . . Look, I'm in enough shit as it is, okay? I just don't want any more trouble.'

As if he seriously thought I might be looking to make some. Was he insane? No, I decided, just the same Aidan he always was. *I don't need this. Okay? I'm in enough shit. Okay? I was in a state. Okay?*

37

Ever on the defensive. Ever redirecting blame. *I didn't mean to hit her. She just really, really wound me up. She made me do it. Okay?*

'I know,' I said briskly. 'I understand your situation. I'm very sorry about your arm. Try to get some rest.'

I left him then, there being nothing else to add. Such conversations as needed to take place about his recovery and rehabilitation could and should be had by whoever took him on. As far as I was concerned, our professional relationship ended as of now too.

'Look, I'm *sorry*,' he said again, to my back, as I walked away. I didn't turn around. I headed straight to the cluster of medics at the other end of the ward and when I got there, motioned to Siddhant that I needed a quick word.

'Listen,' I said, when he'd stepped outside the huddle. 'Is Mr Porter around, d'you know? I need to have a quick word with him about Mr Kennedy.'

'Down in outpatients, as far as I know,' he said. 'Shall I call him?'

'No, no, don't worry,' I said, checking the time. With any luck, his afternoon clinic wouldn't have started yet. 'I'll pop down there. Just give me ten minutes.'

Neil Porter was one of the senior T and O consultants. One of the first I met – he was on the panel when I came for my interview – and, since he was an upper-limb specialist, the obvious colleague to ask to take Aidan on for me. Plus we had a connection – a med school in common – so I was hopeful.

I ran down to surgical outpatients and caught him just as he was returning to his consulting room with a mug of tea and a lurid green cake, presumably from the bake sale that seemed to happen every week at every hospital, in this case part of the push to get their hands on a new MRI scanner. 'Can I ask a favour?' I asked him.

'Absolutely not,' he said. And since he was also carrying a bunch of patient notes under his arm, and I was so wired about Aidan, it took a second before I realised he was joking.

'It's one of my new patients,' I explained. 'Emergency admission and amputation on Sunday morning. I have a personal connection with him.' Neil raised one eyebrow. 'He's my late sister's ex-partner – sorry, bit of a mouthful – and, well, things ended badly between them. It's been years since I've seen him – she died in 2011 – but, well, it's likely to be awkward for him. And for me, of course,' I added, 'so it wouldn't be appropriate for me to continue to treat him.'

'Of course, Grace,' he said, raising the cake as an affirmative. 'No problem. These things happen. Just let my secretary know. I'll pop up and introduce myself soon as I've finished clinic. You okay?' he added, and I realised I must look as flustered as I felt. He grinned then. 'Hey, he's not likely to be problematic, is he?'

I returned the smile. Shook my head. Said, 'For you? No, not at all.'

For me though? I wasn't so sure about that. Because wherever Aidan was, so too *surely* would be his mother; a woman for whom the loss of his arm would be a tragedy of seismic proportions, in a life already rocked to its foundations. As night followed day, if she could be, she would be there. And, as night followed day, once she found out who his surgeon was, she would blame me. Again.

And I did not want to be on the wrong side of Norma Kennedy.

Chapter 4

Almost every life, at some point, is destabilised by seismic shifts. We're all on the same road – the one signposted 'death, eventually' – but for some of us it arrives as an unanticipated wrecking ball, giving us no time to belt up and brace for it.

My sister's wrecking ball, her tumour, became my own seismic shift via the medium, as was Hope's way, of a text. Which wasn't unusual; I'd had a string of them over the previous week – short, excited missives, charting the progress, and emergence, of Dillon's second tooth. It was our main form of communication back then.

This was not that. *OMG!!!* it had read, on that random Wednesday morning. *OMG! OMG, sis! You won't believe this! I've had a FIT!!*

I read it twice. Not least because of the number of exclamation marks – a lot, even by her standards. It had come in while I was standing in my scrubs, slurping coffee. I was a specialist A and E registrar at that time, three years into a six-year/six-hospital rotation, and trying to juggle work, and all the studying, and, by that time, a toddler. Basically trying to be Superwoman, poisoning myself with caffeine instead of kryptonite. It sometimes felt as if coffee was more my life blood than my actual blood.

I read the text a third time. (A fit? What, as in a hissy fit? As in a fit for a job? A flower show? A new client? A life-changing commission? Because when your twenty-nine-year-old little sister sends a text about 'fits', your brain tends not to respond with the immediate thought 'brain'.) Then the next tranche of words came pinging in.

I'm in hospital. Waiting to be seen by a doctor. F***ing STUNNED. Was just soooo lucky Daisy was with me. Why the hell would I have a fit? Any ideas???????

All of a sudden, I had a lot of ideas. Way too many. All of them jockeying for supremacy. On the one hand . . . On the other hand . . . Maybe this . . . Maybe that . . . Highly unlikely, but . . . Perhaps . . . No, not that . . . No, but *surely* . . . Just possibly . . . *But* . . .

I texted back, needing details. *Is it okay to call you?*

Ten seconds went by. Twenty. Twenty-five. Forty. I called anyway. It went straight to voicemail. Perhaps the doctor had arrived. Was already working through all the differential diagnoses. Why, indeed. Why *would* Hope have a fit? She was a mother too by then; Dillon was seven months old. Could it in some way be related to that? Not for the first time, I thought dark thoughts about Aidan. About drink. About drugs. About how relatively little, as far as I could tell, parenthood seemed to have clipped Hope's or his (especially his) wings. Unsettled now, and anxious, I went to see the next patient. A seven-year-old boy with a foreign body up his nose, the extraction of which – it turned out to be a BB gun pellet – would go on to stay with me forever. Part of a cluster of satellite memories that would always orbit around that heartbreaking central black hole.

Then, too soon after – the speed of investigation being its own worrying clinical sign – came a definitive diagnosis. Which shook the ground beneath my feet after just three dreadful days. Days in which, after an examination, then another, then a scan, then another scan, Hope metamorphosed from a young mother who'd had an unexplained seizure to a person who had a tumour inside her head.

A little knowledge, so goes the saying, can be a dangerous thing. Too much knowledge, on the other hand, is often an oxymoron. And being blessed with it, in this situation, *was* a kind of blessing. It blessed me with time to adapt to the reality Hope was facing, when the time came for it to be spelled out to her, in no uncertain terms, three months later. And there really *were* no uncertain terms. Her prognosis, I already knew, was 'death, soon'.

And I needed that time, because by a short process of elimination (my father was by now dead, plus Hope hated him anyway, my mother was in pieces, Aidan stupefied with shock) it was me who went along with her for her reckoning of all reckonings.

I drove there in a state of distress and disquiet, realising that this appointment to discuss her coming death constituted only the fourth or fifth time I'd seen my little sister since Dillon was born. Yes, to be expected – geography, work, family commitments, our very different lifestyles – but it was a number that now took on a shocking significance.

As they'd suspected even before they did the biopsy, Hope's cancer was inoperable, both because of where it was and what it was. She had a grade-four astrocytoma, the consultant told her, or glioblastoma – a tumour that had been growing undetected in her glial cells, probably for many months, even years.

Astro? she'd asked. Was the very first thing she asked him. Not *How long have I got?* Or *Is there anything else that can be done for me?* Or *FUCK*, which is what I was saying as I sat there next to her, over and over and over, inside my head.

Astro, he explained, because the glial cells are star-shaped. I rather like that, she said, to his ill-concealed astonishment. That they're star cells, she qualified. Because we're all made of stardust. And I'm obviously more starry than most.

Which fuzzy logic (fuzzy *ill*ogic) seemed, weirdly, to sustain her. On the way home (via picking baby Dillon up from his Nanna Norma's; it was only the second time I'd ever met Aidan's mother) she even became coolly philosophical about the manner of her impending death. Forget all that nonsense about Jesus wanting kids for sunbeams, she said, wasn't the business of her star cells wanting her body to return to stardust just, like, so much more rational, so much more apt, so much more *pleasing* a notion to contemplate? And since the consultant had made it clear that she was going to die anyway, was there really any point in her having radiotherapy or chemotherapy? In going through it all, in not being fully present for her baby, just to gain a scant two or three extra months?

I told her it was her call. But Mum convinced her. As mums must. *Keep the faith. Because you never know – they might find a cure!*

She had both. Both were hell.

She died anyway.

And every last horrible, shitty, violent, controlling, evil, *evil* thing that bastard Aidan ever did to her – every put-down, every slap, every thump he landed on her, every instance of him having sex with some girl who was *not* her, every day (which was most of them) when he was drunk or high or both, every day, which was *all* of them, when he utterly failed to cherish her – died, as far as I was concerned, along with her. Only Matt knew the half of it, and that was how it would stay.

And not just because Aidan could no longer hurt her. Because I truly believed it was the right thing to do. Let it go, let it go, let it go, let it *go*. Like I was south London's answer to Princess Elsa.

But had that been the right thing to do? In running from the Kennedy family fire, saving only Dillon and letting the rest burn to ashes, had I made a colossal mistake? What if Norma, Aidan's adoring mother, had known the half of it as well? Would things have turned out any differently?

43

It was now one minute to visiting time. And walking back to the ward after seeing Neil, I was beginning to wonder. Because, almost as night followed day, the rule generally held: if a person who'd undergone major surgery had family, then that family would come and visit them as soon and as often as they were able.

So if Norma was able, she would be there today.

Which was why, when I saw her, it wasn't a shock. It wasn't even an unlucky coincidence. Of *course* she'd be coming. She was walking towards the ward from the opposite end of the hospital, with a magazine in one hand and a brown paper bag in the other – fruit, presumably, from the stall down in the main concourse.

The last time I saw Aidan's mother – as opposed to being screamed at down the phone by her, as opposed to being sent sinister 'gifts' – was around four months after Hope's death. So – I did the sums as I walked – around eight and a half years ago. And, unlike her son, she looked remarkably unchanged. In part that was because her hair was still unfeasibly black, but also because of her familiar bearing; she wasn't so much walking as bulldozing her way down the corridor, slight as she was, as if driving geese, or maybe cattle. As if the very air in front of her was out to get her. Never was a person's personality so at odds with the soft pastel hues she'd always favoured.

I checked myself. Reminded myself that life had not been kind to her. In one specific case, by my hand, at least in her view. I didn't break stride, though, because the slightly surreal *High Noon*-ish quality of our situation wasn't lost on me, so reminiscent was it of the circumstances of the last time we spoke. Though being closer, I was going to arrive at the ward before she did, and I couldn't imagine she'd make any sort of scene there.

But I underestimated her. She saw me and sped up immediately, the soles of her shoes slapping audibly down on the supposedly noise-dampening vinyl. So I had no choice but to acknowledge

44

her, though, ridiculously, my instinct was to turn around and run the other way. Ridiculous because she must have been, what, seventy-eight now, or something? An elderly lady, I reminded myself, a diminutive elderly lady, who was upset, and very stressed, and *in extremis*.

But the memory of some confrontations never leaves you. I straightened my back, noted the way she clutched the paper bag against her. Noted the rings she still wore on all eight fingers, like knuckle-dusters. 'Norma,' I began. 'I'm so sorry about—'

'Don't even *speak* to me,' she hissed. 'You fecking *butcher*.'

She marched past me then, on into the ward, and to her son, leaving her long-familiar perfume clinging to the air in her wake. She had obviously already been told I was the surgeon.

I stood in the corridor for a moment, letting the adrenaline rush subside a bit, clenching and unclenching my tingling fingers, steeling myself to follow. Twice now. Son and mother. I was a bitch and now a butcher. Would the third denouncement of my character come by cockcrow? One thing was certain. However much I believed I'd escaped it, my little sister's past had chased me down yet again.

Chapter 5

Most of the time, give or take, I'd have a dozen or so inpatients spread across the two dedicated orthopaedic wards. But as there were rarely sufficient beds, I would also have outliers, who could be billeted pretty much anywhere.

Luckily, it having been a busy night, Aidan Kennedy had been an outlier. So via a mixture of good luck and bed-shortage logistics, I had no need to visit the ward he was on for the next couple of days, which made it less likely I'd bump into Norma again. And with Aidan's amputation having been without complication, by the end of the week he would be gone.

And would that be the end of it? Now he was no longer my patient, I hoped so. He'd made it clear that he wanted that too. However vengeful his mother might feel, and I didn't doubt that for a moment, there was no benefit for Aidan in dredging up the past; he was right – he was in enough trouble already. Although to be sure I heard no more from him, I didn't delete his number. Instead, I kept it and blocked him.

By Friday – my last day in work before Christmas – I had almost convinced myself it would be the end of it, too. But I was wrong. It was only the beginning.

One of the big leaps from specialist registrar to consultant is the appointment of a clinical secretary. Mine was called Jenny, and I shared her with two other consultants. She, in turn, shared an office with four other secretaries, a large open-plan space from which our own offices sprouted.

Bar the cubbyhole that had served me as an A and E senior registrar, it was also the first time in my life that I'd had any sort of office, and though the window, which was draughty, looked out over one of the car parks, and the empty MDF shelves bowed beneath the ghosts of long-redundant medical textbooks, it was such a novelty to have a space that was for my exclusive use that two weekends into my new job I'd declared we were going on a family outing, dragging Matt and both the boys down so we could scrub the pitted lino, and paint the walls a calming shade of pale green.

As theatre started early, I was in before Jenny most days, and today, being a theatre day, it was lunchtime before I touched base with my desk, to find a poinsettia on it, in a tissue-wrapped pot, with petals almost the same colour as my scrubs.

'Daughter of one of your patients dropped that in earlier,' Jenny told me, as she came in with an armful of paperwork. 'The lady whose hip you resurfaced on Friday?' We were still at the getting-to-know-each-other stage in our relationship, but already I had a sense that we were going to get along. We were around the same age, and, even more importantly, were the same gender. A first, she'd explained on my first day in post, in her entire life as a medical secretary. 'Oh, and Grace, I don't know if you've had a chance to check your diary yet, but Dr Shelley needs to see you, so I've put him in for three, right after the clinical audit meeting. Is that okay?'

I nodded. 'Fine. What about? Did he say?'

She shook her head. 'No. But probably just to talk through the winter pressures plan, I imagine.'

As well as being a physician, Dr Shelley was the hospital's medical director, and when he arrived at my office, only moments after I'd returned to it, I was surprised to see that he wasn't alone.

He had a woman with him, who I didn't recognise. She looked to be in her fifties, was carrying a clear plastic slip folder, and had an NHS lanyard round her neck. Like him, she was smiling, but in a way that unsettled me, because it was the sort of smile you adopted when you were hoping to provide reassurance in the face of being the bearer of bad news.

I jumped up from my chair to go and grab the spare one for her to sit on – I had two, but only one was on the other side of my desk – but Dr Shelley beat me to it, obviously reading my intention. 'No worries, stay put,' he said, as he plucked it from the corner. He placed it beside the other one, but before sitting down on it, the woman turned and closed my office door.

'Everything okay?' I asked, looking from one to the other, smiling quizzically. 'This is beginning to feel a bit like a deputation.'

Dr Shelley frowned.

'I'm afraid that's because it is, Grace. This is Carol Lightfoot,' he went on. 'Our complaints officer. I'm really sorry,' he said as he sat down on the other chair, 'terrible timing, I know, but we've had a letter come in this morning.'

It took a nanosecond for me to put the pieces into place. 'A *complaint* letter?' He nodded. 'About me?'

He nodded again. The woman was already pulling something from the slip case. 'Here,' she said, passing it across to me. 'Have a read.'

It was handwritten, the backwards-sloping writing covering both sides of the paper, and as I read it, I had an increasingly sick feeling in my stomach, because I immediately knew who it was about. Phrases started jumping out at me, like snapping piranhas – *known to the surgeon, negligence, highly unprofessional* – as whoever wrote it made it clear that, in their 'firm' opinion, Aidan Kennedy's hand and lower arm should never have been amputated, that a second opinion should have immediately been sought, that my decision to remove it without getting one – my *professional judgement* – was '*substantially compromised by Mrs Hamilton's former relationship to Mr Kennedy*' and that '*given her long-standing personal enmity towards him, she should have immediately understood that it would be highly inappropriate for her to even operate on him in the first place. To have gone ahead with the amputation without declaring her relationship with him was therefore tantamount to gross medical negligence.*'

I expected to see Norma's name scrawled at the bottom, but the letter was signed Mrs J Kennedy. I turned it back over again. Noted the address, which was in Moulsecoomb, on the north-east edge of Brighton. And the date above 'to whom it may concern', which was today's.

I felt heat flood my cheeks. It was part embarrassment – I might be the one sitting behind the desk, but it was the opposite to how this felt – but it was also anger and incredulity. *Seriously?* How did *she* know I didn't seek a second opinion? And '*long-standing personal enmity towards him*' – on what evidence? Did she really think I'd spent the last decade even giving him a second thought?

Stop it, I told myself. See it for what it is. Spiteful nonsense.

But spiteful nonsense that had brought these two people to my office; it didn't matter that it was baseless. It was still humiliating, excruciatingly so. 'Was this delivered by hand?' I asked.

'Apparently so,' Carol Lightfoot confirmed, as I returned the letter into her waiting hand. 'By the patient's wife, when she came to collect him this morning. I'll email you a scanned copy of this, by the way.'

So he'd been discharged. Which at least meant I was spared the constant anxiety of accidentally bumping into Norma Kennedy again. But also denied the chance – and suddenly it felt scarily compelling – to march straight down to the ward and ask Aidan

Kennedy what the *hell* he thought he was playing at. It wouldn't be the first time I'd felt compelled to asked him that question, after all.

I breathed in deeply, then out again, slowly, through my nose. Reassured myself that, actually, this whole thing was risible. That there was absolutely nothing about that surgery I would have changed. 'This is preposterous,' I said. 'The hand and wrist were long beyond saving. There was no question that they could ever have been reconstructed. Absolutely none.' But even as I said that, I was all too aware that the bigger issue here was not the matter of my competence as a doctor. What they were insinuating – and, given the formal language, I imagined there must have been some outside input in the wording, from a personal injury solicitor's website – was that I essentially took his arm off out of some sort of sick desire for revenge.

'I don't doubt your clinical judgement for an instant, Grace,' Tim Shelley said. He couldn't know why, but both the immediacy of his response and the firmness of his tone reassured me, at least a little. 'But I'm sure you know the drill. We will still need to go through the motions, obviously.'

'Of course,' I said.

'Is it true that you know him?' Carol Lightfoot asked.

'*Knew* him,' I corrected her. 'But that was nearly ten years ago. And I certainly didn't recognise him when I examined him in ICU. He was being intubated and his face was swollen and bloody from the collision. I only realised who he was when I saw him on the ward post-op, and once I did, I obviously asked a colleague to take over his care. He's now Neil Porter's patient. In fact, I—'

Dr Shelley raised a hand. 'Don't worry, Grace, we don't need to go through all the whys and wherefores at this point. We just wanted to come up and let you know in person before we put the wheels in motion. I'm guessing you've not been in this kind of situation before?'

I shook my head miserably. 'You guess right, Dr Shelley.'

'It's *Tim*. And, please, Grace, try not to worry too much. I know it's upsetting to have something like this happen, but it comes to us all sooner or later. And please be reassured that you will have our full support. Anyway, what happens now is that we have fourteen days to respond, so Carol will send out an initial holding letter, acknowledging the patient's distress, though obviously not admitting any liability. It'll also confirm that we'll be conducting an independent investigation. Then at some point, once we've gathered what we need from the notes – we've already requested them, yes, Carol?' She nodded. 'We'll interview you formally, and, based on the outcome of all of that, we'll all get together again so we can discuss the contents of our reply, let's hope not *too* long into the new year.'

'And what do I do in the meantime?' I asked. 'Anything? I'm thinking I should contact my medical defence union, shouldn't I?' *And how*, I thought, because I knew the sort of people I was dealing with, and, given the way she'd spoken to me, or, rather, hadn't, I didn't doubt for a moment that Norma was involved. And it grieved me to realise that now this had happened, my colleagues *would* have to know at least some of the whys and wherefores. Anger welled in me. Distressingly, because I couldn't bear to have it happen in front of them, I felt as if I might burst into tears.

'You might want to, yes,' Dr Shelley said. 'Though as I say, Grace, please try not to stress. I have absolutely no doubt that you made the right call. You wait – chances are it'll be over before it's started. Try not to let it spoil your Christmas, okay?'

I nodded, rather than answered, determined not to cry. I saw them out then, and catching Jenny's quizzical gaze over her monitor, raised a thumb to reassure her before returning to my desk, leaving the office door open wide, so I couldn't.

Grace, I thought. *At all times, maintain a state of grace.* A mantra I adopted at fourteen (a silly one, an affectation; I'm not at all religious), because if you have been given a name that demands you live up to it, it's natural, at least for the sort of child I was, to try. Grace, from the Latin, meaning *pleasing*.

Listen, your name's Grace because they knew you were always going to have it. I'm Hope because they took one look at me and it struck them immediately – they could only hope against all hope that I turned out like you. Ha – that worked out well for them, didn't it?

Hope's words had always stayed with me – mostly because of the way she'd said them. Not in anger, exactly, more defeated resignation. She hadn't been dying then, just indulging herself in one of her periodic bouts of self-flagellation. It wasn't out of the blue either; we were tentatively reopening communications, some time after she and Aidan had both got comprehensively trashed at my wedding, and she'd thrown a glass of champagne all over Dad's second wife.

To make matters worse, my mother, who was also drunk (stressed about being 'forced' to be in the same room as my father, she'd apparently started early), had applauded this and cheered, causing a silence so thick and heavy you could have cut it with the cake knife. Matt – who'd shown such incredible forbearance up to that point – lost it then and told all three of them to sling their hooks. And as I watched this excruciating exchange (and that really was the only word for it), I realised it was time to make the same choice. I was done with trying to stitch together the tattered remnants of my family. And as neither got in touch, which added sadness to my anger, it was months before we spoke to any of them again.

Lost months, in Hope's case, which I would never have again. And which I now had a lifetime to regret.

Grace, I thought, as I returned to the paperwork in front of me. I must live up to my name. I must quell the panic, the fury, the still-rising nausea, and remember that I had done nothing wrong.

That I hadn't a shred of concern about my clinical judgement. That the photographs *alone* would be sufficient to confirm it was sound. But how ironic that it should be something like this – a complaint that was so obviously without merit or foundation – when there had been so many occasions when I really had had to make a judgement, and with only a fraction of the confidence I'd had about that arm. When I'd had to make a call, knowing another surgeon might call it differently, knowing full well that I might need to defend it.

But this? I reached out and stroked a finger along one of the raspberry-red leaves of the poinsettia – this tangible evidence that the world was full of good, thoughtful people. A case where there was surely – no, definitely, *unequivocally* – no doubt. Which reassuring thought helped not a bit.

I hadn't been entirely truthful about not having been there, either. Back when I was still a very junior doctor, and on a placement at a GP surgery, I received a letter in the post from a firm of solicitors, acting for a seriously ill patient who was seeking compensation for a delay in diagnosis after a follow-up appointment letter, dictated by me, had been sent to a previous address. It wasn't anything to do with me – it was a mistake in their patient database. And my defence union then, as I knew they would now, made it clear I had nothing to worry about. Writing to me was just standard procedure, due diligence: they automatically wrote to everyone involved. The fear, though, the dread, the sick feeling in my stomach – none of those took a blind bit of notice.

What upset me most was that I couldn't tell anyone, and it hit me hard how alone and vulnerable I suddenly felt. Yes, I could tell Matt I'd had a complaint made against me – oh, and by the way, happy Christmas! – but obviously not who had made it. And this on top of the anxiety that had been stalking me since the moment I'd recognised Aidan. Just the very thought of being embroiled with that family again filled me with dread.

Chapter 6

There was no defined 'palliative care' end-stage for Hope. Despite the gruelling rounds of radiotherapy and the living hell of chemo, with no hope of a cure she was 'palliative' from day one, so, with Dillon to think about, she was encouraged from the start of treatment to think about what she might want to leave for him.

It was usual practice to encourage patients to create memory boxes for their children, especially those with little ones who were too young to understand what was going on. You could put anything you liked in them – letters, photos, poems, keepsakes – but, if they felt able, patients were urged to make recordings as well. Of them singing lullabies, telling stories, reading favourite books aloud. They even had a space at the attached support centre for them to do so. But Hope being Hope, she didn't want to hang around in places that kept reminding her that she was dying, and she certainly didn't want to hang around there with Dillon in tow.

Just people's faces, she said, *when they look at him. It goes right through me.*

No, she wanted to do it in the privacy of her own home. And with Aidan invariably working evenings (or sometimes, as she came to realise, finding solace for his 'dying girlfriend' woes elsewhere), and armed with the voice recorder and stash of memory sticks I'd amassed for her, she'd spend night after night reading everything she could lay her hands on, from the boxed set of Narnia books she'd kept since her own childhood, to Roald Dahl, to Dr. Seuss, to *Little House on the Prairie*. All the special stories she would have read to Dillon had she lived. But none of which (the sadness was still a weeping wound, even now) I'd been able to interest him in listening to in years.

She made recordings for me, too, which she'd put in the post. During those final awful months, they'd regularly plop on to my doormat and, naturally enough, I played the first of them as soon as I got it because I had no idea what it contained.

I don't know what I'd expected, quite, but it made for grim listening. An emotional confessional, which she'd obviously recorded in stages, it was a rambling account of how a pair of my jeans, which had 'mysteriously' disappeared during a weekend home from med school, had (as had been obvious to me at the time, despite her denials) indeed been 'borrowed' by her. And would have been returned too, were it not for the fact that she'd managed to get cooking oil all over them – she was characteristically light on the details of her evening – and dared not admit to it, for fear of my wrath. And also – and here the recording grew even more upsetting – because it went right to the heart of our dysfunction as siblings.

I had, she'd explained, *this sense of validation. This sense that it was alright for you. Not just about the jeans – okay, yes, but only as an example – but you had this thing you always did, which I could never seem to manage. If you wanted something, you made a plan, then you worked till you got it. Didn't matter if it was clothes, or a job, or your GCSEs, or your place at uni. Even to get our fucking father to bend to your sodding will. You applied yourself. You always did. They even told me that in school once. 'If only you could apply yourself, Hope, like your sister.'*

Because I never got that 'applying' gene, did I? You have no idea just how much I resented you for that. How much I hated you that day.

'Hope, please don't do this,' I said when I called her.

'Oh, just ignore it,' she told me. 'Feel free to bin it. I'm just cleansing my soul ready for the great beyond.' She'd laughed then. 'Dying person's prerogative.'

Still she kept sending them.

I couldn't bear to listen to them, but I couldn't bear to bin them either. So, traumatised and upset, I stashed them away – in an old iPhone box, in the bottom drawer of the spare-bedroom desk (long-established graveyard of obsolete tech), never imagining there would be a time when I'd ever want to hear them, but always knowing they were there, a piece of my little sister's soul. So when Matt accidentally chucked them out during one of his sporadic sort-outs, I was devastated. Why hadn't I taken better care of them? Why hadn't I taken better care of *her*?

Perhaps taking care of Mum was my penance. It was definitely why my expectations for Christmas were low – this our first in our new, not-quite-feeling-like-home home. It was becoming all too obvious that the speed of Mum's deterioration had stepped up a gear, the things she did so odd and distressing.

It had started only minutes after she'd arrived, early on Christmas morning. Matt had driven over to pick her up while I showered, and when I came back downstairs she was holed up in the downstairs loo. And had been there a while – 'Is Nanna alright?' Daniel had anxiously asked me – so I went and knocked. 'You okay in there, Mum?'

There was no answer. Nor any sound. I knocked again.

'Mum?'

'Alright, I'm *coming*.' The lock squeaked and the door was finally opened. Mum emerged with her hands clasped together as if cradling a small bird. '*Excuse* me,' she said, then bustled off to the kitchen. I stood aside, peering briefly into the cloakroom, where my gaze couldn't help but land on the poinsettia I'd been given, and which sat, looking festive, on the windowsill.

Or had. Because, for whatever reason, she had removed every single petal.

And the day seemed set to proceed in the same vein. I was desperate to get outside, go for a walk, take the boys down to the sea, but the weather was awful, squally wind and rain thumping regularly against the windows, and they were happier in any case diving into their presents. And to go out alone, wilfully get drenched just to grab a bit of time to get my head straight, would mean leaving Matt to deal with Mum, and I didn't feel I could. Since he'd agreed to move down here – no small thing, for a multitude of reasons – I was about a million marriage brownie points short of enough. The sense of owing him was something I hadn't fully factored into the equation, and though we never discussed it, so I didn't have his take on the massive new imbalance in the relationship scales, it coloured everything Mum-related, and perhaps always would.

Instead, I tried to put the complaint out of my mind, enjoy the boys, and keep Mum occupied by drafting her in to help me prepare our Christmas dinner. Some skill sets, I'd reasoned, both from research and experience, endured because they were so well embedded. My paternal grandmother, for instance, who had also died with dementia, could still, when so much of her was lost (she recognised no one), make a pretty reasonable cup of tea. That she made them endlessly, sometimes lining up multiple cups and saucers for imaginary guests, was neither here nor there. She still understood, and could follow, the basic steps.

I should have known better. While I was in the den off the kitchen, helping Dillon set up his new VR headset, she had, at my suggestion, prepped all the carrots and parsnips – the former into minuscule orange dice, and the latter into tiny diamonds, as if they were runner beans.

Most poignant of all was that she looked so delighted with her efforts, and even as I counted to three in my head and told her what a great job she'd done, I marvelled at the myriad ways a brain could malfunction, at just how complex were the connections that we took so much for granted.

'So, what's next?' she asked brightly.

'How about you lay the table?' I suggested. 'Daniel, d'you want to help Nanna? Put the crackers out and everything?' And to watch them was like a balm for my tense, scratchy mood; her taking charge, and him following along like a loyal foot soldier behind her, quietly rearranging the misplaced cutlery and turning the table mats right side up, and every so often looking across at me and grinning.

What a simple thing it was, I thought, to see life the way a child does. To just see crazy Nanna, doing her crazy Nanna thing. It was just what it was, and that was how we'd urged the boys to see it. To understand that dementia was an illness like any other. That just as a broken leg might mean walking with a limp, so an injured brain was what made her limp mentally. The only difference, we'd explained to them, was that she wouldn't get better, so it was important that they saw the funny side and made the most of her while they could, till such time as she disappeared beyond reach.

Her enjoying spending time with *them*, though, was the greater revelation. One major lesson for me when I'd first become a mother was the realisation that the joy of being anointed as a grandparent was not universal; that no sea change in temperament necessarily occurred. That not all grandmothers called Joy lived up to their names. I'd had high hopes that this new stage would mark a change in our relationship, but soon learned that a distant, self-involved, and not terribly maternal mother could become a distant and self-involved grandmother too.

Which made it sad that it was only now, with her higher functions failing, that she found a pleasure in her grandsons' affectionate, undemanding company that had eluded her much of the time when she was well. Back then, they more often than not had a strictly time-limited appeal for her – after which time they bored her or got on her nerves.

Which I knew wasn't all my mother's fault. I never knew my maternal grandmother because she died in a road accident when Mum was four. She was raised then by a father who, consumed by his grief, could barely function (we learned much later that he had twice attempted suicide), and a grandmother who felt it her duty to counteract the effects of her – to her mind – self-indulgently grieving son, by spanking Mum with a stick for the smallest transgression. She liked her punishments to be short, sharp, and physical. Of physical affection, on the other hand, there was none. When Mum was eleven, without a squeak of dissent from my grandfather, my great-grandmother packed her off to boarding school.

Academically, it was probably the making of my mother (she left university with a first in mathematics, and went on to have a stellar teaching career). Emotionally, it probably destroyed her.

In any merry-go-round discussions about the endlessly debate-worthy subject of my family, this snapshot of my mother's miserable childhood would come up again and again. It seemed to be both the root of why she never really hugged us (or our father, as it turned out; a few months before he finally left her, in one almighty firework-extravaganza of a row, I heard him yelling at her that she had all the warmth of a North Atlantic cod – funny, the things you remember) and the reason she found marriage and mothering such an exasperating business; she'd never had a template to work from.

I kept reminding myself of this, rote fashion, all through the rest of Christmas Day, when, more than once, I was aware of Dillon's anxiety around her. The boys hadn't spent such a lengthy chunk of time with Mum continuously since we'd moved down to Brighton, and where Daniel seemed able to shrug off the odd things she said and did, I'd more than once spotted Dillon appearing tense around her, watchful, as if keeping a wary eye on a dangerous-looking animal, much as he'd always done whenever we'd visited a farm park or petting zoo. As if she might snap at him, or bite his hand, without warning.

But now we were two-thirds done with Boxing Day, and an end was in sight. I was just congratulating myself on a job reasonably well done when, quite without warning, and obviously without meaning to, it was me that she tipped over the edge.

Lunch done, she and the boys were in the living room, watching *Toy Story* (again) while Matt and I finished off the clearing up. I was desperate by now to get outside; just to *be* outside. To feel some cold on my cheeks instead of the warmth of a suffocatingly over-heated house. To be alone for a bit with my still-racing thoughts about the complaint process that was still hanging over me.

But it felt self-indulgent to do so, so instead I put the kettle on, to make tea. And once I'd done that, I popped my head round the living-room door. 'Cuppa, Mum?'

A moment passed, and I wasn't sure she'd heard me. 'Mum?'

Her head swivelled on her neck, almost *Exorcist*-style.

'Will you just GO AWAY, you stupid, irritating woman!'

She turned away then, back to Woody, her dismissal forgotten, and because both boys were now looking at me with their anxious, 'is this just a Nanna thing?' expressions, I pulled a face (eyes crossed, jazz hands, smile-and-wink, in that order) to reassure them that all was well before retreating back into the kitchen, where I was immediately ambushed by such a welling of emotion that a sob, out of nowhere, escaped my lips.

Matt, who'd been unloading the dishwasher, turned around, confused. 'You okay?' he said.

I knew I couldn't speak, so I didn't even try. Just shook my head, left the room and ran up the stairs.

He followed me up there five minutes later, presumably to give me time to compose myself. Matt hated, *really* hated, to see me crying.

I was in the en suite when he appeared in the bedroom doorway, trying to deep-breathe myself back into a state of composure. He had one hand on the door handle, a Christmas tea towel slung over his shoulder, and a look of what I assumed he hoped conveyed husbandly concern, but provided only the thinnest veil over his obvious irritation. 'What's *wrong* with you?'

I stamped on the pedal-bin lever. Not 'What's wrong with you.' 'What's *wrong* with you.' The difference only made me cry harder.

'Nothing. It's nothing. I'm *fine*,' I told him, dropping the piece of mascara-streaked loo roll into the bin, knowing that, as much as him, I was trying to reassure myself.

He walked across to join me in the en suite. 'No, you're not.'

I turned away from him to turn the tap on, splashed some water on my face. 'I am. *Honestly*. I'm just, I don't know . . . I'm just feeling a bit emotionally exhausted. Just Mum snapping at me the way she does—'

'What? What did she say?'

I grabbed the hand towel and scoured my face with it. Tried to still the rhythmic shudders. 'It doesn't matter.' I lowered the towel, met his reflection in the mirror. '*Honestly*,' I told it. 'I'm okay now. I'm fine. Just having a moment. Go back down. I won't be long, I'll just—'

'Will you stop saying you're bloody fine when you're not! And stop it with all this "Mum" business. This is not about Mum. I know it's not. You've been like this for days.'

I dried my hands, then plucked another couple of pieces of loo roll off the holder, and even as I swabbed away at the tears – they just wouldn't stop welling now – the less emotional part of my brain registered that, despite us being so bad at communicating lately,

Matt was no less capable of reading me than he ever was. It was a comfort, but it made me want to cry even more.

And want so much to just *tell* him. Sod it. We'd done Christmas now, hadn't we? I sat down on the edge of the bath. 'I've had a complaint made against me.'

'*What?*'

He was suddenly all ears. Shifting gear, stiffening, as if readying himself for a fight. I had a bad time once, at work, when I was surgical registrar, under a boss who was as much consultant misogynist as consultant surgeon. A shouter. A thrower of surgical instruments. An ageing lion, he had a reputation for taking the term 'theatre' literally, and when stressed – which he often was, as he was going through an ugly divorce at the time – could reduce not just me, but whole teams to tears. I'd often cry in the evenings, too, and I've never been a crier. And Matt would duly bristle. *I don't care if he's having the divorce from hell. I'm going to go up to that hospital and knock his bloody block off!*

Matt, who, to my knowledge, had never hit anyone in his life. But, full of impotent rage, would get so incredibly angry. And I never knew quite how to manage it. I could handle my own anger, refuse to let it rule me, because I had seen and heard, and felt, so much of it growing up. I knew that you could spread a slick of bile just as easily as you could sprinkle fairy dust, that angry feelings could be just as contagious as happy ones. So I'd just grind it out, because what else was there to do? I'd get up in the dark, sick with nerves, a knot of anxiety in my stomach, learn my craft, keep my head down, get through the day, return home. Dogged stoicism was sewn into the fabric of my being. But on some nights I'd get in, and, without even taking my coat off, I'd just lie down on the living-room floor and leak tears. And on those nights Matt had no idea what to do with me either. And I knew why, as well. Because if I crumbled, he crumbled; the whole edifice crumbled.

I could see it in his eyes now. That familiar blend of anxiety and anger. *What the hell am I supposed to do with her?*

'When?' he snapped. 'Who from?'

'Last week. A patient.'

'Why the hell didn't you tell me? What patient? What about?'

'The amputee,' I said carefully. 'That RTC when I was on call the weekend before last?'

'The bloke who hit the lorry?'

I nodded. 'They're saying I shouldn't have amputated. That I should have got a second opinion. That the arm could have been saved.'

'Could it?'

I dispatched the second wodge of paper to the bin. Sniffed. Shook my head. 'Absolutely not.'

'So they're just trying it on, then. After money.'

God, how I wished I could tell Matt the truth. 'Not necessarily,' I felt compelled to say. 'They might genuinely think it could have. They haven't seen the pictures, have they?'

'But they will now.'

'Yes, of course. And they're unequivocal.'

'So there's no case to answer, surely?'

'No. None at all. Not in theory.'

'So why the hell are you in such a state about it? These things happen all the time, don't they? That's precisely why you pay obscene amounts in medical defence insurance premiums, isn't it?'

'It's not that. It's just the *fact* of it. Being so new. Having a complaint made at *all*. Being accused of bloody *negligence*, of all things. Doesn't matter that it's groundless – it's still hanging over me. The embarrassment. Having to be interviewed. Causing everyone so much *trouble* . . .'

This seemed to set fire to something in him. He looked incredulously at me. 'What the hell are you *on* about? How are *you* causing anyone any trouble? And what d'you mean, "in theory"? Do they have a case or don't they?'

'*No!*' But as soon as I said this, something sparked in me too, and the tears I'd been mopping refused to be stopped any more. I tugged at the loo roll again, but did it too sharply, and a ribbon of paper, propelled by its own momentum, waterfalled down and started pooling on the tiles.

Matt put a hand out to stop it. He looked completely exasperated now. 'So why,' he asked a second time, 'are you in such a *state*? What aren't you telling me?'

I ripped another wodge of paper from the end of the ribbon. '*Nothing.*'

'Grace, *tell* me.'

'There's *nothing!*'

'Stop lying to me!'

'I'm *not!*'

But I was, and I couldn't keep it up any longer. Because *he* knew that as well – my snivelling made it all too obvious. 'Look, I can't. Matt, you know I can't discuss any of this with you.'

'Bollocks,' he said firmly. 'They can take their patient-confidentiality rules and shove them where the sun doesn't shine. I'm not having my wife in this state and not know why. Come on, spill, for Christ's sake. What aren't you telling me?'

He'd raised his voice now, which only made me cry more.

Which made him crosser still. 'For Christ's sake, Grace, I'm your *husband*. Don't you think that gives me a right to know the reason why you're in this mess? Look at you!'

I couldn't imagine anything I'd rather have done less at that moment. 'It's not *about* rights,' I snapped back at him, blowing my nose; still, infuriatingly, unable to stop the tears pouring out of me. 'It's about the nature of my fucking *profession*.'

This knocked him slightly sideways. '*Whoa*. Jesus, Grace. Get a grip, will you? And stop being so bloody disingenuous.'

'I'd be able to get a grip if you'd just stop bloody shouting!'

He threw his hands up. 'Okay, *okay*. I'm *sorry*. But I don't think you get that it's hard for *me*, too. I know your work is important. I know it takes it out of you. I know you're stressed about your mother. But hello? I'm *still here*.'

He squatted down beside the bath then, so he was looking up rather than down at me. 'Look, I'm sorry to raise my voice. But you've got to stop shutting me out, okay?' He lifted a hand, traced an arc with his thumb over my wet cheek. 'State of you,' he said. 'You carrying on all the time as if you're Super-bloody-woman, but, trust me, you look more like Alice Cooper's granny right now. More to the point,' he added, his tone softening, 'who the hell do you think I'm going to tell exactly? The *Daily Mail*? The police? Look, is there more to this, or isn't there?'

I wasn't in the habit of breaking rules. I never had been. But there was another rule in marriages, and right now, it felt by far the more important one. So even as I knew I mustn't, I couldn't seem to stop myself.

'It's Aidan. The man whose arm I amputated is Aidan.'

It took a moment for the name to sink in. Then, as if it was too indigestible to swallow, he spat it out again. '*Aidan?* Aidan as in *Kennedy*? It's Aidan Kennedy's arm you've amputated?'

I nodded, and the stream of air rushing out as he exhaled was powerful enough that I felt a ripple cross my forehead. He lifted a hand to his own then, ploughed his fingers through his hair. 'Jesus *Christ*. So this complaint he's put in, it's malicious then? That's pretty rich. Or is he just chancing his arm – ha, sorry, *not* – in the hopes of compensation?'

'It's from his wife.'

He gaped. 'That lowlife has a *wife*?'

'And two children. Two little girls. It's not likely to get that far, because they've already been through the op notes, but I don't doubt they'll try, based on the fact that I knew who he was. They're saying that knowing him affected my judgement. That even if I called it right, I still shouldn't have done the surgery. That doing so constituted professional negligence.'

'What an *utter* load of nonsense,' he said, and I was grateful for his instinctive loyalty at least. 'At six on a Sunday morning? Like they have a cupboard just off theatre full of idling trauma surgeons playing fucking Uno – as *if*! Did you, though?'

'Recognise him? God, no. He was under a mask by the time I got there, and even if he hadn't been, I still doubt I would have because his face was such a mess. No one knew who he was. He had no ID on him.'

'Well, *that* bloody figures. So when did you realise?'

'Not till I saw him on my ward round, post-op. And once I *did* recognise him, I obviously got him transferred to another consultant – for his sake as much as mine. He looked pretty horrified to see me.'

'I don't doubt it. But, *Christ*, Grace, why the hell didn't you tell me?'

'Because I thought that would be the last of it. That he'd *want* it to be the last of it. I never thought for a *moment* that he'd do something like this.'

'You're joking. That's exactly the sort of thing he'd try. He'd be all over it.' He put thumb and forefinger together and rubbed them to illustrate. 'God, that *bloody* family! If I—'

He was interrupted by the sound of elephants thundering up the stairs. 'Da-ad!' Dillon's voice. The boys tumbled into the bedroom, balls of energy in their matching Christmas jumpers. 'Nanna fell asleep,' Daniel said, while Dillon pulled on Matt's sleeve. 'So we've paused the film for later. Can we build my Lego Land Rover now, please please please *please*?'

'Course we can,' Matt said. 'Well, at least make a start on it. And while we're doing that,' he added, glancing out of the bedroom window, 'Mum can take herself off for her walk in the woods before it gets too dark. Plan?'

So we trooped back downstairs, and though professional instinct told me to regret telling Matt about Aidan, the relief at having done so was too immense. I decided I'd just have to square it with my conscience later. And given what they'd done, were clearly trying to do, anyway, weren't all bets – and boxing gloves – now off?

Chapter 7

In the end, because Dillon was keen to go with me, we jumped in my car and drove down to the beach at Rottingdean, so he could practise his stone-skimming technique.

I'd been surprised by his enthusiasm for coming out for a walk at all – though the rain had finally stopped, it was still a dark, chilly afternoon, growing darker, and he usually enjoyed helping Daniel build his Lego. But he clearly had his reasons; he was uncharacteristically quiet during the journey, and by the time we'd parked and put our beanies on, it became obvious he had something on his mind. I knew he'd had a bit of a falling-out with a boy he usually walked home from school with, because Daniel had told me. Was that what he was brooding on, I wondered?

'You okay, bubs?' I asked him. 'You've gone all quiet on me. Something up?'

'I'm okay,' he said, as we set off down the beach. Then he stopped on the shingle and tugged on my hand. 'Mum, why's Nanna always so mean to you? I don't like it when she's mean to you.'

Ah, I thought. *Ah*. So *that* was what was on his mind. 'I know, sweetie. But she doesn't mean to be,' I told him.

'She sounds like she does.' He looked up at me. 'Was that what made you cry?'

I knew better than to try and convince him that I hadn't been. Instead, I squeezed his hand and nodded. 'I don't much like it either,' I admitted. 'But remember what we said about Nanna's brain playing funny tricks?' He nodded. 'That's why we have to remember that it's not really Nanna. It's just her illness. Her dementia. She doesn't mean to be unkind. It just makes her a bit crotchety when she can't remember things the way she used to.'

We'd reached the shore now and I bent down and picked up a pebble. 'You know when you see this?' I squatted down and held the pebble out to him. 'Your eyes, in an instant, send a picture to your brain, and your brain, which is full of all the things you've ever seen, thinks "I recognise that. It's a pebble." But with Nanna, when her wires cross, the messages get muddled. Her eyes send the picture, but her brain doesn't recognise it. Or sometimes it thinks it does, but has remembered it wrong. It thinks "that's a potato" or "that's a plate of spaghetti".'

'Or a snail?' he suggested.

'Exactly. Which must be very confusing, mustn't it? Especially when other people tell you you're wrong, because we expect our eyes and brains to work together, don't we? I'm Mum, you're Dillon, it's Boxing Day afternoon. That's the sea, that's the sky. It's all pretty straightforward, isn't it? But when it *doesn't* work, it's frightening because you don't know what's what. What time it is, what day it is, sometimes even whether you've had your breakfast or not. Or when someone you know well walks up to you and says hello and you can't remember what their name is.' I stood up again. 'Can you imagine how frustrating that must be?'

He slipped his hand into mine again. 'But why does that mean she shouts at *you*?'

'It's just because she's cross, like I said. Not at me. At herself. You know when Dan's playing Fortnite and he's losing a battle, and if you interrupt him when that's happening, he snaps at you? It's a little bit like that, I think. It's not *you* he's cross with. He's just irritable. Snappy. And when Nanna gets snappy, she sometimes snaps at me. Don't worry, sweetie. It's okay. *I'm* okay. Because I know it's not her. It's just her dementia.'

'Do all old people get dementia?'

'No, they don't. Not by a long shot.'

'Will you?'

'Almost certainly not.'

'Why not?'

It was a reasonable enough question. And deserved a decent answer. But he was ten. There was nothing to be gained by making him worry. 'Because it's really, really rare,' I said, 'and by the time I'm Nanna's age, I'm pretty sure science will have found a cure anyway.' I stood up, squeezed his hand, then lifted it up to my lips and kissed it. 'So you don't need to worry, okay? About *anything*. Now then, shall we see if we can find some good stones?'

Dillon nodded, but he was chewing his lip now, and not meeting my eye.

'Are you sure you're alright, sweetie?' I said, crouching down again. Tears had pooled in his eyes.

Now he looked at me. 'Mummy, do you love Daniel more than me?'

I was stunned. Where had *this* come from? 'Not in a million years,' I said firmly. 'I love you both the same. As in billions. As in *squillions*. Why on *earth* would you think something like that?'

'Because Daniel's your *real* son, and I'm only your adopted one.'

'You are *absolutely* my real son. Every bit as much as Daniel.' I swept my thumbs across his cheeks to catch the falling tears. 'That's what the word adoption means. That you *are* my real son. Oh, sweetheart. What on earth has brought this on?'

'Nanna said . . .' He hesitated. Sniffed. Cried some more.

'Said what, bubs?' I pressed, anger sparking now. Of *course*. 'What did she say to you?'

'That you couldn't love me as much as Daniel because I'm not your *proper* son.'

Had my mother been there at that moment, I would have struggled not to slap her. Because this particular beast had reared its ugly head before, too many times. But not in a long time. Why now? '*What?*' I said. 'When?'

'This morning. After breakfast. When she came into our bedroom. She told me I should have a picture of my mummy by my bed. But she didn't mean you. She meant I should have a picture of Mummy Hope there. And when I told her I didn't want to, she got all cross with me and told me off.' He sobbed again, loudly. 'I *hate* her.'

I dropped to my knees and pulled him tight against me, biting down hard on all the words that could so easily come tumbling out because, right then, I hated her too. 'Oh, my darling boy,' I said, 'You *know* that's not true. You're—'

But Dillon hadn't finished. 'She said you'd never love me the way Mummy Hope loved me. Only Daniel. Because he's your *real* son, and I'm *her* son. But I'm *not*! I don't *want* to be! I want to be *your* son.' He let out a great shuddering sob. 'Nanna's horrible and I *hate* her.'

I shushed and soothed him till he quietened, then loosened my hug a little so I could look at him. 'Sweetie, you *know* how much I love you,' I said, touching a hand to my chest. 'Look. Nanna's right about one thing. That Mummy Hope loved you too.' (We had talked about this often, once. Then not so much. Then not at all.) 'And she's a star in the sky now, watching over you, remember? And she always, always will be. But I'm your mummy now. And I could not love you more. The things Nanna says sometimes – you have to understand, she doesn't mean them.'

'Is it just her dementia?'

'Exactly. Just the illness. Just her brain getting muddled.'

'She didn't sound muddled.'

'Ah, well, you see, that's the unfortunate thing about dementia. It gets into brains and it's super, super sneaky. Some of the time it makes people who have dementia sound almost *exactly* like they would if they *didn't* have dementia. *That's* what you must remember. That it's not Nanna speaking.'

Which seemed to satisfy him. But not me. I knew better.

We spent almost an hour on the beach, moving west along the tideline, and I silently found the wherewithal to still my seething brain, and accept that what I'd told Dillon was at least partly true. To inwardly chant *She didn't mean it, she can't help it*. To still Matt's voice, over years now: *Chill, hen. You need to stop overcompensating.* To still the voice that was saying, yes, but, at one point, it *was* true. And my biggest fear then, that it would *always* be true.

But it wasn't true *now*, I told myself sternly. And if any residue of truth still remained, well, I'd just *keep* telling myself that, very sternly, until it went.

We strode on, donning gloves against the icy onshore wind. We found a mermaid's purse, and a tangle of blue plastic fishing net, which was alive with all kinds of tiny crustaceans, drawn to the dead fish that had been entombed inside it, and prompting Dillon, who was studying climate change in school, to start worrying anew. At least, till I distracted him with a particularly good find: a hermit crab who'd made its home in a whelk shell.

Down at this end of the beach, though, I'd become distracted myself. Not by my mother, now – a small mercy – but this time by my father, because we were at the same place I'd last come to with him many years back, when he'd visited (this about nine months after he'd moved to France with Aurélie) and suggested the two of us 'have a talk'. If he had added 'man to man' I wouldn't have been surprised.

I had been seventeen then. My father forty-eight or forty-nine. It felt strange to be around him. He had changed. I also hated that he was taking up space in my head in a way he previously hadn't, and shouldn't. I hated the reality – which every pore of him seemed to make so obvious – that my father and Aurélie were having so much fun, so much sex.

'Your mum,' he said. 'She'll be okay, you know. She'll bounce back – boing-boing-boing – you'll see.' He even mimed it, excruciatingly. Who was this person, who had always been so short and snappy, and now mimed beach balls and took me for walks by the sea? Yet, at the same time, his happiness was oddly infectious. Because the image he'd created, of my mother bouncing along the shoreline like a big happy beach ball, made me giggle. Despite the heavy cloud of gloom under which we were living, or perhaps even because of it, it actually *made me giggle*. I was that much not myself.

'That's the spirit,' my father said, placing a stiff hand on my shoulder. 'In the meantime, Chicken Licken' (he'd always called me that because, just like Dillon was now, I was a child prone to worrying about the sky falling in), 'you look after your mum and little sister for me, eh? I'm relying on you.'

And I was too young to realise what a preposterous thing that was to ask of me. It had taken years, and a great deal of hounding by Matt, to realise just how preposterous. I made a rule from the get-go that as a parent I'd be different. I would never ask Daniel to look after Dillon. Look *out for*. Not after. A massive, massive difference.

I turned to Dillon now. 'Tell you what,' I said, 'it's getting late, and getting dark. Time to head back, I think. Shall we do a bit of fartlek?'

Which made *him* giggle, which immediately reclaimed the space for me. For us. And as we ran-walked and ran-walked our way back towards the car, still giggling, I realised that being back here would require lots of this kind of stuff, of actively smothering the bad memories under a quilt of happy new ones. Dampening down the feeling – already rising, because of Mum, and growing exponentially since my encounter with Aidan Kennedy – that we'd made a mistake of colossal proportions in returning here.

But perhaps it had been inevitable. That I'd end up caring for Mum had always been a given, even before the ink dried on their decree absolute, before Dad had blithely assumed it was a given, and long before Hope's death made it a certainty. That sense of responsibility had begun dogging me early. Not least because, even before I left for uni, I knew the foundations of what was left of our family were way beyond any sort of remedial underpinning, despite my father's highly convenient faith in the idea of our mother 'bouncing back'. Too much said, too much unsaid, too many seams of recrimination and ill feeling having been gouged out of the already unstable bedrock. To create a borehole – suggest, say, that some 'home truths' be aired, perhaps – would be to risk an explosion of dark matter that, with my own life ahead of me, and all that delicious distance soon to be between us, I had little motivation to wade through.

But while I doggedly ploughed my dry, academic furrow, seeking to replace chaos with order by escaping to university, Hope, made of different stuff, thrashed around with her emotional machete, finding order in creating *more* chaos. At least, that's how it seemed, particularly once I had finally left. She never seemed more at peace than when she'd laid waste to something, be it a plan, a commitment, a previously happy gathering, my Mother's Day (the last being her particular favourite). Her meltdowns always felt less like impulsive explosions and more like premeditated therapeutic bloodletting. (Which was perhaps why she and Aidan were so well-suited.)

All of which ensured that my father's favourite child (a construct built on fact; he'd been vociferously opposed to having a second) ended up being my mother's favourite too, simply by virtue of the fact that I gave her no trouble, and she could rely on me to do the ironing and the weekly food shop. *Grace is so good*, she would trill to any neighbour who'd sighted me in Tesco. *I really don't know how I'd cope without her. She's my rock, bless her.* I was set up to become her carer from a very early age.

I hated it. It felt like a curse to be so blessed. An unsolicited 'gift' (what sane child would want to carry such a burden?), being the favoured child had so many strings attached to it that I felt constantly tied up in knots. There was the expectation that I would scrabble up the pedestal my parents had designed for me, and the constant compulsion to tell Hope that the evidence of her own eyes actually wasn't – that black was, in fact, white. There's only so many times you can hear 'it's alright for you, you're the favourite' before the poison in your chalice becomes apparent. Hope never *really* hated me – she couldn't afford the luxury, because I was the only chunk of masonry she had to lean against – but resentment in a family can be a powerful force. Perhaps, if she'd lived, she'd have worked through her demons. Had some counselling, taken up yoga, achieved some kind of acceptance, indulged her inspirational-quote poster quotient to the max and actually come to believe the things they told her.

But she died, so our roles became forever preserved in aspic, the price of my unwanted gift of 'favourite' status being a sense of duty I'd had to haul around with me ever since.

And with adulthood and marriage came a further revelation. That while Hope's blood still ran hot in all parent-related matters, I was done with going over it; the point had already come when it was obvious, at least to me, that Mum would never climb back down from her safe house on the moral high ground. I'm not sure she even wanted to. Being a bitter, abandoned woman who'd been callously cast aside for a younger model was like an old coat in which she'd become way, way too comfortable – so to bring candour into any conversation about our childhood unhappiness, would, I knew, send her into such a funk of self-flagellation that the fallout would be to nobody's benefit.

So we maintained a mutually beneficial disinclination to exhume the truth – and even more so after Hope died. And, since we saw little of one another (my long hours, the distance, Mum's increasing disinclination to leave Brighton), that state of affairs worked for both of us. At least till the spectre of dementia took solid form.

One of my early conversations with Matt around the move – around the 'what to do about Mum' question, essentially – quickly escalated into row territory, as by that time they were mostly bound to do. Yes, leave London – Matt was fully on board with that notion, not least because, as a doctor, I was geographically hobbled there. To continue to work in a central London hospital would, of necessity, mean raising our family in central London too. But could I not accept his argument that we had other, better, options? Why return to Brighton, scene of so many emotional traumas? To a place where he'd never felt at home, unsurprisingly (what home?), and which held so much potential for further grief?

With his own family uncomplicated, intact, and far distant up in Scotland, he couldn't get his head around my belief that I *had* to. I owed Mum nothing – he was frank about telling me that, often. So he had little patience with my endless droning about duty.

He was right, but also wrong, because I wasn't being selfless. It was, and always would be, about what was best for me. Because it turned out that I could no more free myself of demons than Hope had been able to. To remain far from my mother while her brain and body withered, would, I knew, bring about a sense of guilt so pervasive that it would begin to eat away at me too. I needed to go back in order to keep moving forward. I could no more abandon her – set up carers, throw money at it, keep my physical distance – than she could ever (while she still had the cognition to do so) reassure me in the way that most parents ultimately realise they must: that, absolved from any guilt or blame or shame, or, indeed, duty, I should go live my life where I chose.

And besides, with Aidan long gone, and relations with Norma severed, the Kennedys, so went my reasoning, were history. I had put everything to do with them in a metaphorical memory box, just like the one Hope had so painstakingly made for Dillon, but with a padlock and long-ago thrown-away key. They'd been part of Hope's life, not ours. They were *her* Horrible History. They were not part of our or Dillon's lives now, nor ever would be. And if I couldn't quite airbrush them out of my head space, I had put sufficient work in to keep them contained; Aidan still as Aidan – I knew his type, they never changed much – but Norma, despite all the rancour, the deceit, and all the hateful things she'd said to me, as a little old lady who, if I bumped into her in the street, I should, and probably still would feel sorry for.

Except I didn't. Because the box had been opened.

Chapter 8

Hope's funeral had been a minutely choreographed affair. Just a couple of weeks before her sudden death (and many weeks before anyone had anticipated attending it) she had given me a memory stick she insisted I must listen to, because it contained detailed instructions about her funeral. How she should be dressed, what we should read, what we should listen to, what we should wear, and given to me on the basis that, unlike Mum, I would do as I was told. By this time, she was reading me well.

Difficult to hear (she was lying in the mortuary when I had no choice but to get it out and listen to it), it was harder still to put her plans into action, since, like a circus ringmaster during America's Great Depression, she had seemed determined to orchestrate a spectacle.

She'd picked the natural burial site not long after her terminal diagnosis, a complex of nascent woodland and wildflower meadows nestling in the lee of the South Downs. And the humanist ceremony was always a given, since another thing Hope didn't 'do' by this time was 'f***ing deities'. She was adamant – she was simply returning to the earth from which she'd come. And would, eventually, become stardust herself. All that would remain would be the plaque above her – English oak, nothing fancy – which was to read 'Hope Faulkner', plus her dates, plus 'Dillon's Mummy'. One of many reasons, hard though it was to square it with my conscience, why I no longer took Dillon there.

But brain tumours, by their nature, can interfere with personality, and by the time she'd recorded all her must-haves and must-dos, Hope's wishes for her funeral had clearly mutated into the al fresco summer wedding she'd always dreamed of having, but which both Aidan and her cancer had denied her. Now, in death, it seemed, she could finally be the bride.

The sun had shone, if coldly, on that cloudless winter Wednesday, and the grass, stiff and frosted as we gathered at her graveside, sparkled prettily as it crunched beneath our ridiculous heels, lending the funeral a fairy-tale quality. But of all the arresting montages still available to my mind's eye, it was the vision of Norma with Dillon, the closeness of that bond, that was among the most powerful of my memories.

As had been agreed, the day after Hope died we collected him from my mother's and took him back home to London, and did our best to adjust, in a million tiny ways, to the enormity of what we'd committed to take on. Which was a lot. Daniel was just three then, Dillon not quite twenty months, and we both had demanding full-time jobs. But how could we not? If something had happened to us, wouldn't we have wanted the same security for Daniel?

Though not with Hope. Not while she stayed with Aidan. If the unthinkable happened, Daniel would be spirited far away. To live with Matt's sister and her husband and their adopted twin daughters in Edinburgh, where they promised us they would love him as their own.

For Hope, when it came to it, things were very different. There was only one place for Dillon to be after her death, and that was with us. End of. Despite him having a father (if, by now, an absentee, and also manifestly unfit one) and a doting paternal grandmother, who was still very much around for him, during those awful final months Hope made a watertight case – an offer we, or at least *I,* could not refuse.

Which left Matt boxed into a terrible corner. To bring up my sister's child as his own son was an ask of momentous proportions. Yet once it had become obvious that I had no choice, what choice did he have?

We had talked about it, endlessly, exhaustively. Mainly it was a question of talking ourselves into it, as people faced with such a high-stakes fait accompli have to do. It was obviously going to be challenging, because we both understood that the kind of love you automatically feel for your own child cannot just be magicked from thin air. But we had faith that we could will that kind of love into being; it was only a question of degrees, after all. This wasn't some stranger's child. This was our nephew. So I chased all my misgivings away.

And there was also the question of *us.* What 'us' would there be if Matt refused to sign up, given that I knew I had to, heart and soul? Of all the things I could hate Aidan Kennedy for, I despised him most for creating that hairline crack in our marriage, because it could so easily have become a gaping void.

So we practised the art of ruthless optimism. Yes, it would be strange and stressful in the short term, not least because Dillon barely knew us. We lived in London and they lived in Brighton, so we'd shared mutual visits, the odd play date, little more.

Still, we remained doggedly positive. Trusting that, in the longer term, life would just reshape itself slightly, and Dillon would be absorbed into our family bubble. That we *would* love him as our own.

So we were ready. We had to be. Norma couldn't be. And was not.

By the time my sister died there was no love lost between them, yet ironically, partly *because* of Aidan having walked out,

Norma had increasingly become central to Dillon's life, taking care of him while Hope slipped inexorably away, in a way our own mother, stricken by the loss she was facing, seemed constitutionally incapable of doing. Norma loved Dillon – that much was clear. And however Hope might have wished it otherwise, Dillon loved Norma. Aside from Hope, she'd been the one constant in his short, bewildering life, and in a day so chock-full of powerful imagery, the one of Dillon, when we tried to separate him from Norma – howling in anguish, his face smeared with dirt and snot and tears – was the one that haunted me most.

His cries, as he clung to her, cut through me like a knife. She was crying too, distraught, red-eyed, her whole body language pleading. He was wrapped around her koala-style, and as she held him, she swayed and soothed him, one hand gently cupping the back of his head, in a way she must have done a thousand times. 'Please, whatever's happened with Aidan, Grace, don't forget, he's *still my grandson*. Please don't shut me out now. You can *see* how much he needs me.'

I could. So whatever Hope had thought of her – a mother who was blind to her son's multitude of deficiencies – it would be madness to cut her off from him, wouldn't it? It seemed so obvious. She'd stepped in to *make up* for those deficiencies. And long before Aidan had physically left. How could it ever be in Dillon's best interests to lose her? 'Of course I won't,' I said, as I finally went to prise him from her, screaming, kicking, bucking. 'I understand. God, I *know* that. We'll sort something out. Something regular, I promise.'

And I meant it. Yes, making that promise meant breaking another: the solemn promise I had given my dying sister. But surely Dillon's well-being and happiness was what mattered most now? And wouldn't his happiness be what Hope would want too?

I suppose I was as blinded by emotion as everyone else was that day, because I didn't register what should probably have rung some pretty loud alarm bells.

It was something and nothing, or so I'd thought – just a farewell, nothing more. 'Remember, Dilly,' Norma had whispered as she'd handed him over. 'Mummy loves you, okay?'

It was a good while before it sunk in. Many months before the truth dawned. She hadn't been referring to my sister.

The rest of Boxing Day passed without incident. Once the boys were asleep, and Matt was running Mum back home – she refused to sleep anywhere but in her own bed now – I gave Mr Weasley a stray leftover carrot to get his teeth into, and lit the pine-scented jar candle Jenny had given me for Christmas. I then pulled a bottle of red out from the rack in the garage. Now the can had been opened, there seemed little further harm in letting the rest of the worms slither out of it, after all.

At first, my relief at knowing I would now be able to tell Matt the whole story was so intense it must have crowded out my other senses. And having opened the bottle and poured two decent glasses (we both had one more leave day, so could cope with a hangover, I decided), I realised I was in a better, calmer place than I had been in a fortnight. So it wasn't till his car keys clattered down so loudly on to the kitchen island that it hit me that I'd missed a key trick. Which I shouldn't have, because I knew my husband well enough, surely, to have realised that there was a major point at issue here, as yet still unresolved, and that was not anything to do with his anger towards Aidan or Norma Kennedy. To have realised, surely, that he would still be upset with *me*.

'All okay with Mum?' I asked, sliding the glass of wine across the island.

He ignored it. 'I can't believe you didn't tell me about this,' he said.

'Oh, *please*, Matt. Look, I'm sorry. I called it wrong. I thought I was doing the right thing, and I wasn't. I'm *sorry*. You know what I'm like. I just didn't want to worry you if I didn't need to. Put all that extra stress on you—'

'You should have told me.' He reached for his glass. Took a sip. His expression was colder than the still too chilly wine.

'I know, but . . . Look, it's just – well, it's just me, okay? I didn't say anything to you because it's *always* me, isn't it? Always *my* family being the ones causing all the grief. Whereas yours never do . . .' I stopped then and shrugged. We'd been here so many, many times. This business of our respective good luck and bad luck when it came to acquiring in-laws.

He didn't answer straight away. Just swirled his wine in his glass. 'So go on, then,' he said eventually. 'Tell me now.'

So I did. What I knew about the circumstances around the accident. About the point at which I'd recognised Aidan and our subsequent exchanges. About transferring him to Neil's care, about my encounter with Norma, about the contents of the complaint letter, and, because I knew leaving it out, especially given the mood he was in, would be foolhardy, about the fact that Aidan still had my number, and had telephoned me. And, even knowing that it would send Matt into an even greater froth of anger, I told him about the text he'd sent too.

I regretted telling him about that bit immediately. Matt had variously nodded and hmm'd and rolled his eyes as I'd been speaking, taking sips from his wine, seeming marginally less cross – or at least, or so it seemed to me, redirecting his anger – but when I finished telling him about the phone calls and text, his expression changed again.

'You mean that man's been making threatening calls and sending texts to you in the small hours, when you're at home alone with the boys, and you didn't at any point think you ought to *tell* me? Jesus, Grace.'

'They weren't threatening. I didn't even speak to him.'

'Bollocks. You get a text calling you a bitch and you don't think that's threatening?'

'He was twenty-four hours post-op. In *hospital*. How on earth could he be a threat to me?'

'That's not the point and you know it. As far as I'm concerned, he's a threat just by existing on the planet. That *bloody* family.' He slapped his hand down on the worktop, then reached for the wine and topped his glass up. 'Do the hospital know? As in, what's really motivated the complaint against you? You told them that, I hope?'

'Yes, of course. Well, as much as they needed to know.'

He rolled his eyes. 'Of course you did.'

'Matt, this really isn't helping. I. Am. Sorry. I. Didn't. Tell. You. How many times do I have to say that?'

His only answer was to narrow his eyes. 'Tell me something. If they hadn't put that complaint in – say, if you'd patched him up and sent him on his merry way – would you have told me then? I'm serious. Would you have told me at *all*?'

I felt skewered then, because I genuinely didn't know the answer to that question.

But Matt was already one step ahead of my thought process.

'I'm guessing no.' He cast his gaze around the kitchen, and when it returned to me it stayed, even as he lifted his glass and drank his wine. He lowered the glass then. 'You know something? I'm beginning to feel like a visitor in my own house. And that *bloody* family. Just the thought of them having *anything* to do with us. I knew we should never have come down here.'

I didn't know what to say to that, either. Except perhaps that I'd been thinking the exact thoughts he had, with some conviction, for over two weeks now. I didn't though, because I knew it would only inflame him further.

'I know,' I said limply. But he was off on his own train of thought now. 'Your bloody mother,' he said, as if half to himself. And when he didn't continue, I ventured, '*My* mother?'

'Yes, of course *your* mother. *All* of this comes down to your mother. Why else are we here? We wouldn't *be* in this situation – anywhere *near* that poisonous family – if we hadn't let her blackmail us into coming down here, would we?'

I was grateful for the 'we', which could so easily have been a 'you', but less enthusiastic about revisiting that particular conversation. 'We're not *in* a situation. The complaint will be thrown out and that will be the end of it.'

'Christ, how can you be so naive? The guy's lost his *arm*. So he'll also lose his livelihood. And his driving licence – no question about that. And his insurance will be invalid, so he'll almost certainly be charged with causing criminal damage too. And his mother, in case you've forgotten, hates us even more than he does. And you expect me to skip around thinking that will be the end of it? They *live* here. *She* lives here. And now *we* live here too. Jesus, Grace, if you think she'll let this go, you have a *very* short memory. Trust me, she'll be out for your *blood*.'

Chapter 9

Tim Shelley was as good as his word. Though I didn't see him between Christmas and New Year – there were no routine clinics then, so I was only operating on emergency trauma patients – an email from him appeared in my inbox on New Year's Eve, to let me know they'd conducted their investigation and, just as they'd anticipated, my confidence in my professional opinion had clearly not been misplaced. The next step, therefore, would be to draft a robust letter, so did I have any space in my diary on the 3rd?

The letter itself, once it was written and signed (in my case, after I'd cleared it with my defence union, as they'd instructed), was necessarily frank and to the point. There was absolutely no case to answer.

Privately, I would have liked to add a further, pithier paragraph, making it clear that malicious accusations like theirs could be subject to legal redress. After all, they'd tried to smear my professional reputation. But I said nothing. What good would it do, after all? And perhaps, as I kept trying to reassure Matt, this would be the end of it. That realising they'd shot their bolt and missed, they'd see sense, and the whole thing would be over.

But it didn't matter how many times I convinced myself it should be, something told me it wouldn't be.

I was right. Because I was on my way out of outpatients the following Monday, having just finished my morning clinic, when a woman came hurrying up to me. 'Mrs Hamilton?' she said. 'Is there any chance I could have a word with you?'

I didn't recognise her at first. I'd only seen her very briefly, after all. Plus her hair was different; she had it pulled back into a high ponytail, which bounced behind her as she walked. She was wearing an NHS uniform, too. Short-sleeved tunic, black trousers, soft-soled shoes, the usual lanyard. So she *worked* here?

She'd obviously noticed my confusion.

'Sorry, I'm Jessica,' she said. Then added, 'Jessica Kennedy?', her voice rising at the end as if even her own name was up for dispute. Her accent wasn't local. Perhaps Yorkshire. Had she met Aidan in Hull?

Like me, she had a handbag over her shoulder, so I imagined she was either at the end of or perhaps midway through a shift. The badge hanging from the lanyard told me she was a healthcare assistant – the modern equivalent of the old auxiliary nurse.

The word 'meek' came to mind again. Meek, demure, diffident. Perhaps Aidan's tastes had changed. And if so, pretty radically. Hope had been none of those things. But perhaps that was the point.

'Hello,' I said, wondering what was coming next. First impressions (mine was 'brace yourself') weren't always the right ones, after all. But her smile was both open and apologetic.

'I'm so sorry to accost you like this,' she went on, 'but I was wondering if there was any chance I could have a word with you? Either now, or . . .' She opened her palms. 'Well, whenever, really. I'm on a break at the moment, but maybe later, if you're busy now? If that would be better for you?'

Distrustful as I was of her – she was, after all, a Kennedy – both her expression and her body language seemed genuinely appeasing. And she *worked* here. Did that change anything? If so, how?

'Now is fine,' I said, wondering if she'd been keeping an eye on my movements. Had she been watching out for me, waiting for me? If so, to say what?

I took her back into the consulting room I'd just left.

'I didn't realise you worked here,' I said, as she sat down in the chair I'd directed her to. There were a pair of them, so I could equally have sat in the other, but I wanted the security of being behind a desk. She didn't seem in the least threatening, but there was still something about her, an air of agitation she was clearly struggling to contain.

'I don't,' she said. 'Well, I mean, I am this week. A couple of bank shifts. That's what I mostly do at the moment. Mostly nights right now too, so this is . . .' She frowned and bit her lower lip. 'Look, I just wanted to say how sorry I am about everything. About sending that complaint letter.'

Her hands were in her lap and she was rubbing the palm of one repeatedly with the thumb of the other. She looked like she meant it, and, just as had been the case with Aidan, my immediate instinct was to pity her. Not just because it was such a long-ingrained professional habit, but because I knew the kind of man she was married to. But I forced myself to fight it. She had knowingly done something (and her being a fellow NHS employee made it even worse, somehow) that, without a shred of evidence, she must have known would cause me all kinds of grief and stress, and could have seriously damaged my professional reputation.

'The letter that had your name on it,' I pointed out, albeit gently, because old non-combative habits die hard.

She frowned. 'I know, and I really am so sorry. I would never—' She glanced down towards her lap, at her restless, restless hands. 'Honestly, I'd *never* normally get involved in something like that. It's really not . . .' She tailed off, and I wondered if she had ever been on the receiving end of something similar. 'It was just all the anxiety, and the shock – it was all just in the heat of the moment . . . I don't know what I was thinking even *agreeing* to it. I mean, I *knew* it was wrong. I kept trying to tell them . . .'

Again, she let the end of the sentence hang. For me to backfill with reassuring noises?

But knew how? She'd known nothing. At least, not at the time. I could have been a rabid axe murderer in scrubs. There was little doubt in my mind that, for Norma, I still *was*. 'So it wasn't your idea then.'

'No!' Again, she sounded genuine. But then again, I thought, suppose the complaint *had* been considered serious? Suppose I *had* recognised him before I operated on him and had admitted as much? Suppose they'd found a lawyer, who'd dug around into the background and latched on to something they thought they could work with? Suppose the photos had been inconclusive and they *had* made a case? Would this woman be sitting here now, apologising to me?

'Then whose was it?' I asked her. 'Aidan's? His mother's?'

It might just have been the way I said it, but when she met my eye now there was something slightly different, slightly unreadable, in her gaze.

'I'm not exactly sure. Look, I don't want to make excuses for him,' she hurried on. 'But he really wasn't thinking straight. He'd already been through so much, and then for such a horrendous accident to happen to him—'

Been through what? Did she mean recently? Or was she harking further back? If the first, nothing to do with me, and if the second, she was on very stony ground. Not least because the accident hadn't exactly just 'happened'. He'd had significant amounts of alcohol and drugs in his system. Intoxicants *he'd* put there. *Aidan being Aidan*. How many times had I heard those words said? As

89

if 'being Aidan' conferred some special get-out-of-jail-free card. I didn't say it, though. She, of all people, must have known that.

'About which I sympathise, obviously,' I said instead. 'But—'

'Look, like I say, it was a really, really stupid thing to do, and I sincerely regret agreeing to it.'

'Does Aidan?'

'Yes, of *course*. He's just . . .' She leaned forward slightly. 'Look, I just wanted to say that he really is sorry. And that there will be no more of that kind of thing, I absolutely promise. That—' She paused, put her loosely fisted hand to her mouth, and let out a small cough, as if preparing to make a speech. 'Look, I just wanted to ask you, *please*, to not take any of this further. He's already in so much trouble, and if you, well . . .' She left a pause, which I didn't fill, leaving her no choice but to continue. 'Look, I'm sure you'll understand how fragile his mental health is. You know, what with everything, and now all of this on top . . . He's just become . . . you know . . .' (I could tell she was groping for the right word) '. . . you know, a bit emotionally *unhinged* by it all. I mean, I know what you think of him, and I understand why you'd be angry at him. But he's not a *bad* person, honestly. He really isn't. He's just—' Another pause. 'He's just struggling with so many demons. In a really bad place.'

Entonox – or gas and air – is a singular kind of painkiller. It doesn't actually kill pain, but it's great for things like childbirth, because it has the effect of distancing you; making you feel as if you're slightly detached from what's happening to you. I remember it well from when I gave birth to Daniel. As if I was floating above everything, looking down on myself.

I felt a little like that now. Not in pain, but slightly distant, an observer. Observing that I was sitting there with a woman who up until now had been a stranger. A stranger who was talking to me about – of *all people* – Aidan Kennedy, and asking me – *me!* – to care about his demons and 'fragile' mental health. Or at least to accept it in mitigation of his and his mother's actions. Who kept using the word 'everything', as if, where Aidan Kennedy was concerned, *everything* was defensible. Because, 'you know' – and how familiar this territory felt – 'this is *Aidan*.' She might just as well have been my seventeen-year-old sister. The sense of déjà vu was profound.

I wasn't quite sure what to say to her, because I had no intention of taking anything further. Though the suggestion that I would made me angry all over again. As if I was being tarred with the same vengeful brush. 'I'm very sorry to hear that,' I finally plumped for, 'but—'

She obviously misread what I was about to say, because her chin immediately jutted. 'Look,' she said, before I'd even had a chance to point that out to her. 'I'm not trying to make out like it excuses him, I'm *genuinely* not, but he's really not the kind of man you think he is.'

The delicate wire I'd been walking, between objective professionalism and personal irritation, developed a tremor. I wobbled off it now and fell.

'How would you know what sort of man I think he is?'

'Because of what you've been told about him. About leaving his son and everything.'

If she was still hoping to make a case for him, she was making a spectacularly bad job of it. I was beginning to get angrier now. I sat forward slightly.

'I think you mean what *he's* told you I've been told about him, don't you?'

There was a flash of something in her eyes then. Perhaps the realisation that coming here had been an error of judgement. I wondered if Aidan Kennedy's ears were burning. I wondered what he'd have to say about her being here, mounting a case for his defence. I wondered if Norma Kennedy knew she was here. I imagined not. In a million years, not.

'I'm just saying he's not the villain he's been painted as.'

'By who? My late sister?'

She had the grace to lower her gaze for a second. Then met my eyes again. She clearly still had something to get off her chest. And now I'd challenged her to do so, she was going for it. 'Look, no disrespect to the dead, but all the stuff about the way he treated her, none of it was true. She made all that up to get back at him.'

'Back at him for what?'

'For seeing someone else. For not wanting to be with her any more.'

'He'd have barely had to see the New Year out. Did that small fact escape his notice? My sister was dying. Yet he walked away anyway.'

She remained undaunted. 'He left *her*. Not his son. *Her*.' She almost spat it out – this woman who had never even met my sister. 'He *never* wanted to be cut off from his son. Look, I don't know what you've been told – how can I? But I *do* know that.'

But, of course, she would say that, wouldn't she?

'So why didn't he fight for him?'

'Because he knew he'd never win. Because he knew what your sister had told you about him.' Her shoulders stiffened. 'Because he was trying to do right by his son.'

Whoa, I thought. *Enough*. This was my sister we were talking about. My sister, who could not defend herself. 'Okay,' I said, raising a hand. 'I think our conversation needs to end here, Mrs Kennedy. I'm not even sure it's appropriate to be talking to you at all. Your husband is no longer my patient, in any case, and I don't think raking any of this stuff up is going to help matters. In fact, right now, it's making it all feel a lot worse.' I got to my feet, shouldered my handbag. 'I think it's best if we finished this here,' I added firmly.

She half rose as well, flustered now, perhaps realising she'd gone too far. 'Look, I'm sorry. I didn't mean to upset you. I just thought if—'

'Apology accepted,' I said briskly. I was genuinely conscious of the time now. I had a meeting to get to, and was already late. 'But I really do hope this *is* going to be the end of it, because—'

I stopped then, because she had suddenly flopped back down into her chair.

'Are you okay?' I asked.

Her answer was unequivocal. *No.* Because she didn't answer. Instead she leaned forward, placed her elbows on the desk, put her head in her hands, and started crying, her shoulders shuddering as she wept. Which left me little choice but to either ask her to leave or go around to her side of the desk and try to comfort her. Because there was nothing else to do in such a situation (is there ever?), I chose the latter, pulling the adjacent patient chair a little closer, sitting on it, and putting a hand on her nearest shoulder, which seemed to make her cry all the more. Familiar territory again. Horribly familiar territory.

But I wasn't sure quite what to say to her – there, there? – so I got up again. 'Let me fetch you some water.'

I went to the sink, plucked a disposable cup from the stack, filled it from the tap, and grabbed a wodge of paper towels as well. Then returned and, because she still had her head in her hands, placed both the cup and the towels on the desk.

Then waited. It was a full fifteen or twenty seconds before she could pull herself together enough to speak.

'I just don't know what to *do*,' she said finally. 'I'm *so* sorry. I *knew* I shouldn't have come here and bothered you with all this. I just thought I needed to *explain* to you, before things get completely out of hand and he gets into really serious trouble . . .' She started sobbing again. 'And, *God*, his *bloody* mother. And all I've done now is make everything even *worse*.'

'Not worse,' I began.

'But I *have*. And I don't know what to *do*.' She sounded desperate now, and I thought all of a sudden of her two little girls. Innocents, like Dillon, in such a shitty situation. I didn't doubt she *was* desperate, either.

She took a towel from the desk and dabbed at the wetness on her cheeks. 'He's drinking himself to oblivion. I mean, it's always been a problem, but in the last couple of years or so, pretty much since we moved down here, really, it's been getting totally out of control. And Norma winding him up about all this is making everything even worse. She just doesn't *get* it. I mean, seriously, she *knows* what he's like. I keep telling her to leave it. It was his fault, and he knows it – so why can't she just let it go? *God.* I just feel I'm stuck in some horrible nightmare and I don't know what to do to get out of it.'

'Have you spoken to his GP? Maybe if you could persuade him to seek help—'

She shook her head. 'It's completely pointless trying to arrange anything like that. He won't go. He won't let anyone come round and see him either. Not even friends. And I'm having to work night shifts to bring some money in, and I just can't . . .' She faltered. 'Just can't trust him. You know, trust that he's not going to get into one of his . . .' Again she hesitated. *What?* I thought. *His what?* She looked conflicted.

'Trust that what?' I asked.

'I can't trust that the girls will be safe with him when I'm not there.'

Alarm bells didn't so much begin ringing as tolling in my head. 'Trust him how?' I asked. 'You mean you think he might hurt them?'

Again, her chin jutted. And though the message I was getting from her was increasingly becoming mixed, I felt her instinctive loyalty to him tugging at her, like a dog on a leash. '*No.* I mean, no, not intentionally, obviously. But—'

I could tell she was agonising over her words. How to express what it was she seemed determined she must voice.

And voice to me? She stared up at me, her eyes shining with as yet unshed tears. 'Jessica, has he been violent? Towards you? Towards your daughters?'

She looked astonished now. 'No, no, no! You've got it all wrong. *No!* Trust me, the only person Aidan's intent on hurting is himself. That's what I'm *saying*. It's like he wants to destroy himself. How can I leave the girls with him?'

'He's suicidal? Getting drunk? Taking drugs?'

She nodded miserably. 'A couple of nights ago, I came home to find him spark out, completely gone, with a cigarette in his hand still. Burnt right down to the stub. All the ash in one unbroken line on the arm of the sofa. How out of it must he have been that he hadn't even noticed? He could have burned the whole *house* down, and he hadn't even *noticed*. I'd ask Norma to have them but it's such a hike, and—'

'Oh. I thought she lived fairly close to you.'

She shook her head. 'She moved to a bungalow up towards Patcham a couple of years back. Anyway, I won't.' Her voice was firm now. 'It's not fair on them. Since all this, she's just so . . . so . . .' She stopped and exhaled heavily. 'I just wish I knew what to *do!*'

There was so much more I'd have liked to ask her. Particularly about Norma. But I asked none of it. Something told me I shouldn't press her.

'Listen,' I said instead, 'if you think your children are at risk, then you must—'

'Leave him. I know, I *know*. I've been agonising about it for months. It's just such a *massive* step to take . . . specially if I'm going to move back up to Hull. And it's not like I don't love him. I just can't . . .' Her features contorted in pain, and she scoured the back of her hand across her eyes as if exasperated with herself. I had the feeling she'd already cried a lot of tears. 'I've got a friend in Hove who said we can move into her spare bedroom temporarily, but it's such an imposition, and she really doesn't have the room . . . and, God, I just . . . I mean, what's going to happen *then*?'

'Long term? Well, there are options. There are refuges you can go to, and—'

'No, I mean to *Aidan*! I mean, I hope if I *do* leave him he'll come to his senses, realise he can't go on like this – that he needs to sort himself out. But will he? Will he really? It might make everything even worse, mightn't it? And I don't think I can bear to have that on my conscience. He's just so all over the place, so scared. So vulnerable.'

'As are you,' I pointed out firmly. 'As are your children. Look, I'm sorry, but I really do have to be somewhere now. But I strongly urge you to try and get some help for him, perhaps some counselling. Get in touch with your GP. Get a home visit organised. If he's in that desperate a state, I'm sure they'd fast-track him. And most of all, make sure you and your children are safe.'

I stood up as I was speaking, and she seemed to take the cue. Blowing her nose, wiping her eyes again, taking a sip of the tepid water.

'I'm so sorry,' she said. 'I shouldn't have come and offloaded on you the way I have. And I'll do that. Just – sorry – *please* – you won't take this any further, will you?'

'No. *Obviously*, no. I just want it to end now, and—'

'It *has* ended,' she said. 'I absolutely promise. I just—' Her chin began wobbling again and I felt a sudden rush of sympathy.

I slipped my bag from my shoulder and rummaged in it for a pen. Then, having torn the corner off an old receipt, wrote my mobile number down for her.

'Here,' I said, pushing the piece of paper across the desk at her. 'If you need details of a local refuge, get in touch with me, okay?'

'I will,' she said, stuffing it into a pocket as she followed me over to the consulting-room door. 'And thank you. I mean that.'

I opened the door. 'Did you tell Aidan you were coming to see me?'

'No. But that doesn't mean he isn't—'

'And his mother?'

She looked shocked at that. '*Lord, no.* I – look, sorry. Thank you *so* much. You've really helped me.'

And all I could think of as I watched her hurry off down the corridor was her expression when I asked her whether Norma knew she'd come to see me. *Lord, no*, she'd said. And had frowned as she'd said it. No, she'd winced, actually winced. As if she knew as well as I did that whatever she promised, Norma Kennedy's hatred of me was a force outside her control.

Chapter 10

I drove home that evening with thoughts of Jessica Kennedy and what she'd said to me strobing on and off in my brain like neon signposts. She'd by now texted me (a simple *thank you*, followed by an *x*) and I wondered if she'd act on what she'd said. I suspected yes, because, given what she'd told me, it was all so obvious, felt so familiar, the picture she'd painted so clear. She'd married Aidan Kennedy, presumably bewitched by him in the same way Hope had once been, and, one by one, the scales had begun falling from her eyes. Even faster, I imagined, by having put herself in such close proximity to his mother. That he was struggling, and self-medicating with drink and drugs, was no surprise either. However much I wished it otherwise, years of front-line A and E work had chipped away at my relentless optimism about human nature. You saw the very best of people, often, but you also saw the worst, and the histories of so many who regularly haunted the hospital were depressingly similar. And of course he had demons; what he'd done to Hope had been despicable, and he knew it. Though it was no surprise that he'd given his wife a rather different account of the way things had ended.

But though I knew I could (I had plenty of evidence I could show her), I wasn't remotely inclined to try and disabuse her of all the fictions he'd told her. I just felt sorry for her, being in the middle of such a traumatic situation, and for her children, who were clearly at risk. For the decision she was struggling with, about throwing in the towel and leaving her substance-abusing husband. And taking the children back up north to her family. Which, as she'd hinted, would almost certainly have massive implications. And not just for him. For Norma as well. Who she was clearly afraid of.

Déjà vu. I knew all about that, because I'd already been there. And I was still afraid of Norma too.

And with good reason, because on the Tuesday of the following week, she came looking for me. I was on my way to my afternoon clinic when I heard her. First a 'Hey!', ringing out from somewhere behind me, punching a hole through the usual waiting-room torpor and causing a dozen or so whispered conversations to come to an abrupt end. The shrill female voice, in this setting, was noteworthy in itself. While people kicking off in outpatients was an occupational hazard, loud disturbances, at least in my personal experience, were more usually instigated by men. And they were usually much more common to late nights in A and E, not routine afternoon outpatient clinics. By definition, the patients had either generally had enough trauma, or were elderly, polite, and largely patient, as well.

I knew straight away it was Norma. And as I turned around, I saw a small sea of other heads doing likewise, people swivelling in their seats to establish the source of the shout, sensing that a show was about to start. I heard a nervous laugh, the clatter of a crutch hitting the floor, and, as I swept my gaze around, spotted a sprinkling of my own patients, some with their gazes now darting back and forth between us, already coming to realise it was directed at me.

Which was not a great look. She shouted 'Hey!' again, then, 'Stop!' Then, 'You stop right there this minute, you bitch!' And then I saw her, pink-cheeked, in a mustard-coloured raincoat, shimmying sideways, making her way along the last of the rows of seats. There was no sign of Aidan, so I presumed she must be here because he was in having a follow-up consultation with Neil Porter. So had she brought him? And did this mean Jessica Kennedy *had* left him? I had no idea. She might have brought him just because Jessica was working, but my instinct, seeing the fury in her expression, told me yes.

But what the hell to do? Dive into the nearest consulting room and barricade the door? Run? Both options that felt far more appealing than just standing there waiting for the tornado.

Nevertheless, because it felt the only thing to do under the circumstances, I walked back past the rows of startled faces towards her, my wodge of patient notes clamped protectively against my chest. At least I might steer her into a triage bay or something. I saw one of the porters moving towards her too, as if anticipating trouble. Saw heads bobbing up from behind the glass at the reception desk.

I was glad to have the notes to grip, to stop my hands from shaking. 'Did you want to speak to me?' I asked her. 'If so, perhaps it would be better if—'

A bony be-ringed finger started to jab repeatedly towards my chest.

'Don't think for a single moment that you are going to get away with this!' She splayed her fingers with a snap, then, as if trying to dislodge something sticky from her nails. Slapped the index finger of the other hand against each digit in turn. 'You've stolen my grandson. You've ruined my son's life. You've chopped off his *arm*.' I heard a collective gasp at this. 'You've disfigured him. Half destroyed him. And now you've as good as killed him!'

I registered this with incredulity, as dots of spittle hit my cheek. '*What?*'

She was jabbing her finger at my chest now, against the notes I still held there, as if to punctuate her accusations. 'Don't try to deny it! You *Did This*! You fecking *bitch*! Do you want to fetch one of your scalpels and rip my heart out as well?'

'Norma, please . . .' I started to become aware that a silence had fallen. That we had an audience now, a rapt one, who, with nothing else to do, were enjoying the unexpected diversion of an elderly lady with her knickers in a twist about something, shouting abuse at one of the doctors. Nothing to worry about. Nothing they hadn't seen on *Casualty*.

But they, as much as me, underestimated her.

Though there was a nurse hurrying towards us, she was still several metres away when Norma, without any indication that she was about to, stopped prodding me and simply launched her whole body at me, clawing at the notes, which went flying as I tried to protect myself, grabbing at my blouse, my neck, my hair, my face.

I had no idea what to do other than try to contain her, so I attempted to grab her wrists, which felt like bundles of twigs, shifting my weight forward so she couldn't push me over backwards. But my foot slipped on all the paperwork that had cascaded down around us, and though I felt someone trying to grab me – a security guard, come from nowhere – the momentum was too great and, with Norma pushing against me, I overbalanced backwards. Before I could do anything to stop myself falling, I landed, heavily and painfully, on my hip, and Norma – still clinging on to my blouse with one hand, scratching at my face with the other – tumbled down in a muddle of limbs on top of me.

She winded me as she landed on me, still flailing, still screaming. I smelled perfume, and hairspray, and gusts of sour breath, the biscuity sweetness of yesterday's clothes. And a wetness – of tears, snot, or dribble, I couldn't tell – as she writhed against my chest, screaming, spitting, rasping, raging – like a rabid dog, or a tiger, trying to pinion me beneath her; and just as I managed to get a grip on the sleeve of her raincoat, she grabbed hold of the scrunchie that was holding my hair back, and yanked on it viciously, causing me to howl out in pain. 'You bitch!' she screamed. 'If he dies I will *kill* you!'

Then she reared up, pulled her arm back, and punched me in the face.

I heard a shout then. I couldn't see anything, because I'd squeezed my eyes shut now, seeing stars, already bracing myself for a second blow. Then another shout: 'Get her *off*! For Christ's *sake*, get a *hold* of her!' And the weight of her, the rancid heat of her, was suddenly no longer there.

I rolled on to my unhurt side, scrabbled up, and scraped the hair from my eyes, breathing hard, trying not to be sick, trying not to burst into tears. My whole body was now shaking uncontrollably. Someone pulled me to my feet – Siddhant, I realised – he must have run back from where I'd left him, over in X-ray – and as he rootled in a pocket for some tissues (there was blood down my blouse), I saw uniforms. Two police officers, one male, one female, who had Norma clamped now between them; she hung there limply, like a rag doll, like a garment on a washing line. As if her bones had turned to jelly.

Everyone seemed to start talking at once then. Someone fetch another chair. Can someone please pick up those notes? What just happened? Get a *chair*. She needs to sit down before she falls down! Mrs Hamilton, are you alright? Well, it was lucky they happened to be in A and E, to be honest. I *know*. I can't *believe* it! *Look* at her. No, we'll need to take a statement. Who *is* she? No, it's fine, love. I'll see to it. No, no, it's *fine*. Just mind your step there. Mrs Hamilton, are you *okay*? Shall I get you a glass of water? In the sluice room. Behind the printer. Well, she's in shock, obviously. Me neither. I have *absolutely* no idea. Can someone go and grabs some pads, for Mrs Hamilton's nose, please?

And while my ears struggled to make sense of all the jabbering, my eyes met Norma's. Her face was mascara-streaked, lipstick-smeared and blurry, its vertical contours like tributaries flowing down to an estuary. Her hair was a crow's nest of coal-coloured tufts, and her raincoat hung open, her body beneath it a skinny, trembling mess. The low growl from her throat made the wattle on her neck shiver.

Her eyes, though. They stared out at me, exactly like Aidan's. As pale and cold and treacherous as Arctic meltwater.

'How's it doing?'

'I think it's stopped. I need to go. My patients . . .'

Half an hour had passed. The police had gone, taking Norma Kennedy with them. Arrest made. Show over. And Neil Porter had returned, proffering a mug.

He shook his head. 'No, you'll stay right where you are until the bleeding has stopped, and then you're going to drink this cup of tea.'

'I'm fine. I don't need one.'

'Overruled. You're going to sit here and drink a cup of tea and that's the end of it.'

I couldn't remember the last time I'd had a nosebleed. Had forgotten just how long it could take to make one stop. I gently lessened the pressure I'd been maintaining on either side of my septum, but as soon as I removed my fingers I could feel a fresh bubble of blood forming, and, when I swallowed, the coppery metallic tang of it as it slid down my throat. I also had a dull, steady ache pulsating in my cheek. My hip hurt. I pinched my fingers on either side of my nose again. At least I had finally stopped shaking.

'Overdose,' Neil said, as he sat back down across the desk from me. We were in the same consulting room I'd spoken to Jessica Kennedy in a few days previously. Only this time it was me on the patient side of the desk. Fitting. I tested the flow again, gingerly. 'As far as I've been able to find out, he was brought into hospital first thing this morning, after his mother found him unresponsive at his home. I don't know what he took, but he's not in any danger. He's only staying in because of the query hairline ankle fracture he sustained when he fell. Drink your tea. You'll be in shock. And you probably need a biscuit. I'll see if we can find you one.'

'But then I'll be late getting away, and I can't be late getting away today. The boys have a session at the climbing centre booked, and I'm supposed to be meeting my childminder there. So—'

'No, you won't. I'll mop up for you.' He sprang up, went to the open door. 'Mo! Mo, you out there? Any chance of finding a biscuit to go with that tea? So, anyway,' he said as he returned to his seat. 'What was it you said to me about him? Ah, yes. I remember. "Not likely to be problematic." Hmm. Discuss.'

'It's complicated,' I told him.

'I should say so. And I already know. It was me who reviewed your op notes, remember? When it came to illegal substance abuse, he really did taste the rainbow.'

I rolled my eyes. 'Of course you did. Sorry.' I took a sip of the tea, holding the tissue up a little so I could get the mug to my mouth. It was too hot to drink, and my lip was swollen too. I put it down again. 'I think his wife must have left him. I imagine that's what prompted it. *And* this.' I put the mug down and gestured with my free hand to my nose. 'She came to see me last week, to apologise for the complaint they made against me.'

'Don't you mean *she* made against you?'

'She was coerced.'

He nodded towards the open door. 'By that woman? The man's mother? I couldn't believe what I was seeing for a moment there – she looked completely deranged.'

'You've not met her yet?'

'No, his wife brought him in for his first follow-up. But why attack you? What's any of that got to do with you?'

'She thinks I put her up to it, clearly.'

'Did you?'

I shook my head. Told Neil the gist of my conversation with Jessica Kennedy. 'Though of course Norma would think I had something to do with it. She thinks I'm the devil incarnate.' And, I realised, might have found out that Jessica had been to see me.

'Why?' Neil asked. 'Isn't her son the one who's the black sheep in this equation?'

'Like I said, it's complicated, at least where Aidan's mother is concerned. She lost her elder son when he was still very young. Aidan's half-brother, that is, from her first marriage. I never met him. He died in an accident when he was home on leave from the army. So with Aidan losing his arm too – well, I'm sure you can imagine how that must have affected her. And if his wife's left him now, and taken his children too, well, what with already losing Dillon—'

His eyebrows rose. 'Hang on. Dillon? As in *your* son?'

I nodded. There was no point trying to pretend any more. 'He's also her grandson. At least, he was.'

I watched him try to join the dots. 'O . . . k*ayyyy*,' he said eventually. Then frowned at me. '*Was?*'

'He was my sister's son. *Aidan's* son. But Aidan walked out on them. And when Hope died, Matt and I adopted him – as per her wishes.' I paused, instinct kicking in. Unwilling to elaborate further. 'Well, perhaps naively, we thought, you know, that that was going to be the end of it.'

Neil was nodding. '*Now* I get it. No wonder you wanted shot of him.'

The tea was cooler now, so I took another sip, to show willing. Smiled a grim smile. 'Exactly. Welcome back to Brighton, eh? God, let's just hope this *is* the end of it.'

'Well, they've arrested her, so that should at least give the woman pause for thought. And you be sure to fill in the incident report for HR here as well – and while it's fresh in your mind, too, ready for when you make a statement to the police. They're going to come back tomorrow, by the way, and speak to you then. Oh, and let me take some photographs,' he added, picking up his mobile off his desk. 'Because you know how these things go. Given her age, they might be inclined to let her off with a warning. But you shouldn't let it go. She could have broken your nose. And I'm not at all sure you shouldn't get your things and head home. You look like you've done a round with Ronnie Kray.'

I smiled. Lowered the tissue. The flow had finally stopped. 'No, just Vi Kray,' I corrected, as Mo appeared with digestives.

Though as I returned to work (on which we compromised: Neil would see my last three patients), the similarities between the infamous gangsters' mum and Norma felt all too real. Both were famously blind when it came to their precious boys. Which perhaps made her all the more dangerous.

I did a stupid thing then. With a little time to kill before I'd need to leave to meet Isabel and the boys, I decided – no, felt compelled – to go and see Aidan.

I didn't know what I hoped to achieve. Even more grief, most likely. After all, Norma could have been released by now and be perched at his bedside. Or Jessica might be there with their girls. But my hunch was that the former was logistically unlikely (and after all, she must surely have known he wasn't in danger by the time she attacked me), and if the latter, so be it. I could always walk away again.

It was close to five, and the ward I had tracked him down to was still busy, but a quick visual sweep revealed him to be alone. And bar the nurses, who greeted me incuriously as I passed, every other occupant was otherwise engaged, some with visitors or magazines, others scrolling through tablets and phones.

Aidan was awake, but doing nothing. Just staring up at the ceiling, though when he sensed me approach he turned his head. And did nothing to temper his expression when he saw me, which was one of intense exasperation. He looked, to use the off-duty technical term, like shit. He had one leg outside the covers, the foot and ankle thickly bandaged, but the sheet and blanket were pulled up to his chin. By a sympathetic nurse, I suspected. He lay still, like a corpse, his stubble thick and oily-looking, as if painted on for a part in a play. He'd also had a recent haircut, which had aged him. Or perhaps life had done that on its own.

'*What?*' he said, as I reached to sweep the curtain around the bed. 'I'm not receiving visitors. Didn't anyone tell you?' Then when I didn't answer immediately – I wasn't even clear what I wanted to say to him – he added, 'Come here to gloat, have you? Go ahead. Don't mind me.'

Then he turned his head dismissively so he was back staring upwards. As disabled as he was – by the drugs, the missing arm, and now by an injured ankle – I supposed it was all he could do. His mobile was by his bed. I wondered if he'd heard that his mother had been arrested.

'Aidan,' I said. 'Look at me.' He didn't. 'Do you see this?'

I put a finger to the side of my nose. It was sore and swollen now, and the skin of my cheek and right eye socket was already darkening with subcutaneous blood.

'Your mother attacked me in outpatients earlier. *She* did this. Look, I'm sorry for what's happened to you, and I genuinely hope you and your wife manage to sort things out. But all this stuff with Norma, it has to stop, okay?'

He turned his head then, finally. Cast his gaze over my face. A part of him, I realised, seemed to be enjoying this.

'You honestly think I can stop her doing *anything*?' Those pale eyes, so reminiscent of a Siberian husky's, bored steadily and unblinkingly into mine. A whisper of a smile then. 'You honestly think I even *care*? Tell you what, why don't you just fuck off, Grace.'

It wasn't a question.

And as I left him, cursing myself for having gone to see him – what else *had* I expected? – he was already reaching across the bed for his phone.

Chapter 11

I looked, no doubt about it, a bit of a state. Though my patients, every one of them, had kindly refrained from passing comment (presumably because they didn't need to – news travels fast in waiting rooms), a quick inspection in the wing mirror before I'd climbed into the car had reminded me why I should always keep sunglasses in it, however dark and overcast the day. My upper lip, though still swollen, was looking slightly less alarming, but I'd obviously burst a tiny capillary in my sclera, because there was a smear of bright red in the white of my eye. And the bruise that was forming between my nose and right eye socket was still at the start of its journey. Soon, it would darken to a deep navy-purple, where the haemoglobin in my blood, starved of oxygen, broke down, and within a week, it would be green, and then yellow.

Right now, though, it was an arresting shade of raspberry-red, and as I walked into the climbing centre to meet Isabel and the boys, I was aware of the stares it couldn't help attracting, and the presumptions of violence (people always assumed violence) it no doubt inspired as well.

I had already texted Isabel to warn her, so she knew what to expect, alluding to a misjudged intervention when helping a colleague with a distressed and angry patient. *Occupational hazard!* I'd finished it, jauntily.

Matt I'd told the truth to, between patients. Well, a version of it – a milder 'holding' one, at least till I saw him on Friday, because there was no sense him fretting and fuming in London. And, for once, I was glad I wouldn't see him till then. Give it time to go down, so he wouldn't overreact.

Which, of course, the boys did, because I looked such a fright. And more down to that, I judged, than concern for my welfare. Which was good. I didn't want them worrying I now worked in a war zone.

They had just finished their session and were emerging as I went in. 'Oh my GOD, Mum!' Daniel said, characteristically mindless of his decibels. 'You look like you've been in a punch-up!'

'It feels like it, too,' I said, 'but thankfully not. Just accidentally ended up at the sharp end of an elbow.'

Dillon looked anxious suddenly. He pointed towards my chest. 'Is that *blood*?'

'It is,' I said, nodding. 'I had a nosebleed as well.' I smiled broadly, which hurt. 'A rather spectacular one, too.'

Isabel, off to meet her boyfriend, was pushing her arms into her coat sleeves. 'You sure you're okay?' she asked. 'That looks majorly painful.'

'I'm fine,' I reassured her. 'Only seeing the odd star now. Nothing a large gin and tonic won't remedy later. One of those things. You get off. Honestly. I'm absolutely *fine*.'

'How did it happen?' Dillon asked now. 'Did he, just, like – oof!' (he did the mime) 'and try and use it to smash your face in?'

'*No*,' I said firmly. 'Not at all. He didn't *mean* it. It was an accident. It was just one of those things. Being in the wrong place at the wrong time.'

Isabel frowned. There was more to it, and she knew it.

Being in the wrong place at the wrong time was a familiar feeling; where Hope was concerned, I'd found myself there a lot. First as an observer – of her being left, of her dying, of my nephew being as good as orphaned – but then, with an inevitability that I had somehow not factored into any of those events (how?), for me and Matt, it stopped being a spectator sport.

Yet, in my naivety, I'd thought I could make everything work. It was one of my core character traits, after all, hewn over years of conflict and insecurity. I *had* to make everything work, because if I didn't, who would?

Though there were ground rules, Matt's red line – a clean break from the Kennedys – being one of them. No half measures, no guardianships, no shared responsibility. In joining our family, Dillon must, definitively, be leaving theirs, so we began the formal process of adoption immediately. And with Aidan's affidavit (signed and witnessed at a law firm up in Hull), a formality was all it was ever going to be. He'd wanted out. He'd already proved it. Had voted with his feet. Now he had formally, legally, confirmed it. So, out in the real world, just as I would be Dillon's new mummy, Matt, his former uncle, would become his legal dad.

And, at first, it did work – at least, as far as it was able, given how painful her son's disappearing act must have been for Norma to process. And not least – Aidan's willingness to walk away notwithstanding – because of all the things I knew about him and she didn't. (And wouldn't. Not from me. She had suffered enough, hadn't she?) It worked because Norma loved and needed to see her grandson, and because I fully accepted that the same was true in reverse.

But I had badly overestimated the extent of her acquiescence about her role in the new family dynamic we'd agreed on. Perhaps I'd been hopelessly deluded to think it ever could work.

Because it was a dynamic that, of necessity, airbrushed Aidan from Dillon's future. That had been his choice, after all. But what was true for us could so obviously never be true for Norma. So while we'd agreed that Aidan would play no further role in Dillon's childhood, for Norma, though he was absent, he was always fully present.

First in small ways. A couple of little wooden trains I found in the bag I would always pack for him when I took him to visit her.

'Ooh, this is nice,' I said, when I found the first, thinking Norma must have bought it for him. He pointed. Said 'dad-dy'. Said 'train' and said 'dad-dy'.

'Oh, *that*,' she said, her voice light as cotton wool when I mentioned it. 'Well, I thought I might as well get Aidan's train set down from the loft. Lovely to see it being played with again after all this time,' she'd added brightly. 'They made toys to last back then, didn't they?'

I let the 'daddy' thing go. After all, I was feeling my way through all this as much as she was. At some point we'd perhaps have to have a difficult conversation about Aidan, and the business of how he was referred to around Dillon, but not till he was old enough to understand a little better. And with Aidan out of the picture, that time wasn't yet. In the meantime, I didn't want to go there.

Three weeks later, however, Dillon emerged on to Norma's doorstep with a teddy bear clutched in his hand. An expensive Steiff teddy – it had the little trademark button in its ear – but old and balding; it had clearly seen much better days. And to which, Norma explained, Dillon had 'taken such a shine', which was why she'd told him he could take it home.

It was clear he had, too, so I automatically made the right noises. But my instinct said otherwise. And my instinct was right. Almost the first thing I noticed, after Dillon pressed the bear on me so I could kiss it hello, was that it had something written on one of his paws. It was faded, but not so much that I couldn't work out what belonged in the gaps. Fill them in and it was obvious. Aidan Kennedy. And I couldn't help it. I thought of Hope, and all the horrible things he'd put her through. I didn't want the thing in my house. 'It has to stay here with Nanna Norma,' I told him firmly.

'Oh, bless him,' she said, as he went into meltdown. 'I don't mind if he wants to hang on to it, *honestly*.' She squatted down to him. 'As long as you take *werry* great care of him, Dilly. Because Daddy's teddy is *werry werry* precious.'

Again, I said nothing. This was not the time or place. But as our eyes met, the defiance in Norma's was obvious. As far as she was concerned, the fact that Aidan had formally relinquished him was neither here nor there. He would always be Dillon's father, end of.

I stood my ground. Politely. Made Dillon hand back the teddy, and drove back home with him screaming blue murder till Gatwick. Where he finally fell into the sort of deep, exhausted sleep that I knew meant he wouldn't settle again once we were home and another fractious evening was in prospect.

I was brimming by now with anger – that '*werry werry*' had set my teeth on edge – and, alongside that, a growing sense of hope-lessness and panic that I knew had been brewing since we'd first taken Dillon home. Not so much about the chaotic new dynamic we were struggling with, profound though that was, but about *me*. About the rogue thoughts that were beginning to ambush me, almost hourly. That the child sleeping in the back of my car wasn't *my* child. That I had willingly invited a cuckoo into my nest.

That while I was trying to navigate a situation I had no part in creating, my own son – already so confused and disorientated by it all – had been denied his mother on her day off, *again*, so that a child I barely knew could spend time with a woman I barely knew, and where both – there was no getting away from this truth – would far rather be with each other. Dillon was far too young to understand, and thank God for that, but Daniel's bewilderment and distress at the invasion was palpable. Only two days before (the only positive being that Matt hadn't been there to hear it), he'd asked me outright. *Can Dillon go home soon?*

I carried regret around like Atlas, a world of 'what ifs' on my shoulders. Guilt and shame like an unexploded bomb tied to my chest.

Matt, understandably, felt even more agitated than I did. 'We need to address this,' he said. 'Nip it in the bud. We don't have the first clue what she says to him when she's alone with him, do we? We need to make it crystal clear that Aidan is no longer Dillon's daddy and that she mustn't refer to him as such. I mean it, Grace. If we don't, this could all become too messy to be viable. Just remember whose mother she is. D'you want me to speak to her?'

No, I thought. Thank you, but definitely not. Because it would require a level of diplomacy my straight-talking Glaswegian husband simply didn't possess. I fretted then, for days, about how best to approach it. But then fate took it out of my hands. I'd planned to visit Mum a couple of weekends later, and drop Dillon at Norma's for a couple of hours, when a crisis at work meant I had to take on another doctor's on-call shift and cancel the trip at short notice. Norma was fine, if a little terse, pointing out that she'd already booked a slot at a soft-play centre. Then suggested that perhaps she could come to us instead.

To which I had to say no, another red line having been that, for all that we'd try to support Norma's relationship with Dillon, this didn't include the whole extra layer of complication of her – Aidan's mother – coming to our house. Which was not what I said. I had no desire to hurt her further, so I explained that I'd already now booked both boys into their usual nursery – but when I told her that I wouldn't be able to make it down for at least another couple of weeks now, she said, 'Ah, so this is how it's going to be, is it?'

'I'm sorry?'

'That it's going to become too much of an inconvenience.'

'Norma, it's not an inconvenience. It's just difficult to organise. I have a busy job, and—'

'And you have to shove my grandson into a fecking nursery so you can do it. It's not right.'

I was shocked by her sudden vehemence. 'Look, I realise it's disappointing, but there's nothing I can do about it. I'll bring him down to see you again as soon as I can.'

But had I subconsciously wished just a little too hard? Because fate stepped in again then, perhaps to accelerate what would always be inevitable; two weeks later, both boys went down with chickenpox, just a day before I'd arranged to take Dillon to see her.

This time, she was angry from the outset. *So* angry. It was a side of her Hope had alluded to but which I'd never seen before.

'I understand that you're upset,' I said. 'But—'

'You understand nothing! What the hell do you think *you* know about my feelings?'

'Norma, I appreciate just how hard all this must be for you, but they have chickenpox.'

'So *you* say.'

'Please, Norma, stop this. I'm trying to do my best, okay?'

'Yes, your best to deny me my grandson. Don't deny it. To estrange me from him, to deny me a part in his life, just like your sister did to his father.'

'That's not fair, Norma. Aidan left *her*, remember. Left both of them.'

'Because she gave him no choice! That was the plan you cooked up together, wasn't it? Don't think I don't know what you and that lying bitch were up to.'

'I don't know what to say to you,' I said, because I didn't. But by the time I'd drawn breath to try, she'd slammed the phone down.

And even then, we might still have patched things up. After all, patching stuff up was my default setting, wasn't it? Doing things for the best. For the good of all concerned. I'd half expected her to ring me, to apologise for what she'd said, and even when she didn't, *still* I hoped we'd smooth things over. I'd had more than enough bile and bitter conflict in my childhood, and fallings-out made me anxious and stressed. But a week later, just at the point when I'd steeled myself to call her, I returned home from work to find Matt almost apoplectic with fury, after a lengthy conversation with the adoption agency.

We were still only at the beginning of the process at this point so, though we'd been assured that it would involve little more than box-ticking, given we'd been named in Hope's will, it most definitely wasn't a given. And it seemed Norma had other ideas.

'She's contesting the will,' he said.

'What? Can she even *do* that?'

'Apparently. She has six months. And it's not been six months yet. And there's worse. She's been in touch with the adoption agency and is trying to block it—'

'*What?* How? On what grounds?'

'On the grounds that Aidan only agreed to it under duress, and that we're "not appropriate" people to be adopting him in any case. And that, bottom line, she is. Because she can look after him full-time, whereas we both have full-time jobs. Because she's cared for him on a regular basis since his birth. Which she has. And we haven't. Because she strongly considers it to be in his best interests.'

In short, she had fired an arrow right through my Achilles heel.

Which was why, during the short, stressful business that followed, I more than once found myself questioning whether we were doing the right thing. All I knew of Norma Kennedy was that she was Dillon's gran and Aidan's mother, and all of that, bar the few occasions we'd spent any time together, had been through the understandably distorting filter of my abandoned sister. And though my every instinct still told me Dillon's place *was* with us, another voice niggled constantly – that she had raised valid points. Unlikely as it seemed that she'd be successful (the solicitor had been reassuringly firm on that), it didn't mean that her case, despite her age, despite Aidan's absence, didn't hold at least some merit. Even my own mother had commented as much. No, she didn't *agree* – Dillon obviously belonged with his cousin – but her sympathy for Norma's case was clear.

And I was sympathetic too. For her terrible loss, the heartbreak of which I couldn't begin to imagine. And when her appeal was dismissed, as everyone knew was going to happen, I even suggested to Matt that I write to her.

He'd been incredulous. '*Why?*'

'Just to say how sorry we are. None of us wanted this, did we? Her included.'

'Hen, *don't*. Just let it lie now. There's no point stirring this all up again. You don't want to go giving her any reason for false hope. Because that's all it will ever be now. In doing what she's done, saying the things she's said to you, she's made sure of that herself. I mean it, hen. *She's* the one who's burnt her bridges. We are *done* with her.'

But, ironically, that ensured that I would never be done with her; with the sense of the sadness and tragedy that anyone had to suffer what she had suffered.

At least, till the morning of Dillon's second birthday, when it was clear it would never be done for her either.

It came in the shape of an unexpected delivery: a tall cardboard box, addressed to me. We'd assumed it would be for Dillon, but what was inside perplexed us. A large flowering perennial, in a pot. It was still in bud, though the tag showed a photograph of it in flower – beautiful spikes of a deep purple-blue. An *Aconitum*, apparently, with the common name of monkshood.

But a note at the bottom of the laminated card held a caution: *All parts of this plant are highly poisonous. Keep away from pets and children.*

There was nothing on it to tell us who'd sent it, or why. The only note on the dispatch slip was a generic 'Enjoy your gift'. It was only later that night, when Matt googled it, that we recognised it for the sick joke it was. Full of deadly toxins, the *Aconitum* was also known as wolfsbane. 'Get this,' he'd said, 'because, historically, it was used to *kill wolves*. What the *hell?* What kind of lunatic sends a poisonous plant as a present? The woman's fucking *insane.*'

We duly burnt it, and dismissed it; refused to grace it by reacting. Decided to see it for what it was – a particularly vindictive species of poison-pen letter. If anything, it felt more like the sort of thing you'd find in fairy tales – the forgotten godmother in *Sleeping Beauty* who, enraged at being excluded from the party, lays the fateful, vengeful curse.

But it was more than that. She had sent it to the home Dillon lived in. Chilling evidence that we *had* done the right thing.

PC Wallace, who arrived in my office, as had been arranged, the following lunchtime, wasn't in fact a PC at all. 'These days, I'm a police community support officer,' he said, gesturing to the embroidered patch on his chest pocket. 'Or PCSO,' he added, 'for my sins.' His role, he explained, as he lowered himself on to one of the chairs, was to practise 'the dark art of diplomatic dissuasion'. 'To defuse things,' he explained, looking very pleased with himself, 'ideally, before they become things.'

He was short, and rather portly, and looked close to retirement, and I wondered if his vision was the reason for the career shift, because he'd yet to indicate that he'd even noticed the state of my nose. I touched a finger to it. Thought about that long-ago sinister floral gesture. 'This is already a thing,' I pointed out. 'Trust me.'

PC Wallace remained unperturbed. 'So I see,' he said, belatedly seeming to notice, 'but you'd be surprised by the effect a little visit from me or one of my colleagues can have on a person. Anyway, I've taken witness statements, and I understand you wish to press charges. But I must advise you that we'd only consider submitting a case like this for prosecution if certain criteria are met. And given Mrs Kennedy's age, and her health, and the circumstances around the assault . . . the unfortunate situation with her son, of course—'

'So you're not going to charge her.'

'We haven't ruled that out. It's just that in the *first* instance, it might be more expedient to take a more softly-softly approach. As I say, given her age, and the fact that she has expressed remorse about her actions . . . would you at least agree that a sensible first step in this case is for us to go and have a word with her—'

'You mean give her a caution?'

'No,' he said, stringing the word out as if gently chiding an errant toddler. 'Not formally. As I say, in situations like this, we usually find a little chat is sufficient. Which is not to say that we wouldn't hesitate to take further action, if—'

'If she comes rampaging into the hospital and attacks me again?'

'I'm sure that's not going to happen, Mrs Hamilton.'

He rolled his eyes as he spoke. Only by the smallest amount, but enough that I caught it even so. I was also pretty sure I knew exactly what he was thinking. That I was mildly hysterical, that my choice of words was melodramatic, and that attacks by rampaging pensioners weren't something that generally happened in Brighton.

But I knew something else. That it wasn't up to me anyway. And even if they did submit a case, it wasn't up to the police either. No, that would be a decision for the Crown Prosecution Service. Who would almost certainly consider putting someone like Norma Kennedy in the dock to not be even remotely in the public interest.

In short, I was scuppered. She'd get a ticking off. No more. That was likely to be the most I could hope for.

I spent the next couple of days deep in thought. As my bruise began its inevitable rainbow metamorphosis (which I continued to document via badly focused iPhone selfies), so my brain spooled through what had happened and the memories that had been stirred, and I kept coming back to the same thought. Twice now my sister had been called a liar. First by Norma, and then again by Aidan's wife.

I had expected the former, but I couldn't help but keep going over and over the conversation I'd had with Jessica Kennedy. Yes, it was to be expected that Aidan had rewritten history for her (and his) benefit – that he'd painted a picture of my sister as some vengeful woman scorned. Yet something else began nagging at me too, and continued to do so. I lay in bed sleepless that night, going over and over it, because the nagging simply wouldn't go away. I thought about Mum, and her addled mind, and the things I'd said to Dillon over Christmas. About how hard it must be to spend a lifetime relying on the information your brain gave you, and then to discover it was constantly misleading you. How hard it must be to accept that it was getting things wrong, even when the evidence was presented as incontrovertible.

Was it nagging at me because there was another potential narrative? A differential diagnosis that I'd yet to consider? Was my 'truth' about Aidan, what he'd done to her, the way he'd treated her, so embedded that I was unable to see what might be staring me in the face? Was there more substance to Norma's vendetta than I'd thought?

Hope's tumour had come with a long list of potential complications. Death, obviously. It was a particularly aggressive cancer; a swift and merciless killer. But before that, and in common with brain tumours generally, it could cause all kinds of progressive brain-related malfunctions, depending on where it was growing: some disabling, some distressing, some completely unpredictable.

I'd researched all of this early on, even discussed Hope's scans with her consultant, so I knew what sort of changes we might expect. And at the time, though we were all gripped with hopelessness and terror, it seemed possible that, with luck, because of the position of her tumour, my sister's route to the destination she had no choice but to travel would at least not be complicated by the sort of wholesale mental fracturing that would effectively see her lost to us long before that.

In simple terms, there was at least a fighting chance that she would not lose her marbles till towards the end.

And so it had seemed, at least on the surface. But was that true? No amount of scans could tell us definitively. Brain tumours tended not to be accommodating like that. Perhaps changes had been taking place that were too subtle to be noticed unless you were constantly with her, which I hadn't been. Suppose they *had* been happening? And no one had picked up on it? I thought back to that first recording Hope had made for me when she was putting Dillon's memory box together. How she'd talked about the business of cleansing her soul.

It was such an odd term to use, even for Hope. And what if it hadn't been just about explaining all her childhood transgressions? What if she'd taken the process further? What if it had become part of some bigger project, some obsession, aided and abetted by her tumour – some mania to get Dillon away from Aidan? But could that really be so? She had still seemed so, well, sane.

I was leaving the hospital on Thursday afternoon when I realised I could push away the nagging thought no further. I had emerged from the hospital to a particularly brilliant winter sunset, ablaze with the same ochres and purples and yellows that were currently trying to outdo each other on my face. I stopped to take it in – it was too arresting, too beautiful, not to. As if some celestial impressionist painter, blessed with a sudden creative urge, had been let loose with their paintbrushes and liberally daubed the whole sky with great sweeps and whorls in magnificent hues. And at its centre, beyond the skeleton of the former West Pier, the sun blazed so huge and orange that I could barely see. It was then that I had my own blinding revelation.

What if everything I'd accepted as fact in fact wasn't?

What if Jessica Kennedy was the one telling the truth?

Chapter 12

'You want my honest opinion or the edited-for-a-family-audience version? If it's the director's cut you're after – and bear in mind that doesn't mean he's not still a complete piece of work – yes, knowing your sister, yes, I'd say it could be. I'd go even further, actually. I mean, I understand about the tumour and how that could have affected her personality, but even *without* the tumour, I can see how she might have done something like that. Can't you? Seriously, you've got to know how manipulative she was.'

It was Thursday evening now, and Matt and I were talking on the phone. We usually FaceTimed, but because I didn't want him to see my face before he had to, I pretended I was having problems with my connection.

'But to be that vengeful?' I said. 'That determined to stop Aidan having access to Dillon, knowing how huge the implications were?'

'Absolutely. In fact, maybe she'd be that determined *because* of the implications. Look at it this way. However she felt about Aidan by the time she knew she was dying, she had a zillion reasons for wanting us to adopt Dillon *anyway*. Financial security. Stability. A safe, decent childhood. Not to mention making sure he'd still have a relationship with Daniel. Because be honest, would he otherwise? Almost certainly not. Can you imagine how it must have looked to her when she worked out her options? More than likely she'd have been all too aware what would most likely happen – that he'd be off living with a father who was sniffing lines of coke for breakfast. And maybe shacked up with the girlfriend he'd been having the affair with. And, who knows? A couple of step-siblings – and, down the line, maybe half-siblings. And that poisonous witch of a grandmother in the picture, to boot. Don't forget, she knew her far better than we did. And it wasn't like your own mother wasn't a factor in any of this, was it? No, I'd say it was highly possible that she embroidered it a little, just to make sure we didn't feel we had a choice in the matter. There's maybe no smoke without fire, because we knew what he was like, and, to be fair to her, it might not even have been primarily about revenge. She might have *genuinely* thought she was doing the best thing for Dillon. And you've got to admit, given everything that happened afterwards – everything that's happening *now*, she was right, wasn't she?'

Hope's long-ago words about cleansing her soul came back to me again. *Had* deceiving us for the greater good all been part of the process? 'But what if *none* of it was true?'

'How can that be? We already know that's not the case. They were possibly the most dysfunctional couple I've ever met. Was there ever a time when they weren't tearing lumps out of each other?'

'No, but specifically. Not the infidelities. We know they were all true. I mean the cruelty, the controlling behaviour, the violence. What if she *had* made all that up, because she knew it would jerk my strings? That's what I keep thinking back to. That because I knew what he was like, I just automatically believed her. Because you would, wouldn't you? Especially given the stress they were under. With her illness, with a baby, with all their money worries – you just *would*.'

'And his conviction for GBH or whatever it was. Course you would. And perhaps that *was* her plan. And it worked, didn't it? But don't forget, he still walked out on her. He can't airbrush that away, can he? And he didn't even try for contact. He didn't even stay in the same *city*. If he was innocent of all the things she accused him of, he would have stuck around, surely? Put up a fight. Why didn't he do that?'

'I don't know. That part of it doesn't make any sense to me. Well, it does if you believe the noble-sacrifice narrative, but I don't. But that's not even my point. My point is what if she *did* do all that, drag us into it – God, not that I'd change anything, obviously – just to get back at him for being unfaithful? What if she did do it primarily as a final act of revenge? I mean, she's my sister, and I hate even thinking it, but, Matt, if she did do that, that's *terrible*. It means she knowingly engineered things to steal Dillon from his own father, *and* his grandmother, don't forget, against their will.'

'*If* it's true. You don't know that. And even if it was, he obviously accepted it as a fait accompli pretty quickly, even if his mother didn't, so my heart's not exactly bleeding for him right now.'

'Nor mine, obviously. But that doesn't make it *right*, does it? And if she did, then it's no wonder Norma hated her. Hates us still. Hates *me*, specifically. I mean, we cut her off, completely, from her own flesh and blood.'

'Hang on – *we* didn't do that. She brought that on herself.'

'Yes, but perhaps it was always going to end up like that eventually. Because it could never have worked, could it? Not once Dillon got older, even if she hadn't done what she'd done. And, let's face it, we were only too happy not to have anything to do with her any more.'

'Too right we were. But you need to stop feeling bad about it all. None of it was our fault. And these sorts of rifts and forced separations happen all the time. Death, divorce, whatever. It's not like she's the only grandparent in the world this has happened to. And you're still missing *my* point. About Aidan. He didn't even *try* to argue his case, did he? If he'd cared that much, he would have. And he didn't. He ran away. Only one person deprived Norma of her grandson and that was Aidan. If he'd stepped up to his responsibilities, we wouldn't be where we are now, would we? The idea of *us* taking on Dillon wouldn't have even been on the radar. No, if you ask me, it all worked out exactly as he'd hoped. I think they probably had a big bust-up over that girl he was seeing, and while she saw it as the writing on the wall for Dillon's future, *he* saw it as the perfect opportunity to walk away, start again. If anyone needs to feel bad about his mother, it's him.'

'God, I *hate* talking about Dillon like this.'

'I know, hen. Me too. But you have to separate where we are now from how we ended up here. And be honest. Isn't that the more likely truth of it? And we're never going to know now. And I'm not sure I even want to. I'm much more concerned about the here and now. What that lunatic bloody woman might do next.'

'Exactly. That's *my* point. I can't stop putting myself in her shoes – thinking how *I'd* feel if someone tried to take Daniel or Dillon away from me. I'd be beside myself. I'd be *raging*. So can you imagine how much anger she must have carried around with her all these years? Especially given that she'd already lost a son. Especially since Aidan then disappeared. And don't forget, even if it isn't true, to her it must have all seemed premeditated. She probably thinks we cooked the whole thing up together.'

'Which isn't terrifically far from the truth, is it? But listen, I need my bed,' he added. 'And by the sound of you, so do you. Oh, and by the way, I have an afternoon site meeting tomorrow, so I'll probably go back to the office and do some work before I head back, rather than sit on the M25 for three hours. And listen, in the meantime, you be sure to chase the police. Make sure they *have* been to give her a warning. And make sure you're on your guard at work, okay?'

'God, Matt. Shut *up*. You're scaring me.'

'Welcome to my world. I've been terrified of your entire family since the day I first met them. No disrespect, but especially your bloody sister.'

I lost another hour to brooding on it before I finally fell asleep that night. Had my little sister knowingly brought all these awful consequences upon us? My sister, who I'd thought I'd *known*? I'd had many years of exposure to her mercurial nature, after all. But the loss of someone tends to shave the rough edges off their memory, because just as it's human nature to try not to speak ill of the dead, it's human nature not to *think* ill of them either.

Because, in reality, how well had I known her? How much detail could I have seen from such a distance? Six years is a big age gap when you're growing up and, in our own ways, we'd both had lonely childhoods. By the time I left primary school, Hope was still in the infants. By the time she arrived at high school, so tiny in my cast-offs and bits of bought-to-grow-into uniform, I was already in the upper-sixth form. Same school, but I might as well have been light years away. By the time she met Aidan, six weeks into her short spell in catering college, I was already in the final year of med school.

So, though the young adult me hoped that one day we perhaps would be, at that time we weren't really close; Hope was just a *fact* of my life, rather than a part of it. Yet every bit of evidence, scant though it was, seemed to suggest that, as death began to claim her, she had known me – and Matt – only too well. That her mind, though inexorably being swallowed by her tumour, was, in that respect, as sharp as it had ever been. Though Matt was right – there was no point going over everything and apportioning blame. It wasn't the past we had to worry about, it was the here and now, and Jessica Kennedy leaving Aidan had already had painful repercussions. How much more loss was Norma going to take before she snapped again?

Chapter 13

The brilliant sunset the previous evening had lied about its intentions, because Friday morning dawned cold, dark and sleety. It felt as if we'd been plunged back into midwinter, spring nowhere near coming, and the clouds rumbling over the sea as I drove into work felt like a physical manifestation of the ones gathering in my head.

I knew Aidan Kennedy had left hospital – he'd been discharged the morning after I'd seen him – but I still had no idea what had happened to Norma. It would only be my business if I proactively made it my business, a course of action (despite Matt urging that we should pressure the police to throw the bloody book at her) about which I now felt increasingly uncertain. I didn't *want* it to be my business. Didn't want any part in making everything even worse, and it might. And there were also Aidan's children to consider.

Perhaps Norma's arrest would have been enough to warn her off in any case. And perhaps I should try and see it for what it might have been – a woman on the edge again, temporarily lost to reason. Perhaps now, even if all they had done was give her a warning, she'd see the sense of leaving me alone.

I would call the police, I decided, if I'd heard nothing by lunchtime. Just to be reassured – as I hoped would be the case after I'd spoken to them – that a stern word from PCSO Wallace had been enough. In the meantime, it seemed the perfect day to be holed up in theatre, and away from yet more of the curious stares of colleagues and patients, and endless questions about how I'd got my black eye. Which, happily, was what at least my Friday morning had in store.

Or so I thought.

When I'm in theatre, my phone sits on the top of the trolley with the computer on. Mostly I ignore it when it buzzes, for obvious reasons, but if it becomes insistent, skittering around so much it's in danger of falling off, I usually ask either Siddhant, depending whether he's assisting or just observing, or one of the ODPs if they can check if it's important.

Back in the day, things were different; when in theatre, we were effectively incommunicado. The only exception would be in the case of an emergency, which would require whoever needed to get in touch to call the hospital landline and, via the switchboard and whichever secretary, send a message.

The last time that happened to me was in February 2011. I was still a junior doctor then, and was assisting with a rotator cuff repair when an ODP pulled me aside to take a call from my mother, who told me my little sister had passed away.

So, not an emergency, not in the sense that I could down tools and rush away to help. Just a terrible, heart-wrenching fact. And, despite knowing it was coming, a massive shock. I'd seen her only a week previously, spoken to her only a day previously, and, illogically, because I of all people should have known better, I just couldn't get my head around it all being so sudden. As if 'probably months yet' or 'probably weeks yet' or 'probably days yet' or 'probably hours yet' were set in stone. A kind of death's Greenwich Mean Time, to which everyone adhered.

In contrast, this was something that clearly needed my attention, because when my phone started demanding that I look at it,

I found a missed call, and a voicemail, and then a text from Holly, asking if I could give her a ring as soon as I was able.

Fortunately, I was operating on the last patient of the morning, so twenty minutes later, having had the ODA text her back and let her know, I was able to call her.

'I'm so sorry to bother you at work,' Holly said. 'It's just that your mum's gone on a bit of a wander. I've put the call out' (to the local police, I presumed – their usual protocol when this happened) 'but I thought I'd ring and check that she hasn't been in touch with you. Though since I called you I've been up to her flat to look for clues, and I suspect she might have gone up to the cemetery. I mean the burial ground,' she corrected. 'She's been – ahem, understatement of the century – turning things out. And I don't know if you remember, but she had that big bag of bulbs delivered, and from the looks of things, she's had it out and taken most of them with her.'

It took two goes to work out what Holly meant by bulbs. Then it clicked; Mum had been on at me more than once about us going together to plant new spring bulbs on Hope's grave – though this had been back in October. And I had put her in a holding pattern – yes, soon, maybe next week, I'm just a bit busy at the moment – because I didn't want to go there. I hadn't for a long time. And if she no longer remembered why, I certainly did.

'In this weather?' was all I could think of to say.

'I don't think your mum worries much about what the weather's doing these days. But her raincoat's gone, and her handbag, so she presumably has her bus pass. Though whether she still has the wherewithal to know how to use it is obviously another matter. I'm not sure she's been on a bus on her own since November. But, look, let's not panic. The police have her picture, and you never know, given the sleet, she might come back of her own accord. And in the meantime, I'm going to call them – the burial place, that is – see if they can have a look around, see if they can spot her, and let me know.'

'What can I do, Holly?'

'Not a lot. I just wanted to keep you in the loop. And don't worry. Sure we'll have her tracked down in no time. Your mum's not a wanderer, and she has ID with her. Just, if she gets in touch, says where she is, let me know?'

I disconnected, feeling the storm, for so long just a suggestion of clouds in the distance, now approaching at speed. Mum had never wandered off like this before, not as far as I knew. But now she had, and the immediate future spooled out before me. Were we entering a new and even more stressful stage? I had a friend in London whose father had been in the SAS. When he took to wandering, he took it seriously. He'd hike twenty or more miles in whatever direction he was facing and was more than once inter-cepted crossing a motorway.

I tried to still the waves of anger that couldn't seem to help rising, and locate a shred of some more appropriate emotion. To remind myself that coming down here had been for precisely this reason, so we could firefight in person, not remotely. But with thinking that came another realisation. Despite Holly's composed, breezy tone, wasn't it *in*appropriate to calmly get on with my day when my mother might be intercepted on a motorway herself, pos-sibly even mown down by a lorry? So though I couldn't stop feel-ing resentful – I was still smarting about the things she'd said to Dillon – I couldn't see any option but to rearrange my afternoon, which, having checked all was well with the lady whose hip I'd just replaced, I duly went and did, feeling terrible.

It wasn't as big a deal as it might have been – I was down for an afternoon of telephone triage, which could be covered – but as I walked out to the car park, sleet swirling wetly around me, I wondered quite what it was that I *could* do. Drive round Brighton trying to spot her spotted Pakamac?

I was just getting in the car when Holly provided me with an answer. 'They have her safe,' she told me. 'She was at your sister's grave, bless her, exactly as I suspected, trying to plant bluebells with her bare fingers.' She sounded justifiably pleased with her detective work. 'Though it's a miracle she made it there when you think about it, isn't it? I checked on Google. I hadn't realised how far away the place is.'

I felt a not entirely unwelcome ripple of instinctive loyalty. It was no miracle. Mum had made that journey (or, perhaps more accurately, pilgrimage) at least weekly, sometimes more, for nearly a decade now. She might make it no longer – well, this unexpected aberration aside – but its logistics were on the hard drive of her still robust long-term memory, so she could probably do it on autopilot. Besides, this was my mother, who was fearless about travelling; a woman who'd think nothing of taking thirty teenagers on a school trip, often almost completely unsupported. Much was taken from her when my father left – her sense of worth, her status, what little joie de vivre she had – but there were gifts, too. Not least that of bullish independence. She may have wanted to hang on to him, but she most definitely didn't *need* him.

'Anyway, here's the thing,' Holly went on. 'I know you're probably busy, but is there any way you could drive out there and collect her? I can't leave here – we have chair-a-cise in the lounge at two thirty – and they say she's upset – understandably – and wet through, to boot. And the girl there's on her own today, so she can't. I was thinking a taxi, but—'

'I'll drive straight up there now,' I cut in. 'It's the least I can do.' Though as I pulled out on to the road and headed north, under a malevolent-looking sky, it was with a profound sense of gloom. Beautiful as the site was as a resting place, there was no rest for me there; no quiet times of peaceful contemplation.

I'd taken the boys there only twice since the day of Hope's funeral. The first visit had been when Dillon was three, and his adoption was finalised. I hadn't wanted to, but it had been suggested that a visit, to mark the end of the process, might help give us all 'closure'. He'd been oblivious then, obviously, to both the occasion and the place. Just content to run around after the long, boring drive. Only Daniel – four and a half then – had seemed to grasp any deeper meaning, suddenly tugging at my arm on our walk back to the car. 'Mummy,' he'd asked me anxiously, 'are there *dead* people under the grass here?'

He'd had nightmares for days after that.

I took them down again when Dillon was five. I'd had some leave to use up between jobs and had taken the boys down to Brighton for a couple of days, and Mum, who was still visiting Hope's grave on at least a weekly basis, was determined he should visit her too. 'It's been *too* long,' she'd said. 'It doesn't matter what *we* want,' (i.e. what *you* want) 'we have a responsibility to make sure Dillon doesn't forget her.' And despite my misgivings (this was something for the future, surely – when he was older, could make more sense of it, make his own mind up about it), guilt and some hardcore emotional blackmail made a wimp of me, and I finally agreed.

It was a mistake. Faced with the words on the plaque, which he solemnly sounded out, Dillon had made a perfectly reasonable point. 'But how can *she* be my mummy?' he asked. '*You* are.' He took it in, too, when I explained (following all the advice I had anxiously scrabbled around to find for just such moments) that I was absolutely his mummy, just as he was my little boy. But he was special. He'd had another mummy too, once, I reminded him, who'd loved him dearly.

'But she died,' he said. And matter-of-factly, because we'd drip-fed the story to him constantly. 'So you're my *proper* mummy.'

And even as I'd reassured him that was exactly how things were, my mother blurted out that, no, Hope was his *proper* mummy, scowled at me as if I had spat on Hope's grave, then, to my utter astonishment – there had been absolutely no hint that this was coming – grabbed his hand, and said, 'Dillon, your *real* mummy is down *there*, under the ground!'

Out of the three of us – Daniel was by now at the lake edge, squatting down, looking for frogspawn – I don't know who was most shocked by this outburst. Mum immediately began apologising, spewing sobs, looking mortified, while Dillon, speechless now, just stood and gaped at the flower-speckled grass beneath his feet. It took a long time to make it right and, for me, an even longer time to process. Had the then apparently sleeping dementia beast already been stirring? It was expedient to think so, so that's what we went with, but, for me, it wasn't just that. It hinted at something much darker. Some complicated rift between *us*.

The sky, too, was growing darker as I swung into the car park. Which, unsurprisingly, I had almost to myself. The only other vehicle in evidence was a muddy white minivan, which was parked over by the small wooden building that acted as both reception and the administration office.

I climbed out of the car, and as soon as I was back out in the elements I felt the ice-laden air swipe my face. And now I was here, a part of me felt a grudging respect for my mother. This was a remote spot, outside Hassocks, some distance in itself, and a long walk from the closest bus stop, too. Yet at no point, apparently, had she faltered. She'd made a plan, prompted by a compulsion born out of whatever had triggered it (seeing that bag of as yet unplanted bulbs, perhaps), and had made it here, on her own, in filthy weather. There was actually something faintly heroic about what she'd done, which made me feel slightly less resentful.

Which magical thinking was obliterated in an instant, just as soon as I entered the reception building and saw the tiny figure hunched by a blow heater in the corner, a forest-green blanket thrown over her shoulders, and her bony fingers – even from a distance I could see her nails were caked in mud – clasped around one of their white branded mugs. Here was no intrepid adventurer – at least, not any more. Just an elderly lady, with dementia, and not a clue where she was.

Mum barely registered my arrival. When the inrush of cold air made her aware of my presence, she didn't so much turn and look at me as through me. The girl behind the desk, however, stood up, pulled out her earbuds – she'd been working on a laptop – and hurried across.

I gestured towards Mum, introduced myself, and she nodded sympathetically. 'She's not making a lot of sense,' the girl said. 'She has dementia, right?' I nodded. 'And she's wet through. Completely sodden. I have no idea how long she'd been out there before I found her. I must have missed her when she arrived, or I'd have spoken to her, obviously. Not really the day for it, is it? Anyway, she's had some tea and she'll have hopefully thawed out a bit by now. I hope she's going to be okay,' she finished. 'Poor thing.'

'I'm sure she'll be fine,' I reassured her. But, privately, I wasn't so sure. Because although Mum seemed to recognise me when I squatted down in front of her, as soon as I touched her – a hand on her arm, as I told her I'd come to fetch her – she flinched and started babbling apologies, evidently much distressed about something, and continued to do so all the way to my car – something that, given her reluctance to be shepherded anywhere, by anyone, was in itself no mean feat.

The girl in the office had been right; she wasn't making a lot of sense. Talking nonsense, for the most part, as I herded her into the passenger seat, no less agitated than when I'd first arrived. Yes, she talked a lot of nonsense anyway, but it was generally a specific kind of nonsense, in the sense that you could work your way back to its root, and, for the most part, it was delivered in sentences. This was not that. Incoherent as she was, she was definitely trying to communicate something important to me.

'It just all got out of *hand*,' she said, more than once, as I clicked her seat belt into place. 'I *told* her. Grace, I *told* her.'

'I know, Mum,' I soothed. 'It's okay. You're okay now.'

She grabbed my wrist then. A sudden icy clasp. 'But you *don't*!'

But whatever she was on about, this was clearly not the moment to dwell on it. Because given that her hands were the colour of raw beetroot, and every single stitch of clothing on her was soaked, there was a genuine risk that she might be developing hypothermia. So I dared not take her home, because her life might be in danger. I needed to take her straight to A and E.

Chapter 14

Because I'd called ahead, a team were ready and waiting, and with minimal delay Mum was allocated a bay, where, between us, we stripped off her scraps of sodden, freezing clothing. I knew there was little I could do about her dignity – she would be absolutely mortified to be so intimately manhandled – but in being there, assisting, just being a presence at the bedside, I could at least cling to the illusion that I was contributing.

In reality, I knew I was only still here because no one wanted to be the one to tell me not to be. Perhaps partly because I was entirely superfluous. Scissors do the best job of these kinds of disrobings, so it was a straightforward business for the charge nurse to slice her clothes off, from foot to head, including the top she was currently wearing more than any other, and would put on every day if she could. A top she'd miss. Which made me think about Daniel, who lost his favourite blanky toy when he was two, and I'd already had the foresight, once it became 'the' toy, to go back and grab a second. I could so easily have done that for Mum, but I didn't. Why didn't I? Why wasn't I better at all this?

Once Mum was free of her clothing, she was covered in a Bair Hugger – a big plastic bag, essentially, into which hot air was pumped – before being transferred on to a bed bound for a ward, leaving the shredded clothes behind on the trolley. They no longer looked like clothes. Just components of clothing. As if laid out in a factory, waiting to be machined. But at least she was a less alarming shade of pink. Though no less incoherent. It was sobering to think that had Holly not been able to put two and two together so quickly, she could so easily still be up there. Could have died.

In the privacy of my head, I'd prepared for my mother's death often. The unanswered phone call. Holly's name popping up unexpectedly on my mobile. A random visit to the flat, to find her lying on the floor. The mental leap. The acceptance. The getting into gear. But not, strangely, this. This more humdrum, much more likely, perhaps, crossing of the Rubicon. Her being hospitalised. Reassessed. Declared moved-up-a-level. To the nursing home. And then to the top floor of the nursing home – the secure floor. The one with window bars and wall-to-wall hygienic easy-clean surfaces. The stage no one wants, but so many get.

Momentarily, because my mum was that no one personified, I considered the benefits of it all ending here, now, today. Of all the things I was least prepared for – with Mum, in life generally, in my relationship with death – the detachment with which I seemed able to process this potential scenario was frightening in itself. That I could do it without feeling bleak felt all *too* bleak. Was such a horrible thing to admit, even to myself.

There were countless staff I didn't yet know in this huge teaching hospital, and once Mum was finally settled on a geriatric ward, to be rehydrated and treated for what they suspected was an acute kidney injury, and would very likely lead to infection, I was just another anxious relative, taking up space. Which was why, when a nurse asked if I had details of Mum's usual medications, I realised I'd be more useful if I actually went to get them, along with her toiletries and night clothes.

Back when Mum first moved into her flat at The Beeches, she would laughingly refer to herself and her fellow residents as the 'inmates'. Though it wasn't a nursing home, or any other kind of institution. They were all privately owned apartments, albeit ones sharing a 'support' umbrella. They had care lines, a social programme, Holly. It was one of many such developments springing up everywhere in recent years, a practical, pragmatic way for the over fifty-fives (the usual watershed) to throw off many decades' worth of material shackles, as exemplified by the hoardings that advertised them – heavily emphasising the silver-surfer benefits of constructive downsizing, freeing up cash, and precious time, to go on cruises.

I'd never seen any evidence of that here. Beguiling though the pitch looked, the reality was very different. Yes, pragmatic (definitely in Mum's case), but usually for different reasons. Most were women here: divorced women, widowed women, women without families. I knew of at least two who hadn't a single living relative. Being around for Mum, therefore, lent me an unsolicited status here too, because it formalised the one I'd been bucking against all my adult life – that of dutiful, to-be-relied-upon daughter.

It looked like a home, though, despite the marketing message. So perhaps someone didn't get the memo. The carpet was burnt orange, the furniture 1970s; the chairs – a variety of wing-backed, easy-rise ones – were all upholstered like train carriages, in cut moquette.

I was keen to hurry past; get what I needed, get back to the hospital, check all was well, then run away, to my own life, and my own home. But I'd arrived during 'Friday Night Fun', their regular weekly early-evening get-together, and Isabel's gran was already rising from her chair. 'How's your poor mum?' she asked. Then took my hand and squeezed it. 'More importantly,' she asked, 'how are *you*, dear?' And I was struck by how I honestly couldn't remember a single time since my childhood when my own mother had ever asked me that question. 'Your *eye*—'

'Oh, it's nothing,' I said, 'just had an altercation with a swing door at work earlier in the week.' Then before the emotions of the day threatened to give me away further, I reassured her that Mum would be fine, told her Isabel was an angel, then made my excuses and headed on upstairs.

Where, as soon as I entered Mum's flat, I remembered Holly's comment about the mess. She was right. The living room looked like a crime scene. There was barely a patch of carpet visible. Just piles and piles of paperwork, seemingly pulled out at random, from various boxes and carrier bags and plastic lidded trays, which she'd presumably dragged in from her bedroom in stages. I stood in the doorway, thinking she was right – things definitely *had* got out of hand here. What on *earth* – *who* on earth – could have prompted her to do this?

It was probably pointless to speculate. It could have been something completely innocuous, after all. A feature on gardening on *This Morning*, or something like that. It wouldn't be the first time she'd latched on to something on television and become obsessed with some tangentially related scheme or search. Equally, she could have stumbled upon the cache of bulbs as a by-product of rummaging around for something else, and remembered what she'd bought them for.

I spotted something else too, which did seem to make sense. In the middle of all the muddle on the floor was an empty photo frame. One I recognised because I'd recently given it to Mum myself. Dillon's latest school photograph; I'd put both the boys' most recent ones in frames for her. I didn't know which was the chicken and which the egg in the bulb/Dillon equation, but she'd obviously decided, since I could 'never be bothered', that she'd take him to visit Hope's grave herself. Well, at least his image. Which was presumably still there, no doubt sellotaped to the plaque, and flapping wildly in the sleety, scouring wind.

Till one of the staff took it down again, at any rate. Which they would: bar the native flower species on the approved list, any kind of adornment to the graves was strictly banned. And Mum, never happy with Hope's choice of resting place and all its 'daft, happy-clappy' rules, was already known as a serial offender.

I stepped over the mess and went into the kitchen, where she kept her stack of plastic trays of pills, one tray per week, four weeks' supply, pre-sorted by the pharmacist into individual daily doses so she didn't get muddled up. Those safely in a bag, I then made my way into Mum's bedroom, to fetch some nightwear and slippers and toiletries.

If anything, the mess in here was worse. There were drawers half pulled out, contents riffled through and muddled, and for a moment I wondered if my first impression had been the right one – had someone broken in after she'd left and turned everything out in search of loot? But nothing of value had been touched – her padded jewellery box still sat where it always had, and its contents appeared undisturbed. In the middle of her bed, though, squatting like a huge sulking toad, sat a holdall I immediately recognised. It had been Hope's, and Mum had obviously dragged it out from the bottom of the wardrobe, because that too was open, and the shoes, boots and sandals that normally sat in a jumble on top of it had been distributed around the carpet in front of it.

I was in a hurry – to do what was required of me and get home to my boys – but something about the scale of the mess of stuff in front of me made me actively want to scan it for clues. There was just *so* much – as if part of a sustained search for something. Not in itself unusual – not at this point in Mum's dementia, anyway – but there was just so much of it, as if she'd been trawling for hours. For those bulbs to plant? No. I didn't think so. This was much more like a palaeontologist digging down through rock strata; an unpeeling of historical layers.

I saw things I'd not seen in years, and, in some cases, decades – possessions and records I'd imagined I wouldn't see again till she was gone and I was sorting out her belongings to settle her affairs. And not just all the well-thumbed bank statements and fuel bills and phone bills. What looked like the contents of the expanding file she bought when my dad left had also been dug out: her passport, her National Insurance card, a cache of long-expired bus passes, plus the old NHS baby books in which she'd recorded our milestones and vaccinations. Marked our steady progress along the centile charts with tiny ballpoint dots.

There were several bundles of letters strewn on the bed too, all categorised and contained by coloured elastic bands. Some I recognised as predating her. Some harked back to her childhood. Some were familiar from my own childhood as bitter-sweet heirlooms: the handful of letters from her father, when she was packed off to boarding school; the rather thicker wodge from a penfriend in Bonn.

One bundle of letters, however, was unfamiliar. And though there was no reason why it shouldn't be – I had power of attorney, but that didn't mean I was my mother's keeper – I found myself immediately drawn to it. The letters were all still in their envelopes – rather large ones, just for letters – with Mum's name and address handwritten, in business-like capitals. And once I liberated them from their elastic band I saw there were ten or twelve of them, and that the most recent – one of only two addressed to here, rather than her old place – had a postmark some three years old.

They were private, no question. Absolutely none of my business. And were it not for the situation, I probably wouldn't have given them more than a fleeting thought. Another penfriend, perhaps. A similarly retired colleague. An unlikely correspondence with Aurélie.

But the postmarks were all Brighton – I flicked through to check them – and though I felt grubby, like a snooper invading her privacy, there was something about the handwriting that was worryingly familiar. There was also something with them, which explained the large envelopes – a folded supermarket carrier bag, corralled within its own elastic band. And within *that*, there was another pile, of this time unopened envelopes. One was white, two were blue, one was red, one was lemon. And all different sizes, because they were greeting-card envelopes, but all of a size that would allow them to fit into the ones that had been addressed to her. And on each, in the same handwriting, was written the same name.

Dillon.

My brain already off the blocks and careering away from me, I picked one at random and slid a finger beneath the as yet unopened flap. Pulled out a birthday card. (Cartoon superhero. *Kapow! Wow! You're FIVE!*) Read the words inside the card, both the printed – a much exclamation-marked poem – and the handwritten; *to Dilly Dilly, lots of love, Auntie Mary xxx.*

Mary? I thought. Was this the Mary she'd mentioned before Christmas?

I picked up a letter, then. The one on top, the most recent one addressed to here. It was postmarked August 2017, a couple of weeks after Dillon's eighth birthday.

Inside the envelope was a single sheet of folded paper. The ink was black, the pen a ballpoint, the handwriting hurried. Not quite dashed off, like it might be on a shopping list or note. But there was no return address, and it seemed written in the heat of the moment. Without pause. Without thought. Only emotion.

It began '*Joy*'. Not '*Dear Joy*'. Just '*Joy*'. Underlined.

I truly cannot believe – double underlined – *that you've done this. After everything you promised me. WHERE* – treble underlined – *WERE*

YOU? Please call me immediately to explain what's going on. I waited an HOUR for you. Why didn't you phone me?????

CALL me. Please don't make me come round there.

So was this from Mary too? *Yes.* The handwriting was the same.

A sickening realisation began to mushroom up inside me. I thought back again, to the evening after I'd operated on Aidan. She'd been looking for something. For someone called Mary. Been triggered to do so by a call from someone called Mary. But I'd checked. There hadn't *been* one.

Then I realised my twenty-first-century error. It had never even occurred to me to check the landline. Mum's meds forgotten now, I tore open the red envelope. (*To a special boy. Merry Xmas! Lots of love, Auntie Mary.*) Then the lemon one. (*Birthday Hugs. Lots of love, Auntie Mary.*) Then another of the letters. An older one, this one. Another single-pager.

Dear Joy, it read. *It was lovely to see you. And thank you so very much for the latest photos, which I'll treasure. As promised, here's the card. (I popped ten pounds in it for him.) Let me know when we can sort something out next. And, as I said, please don't worry if it's short notice. I'll get there.*

Till then, all the best to you, and fingers crossed for Easter, N x

I sat back on my heels, read the letter again, reeling. What the *hell?*

N. N for Norma. My mother *had been corresponding with Norma.*

Corresponding *secretly* with Norma, about Dillon. My own *mother.*

And then something else hit me. This latest colossal 'sort-out'. Was this what Mum had meant about things getting out of hand? Could it have happened because Norma had *been* here?

I'm not easily shocked, but I was now, to the core.

Holly only worked from eight till three, so she was, by now, long gone. And when I left Mum's flat – having thrown everything, plus all the evidence, into Hope's battered old holdall – the sitting room downstairs was dark and deserted, Friday Night Fun being a strictly time-limited affair. I dithered over doing so – Holly was as entitled to her time off as anyone – but in the end, once I was on the road back to the hospital, I decided to call her. I might just as well get her up to speed about Mum now, in any case.

'Just one thing that's struck me,' I added once I'd updated her. 'About what might have prompted all of this. Do you know if she's had any visitors in the last couple of days? There's an old friend of hers. Mary. Elderly. Black hair. Petite. Only, looking at some of the things Mum's turned out, I'm wondering if she might have been round to see her.'

'Not that I'm aware,' Holly said. 'I can ask if anyone else knows, but people come and go all the time here – including dozens of carers. And though a lot of them seem to think I should be, I'm not a sentry. She could well have had a visitor. Could have had several, in fact. I'll ask around if you like, but I wouldn't get your hopes up. When do you think she'll be back now?'

'I have no idea,' I said. 'Now she's in the system it could be days, or even weeks.'

'More likely weeks,' Holly said. 'Now she's in the system, they'll need to put a care package in place before they can let her out again. Still, she's safe. That's the main thing. Give her my love, won't you?'

I told her I would, but as I drove back into town, I wondered just how much I'd be able to summon of my own.

Chapter 15

Mum was asleep, the sister told me, when I returned with the pills and her clothes, the latter of which I'd packed assuming my instinct would be sound – that it would more likely be a three- or four-day stay, minimum.

I gave her Mum's pill packs, then went over to her bedside. The ward was quiet now, the lights dimmed, the nurses padding around silently, and as I walked I could feel the weight of my new knowledge like a ball and chain dragging my feet.

Mum's colour was better now, her hair dry and brushed, and I was pleased beyond measure that her eyes were closed. Because right then, I couldn't even bear to look at her, let alone, as I had seen on my way past the other beds, place a comforting, loving hand over her own. So I didn't linger. Just put the case by her bed and left for home.

Then, on a whim, or perhaps an instinctive compulsion, I dived into the big Sainsbury's on my way. I had a powerful need to separate myself from the clouds gathering around me. To simply bolt. Try and outrun the emotional storm. To get back to my own family, my own life, my own routines. To reassure myself that what was going on – *had* been going on, and for what appeared to have been for years – was something apart from me. Wholly separate. Ditto my mother's astonishing complicity, another product of my dead sister's legacy, the tentacles of which were still reaching out beyond her grave. In that moment, I wished one thing above anything – *anything*. That I could wave a magic wand and wipe the Faulkner family hard drive. Overwrite the past with a completely different story – one where my dad hadn't left us, where we hadn't imploded, where the Kennedys were erased at a stroke. I wanted to scream, just as I had during that final grim encounter with Norma, that I didn't ask for, didn't want, didn't *deserve* any of this. That none of this mess was of my making.

I went straight to the bakery, bought a gingerbread man for Daniel, an iced bun for Dillon, a cinnamon swirl for Isabel and an éclair for myself. Sugar and spice, all things nice, to take away the bitter taste. Then, deciding to abandon the bolognaise I'd got out of the freezer that morning, I swept along the pizza aisle, choosing the biggest I could find.

And all the while the holdall in my car hummed with menace.

By the time I arrived home the sky had cleared, revealing an almost full moon, and where patches of the earlier sleet had now settled, it bathed the ground in a pale, blue-ish light. It almost looked like snow – the air even smelt of it – and though even if it did come I knew it wouldn't last (this was Brighton; snow and sleet rarely stuck), the unexpected brightness, after a day that had been so dank and dark, immediately lifted my spirits.

Though the tableau that greeted me when I entered the kitchen had the opposite effect. It wasn't maternal FOMO exactly, because it wasn't a fear of missing out. It was the *fact* that I'd missed out that really upset me. I wasn't given to sentimentality, because my career mattered to me hugely, but I was emotionally exhausted and it hit me really hard that while I'd been running around after my own treacherous mother, my children were having fun without me.

Or had been. I'd texted to say I was on my way when I left the hospital, so by now everyone was busy, bustling around, clearing up. They'd obviously been engaged in some sort of artistic activity, because tubes of acrylic paint I'd never seen before were lined up on the windowsill, and Isabel was wearing Matt's chef's apron.

'I've done Nan a picture of Spitfire,' Dillon declared, thrusting one of his finished paintings at me. 'He's a soldier, and he has a gun that shoots fire. See? I made a flame print to show it.'

Daniel, more pragmatically, had gone down a different road. His work of art was a vase full of sunflowers, my mother's favourite.

I felt emotion welling dangerously in my throat. My own *mother*. To avert an overflow, I hauled my shopping bag up on to the counter. 'I have cake.'

'Ooh, that sounds good,' Isabel said. 'But how's your poor mum doing?' She was bending down, busy rinsing paint palettes and jam jars, dipping intermittently to place things in the dishwasher, and talking to me over her shoulder.

'So-so,' I said. 'As well as can be expected, I guess.'

Isabel turned around then, hooking a strand of hair behind an ear and wiping her wet hands on her apron. A smiling sun in the centre of a calm domestic universe. The person my children came home from school to.

Something Hope and I had never had. Not, at least, as far as I could remember. Perhaps at one point, before Hope arrived, before her marriage had ended, perhaps my mother *had* been such a warm maternal presence. But my memories said otherwise. All they seemed to register was absence. Sometimes she wasn't there simply because she wasn't home from work, and I would look after Hope (at what now seemed an astonishingly young age); would be her Isabel. Or, much worse (and this became truer as I got older,

148

and my journey to school longer), she would be home but not present. As in not seeming even the tiniest bit pleased to see me – my 'favourite' status still no match for her true love, her work. I could hear the blare of the television in the living room – Hope banished to her electronic childminder, as per – and see the teetering piles of exercise books that always littered the kitchen table, bristling with childish errors that Mum needed to correct. See the irritation on her face as she jabbed her red ballpoint in my direction. For goodness sake, Grace, I'm *marking*. Can't you *see*? Just because I'm home doesn't mean I've finished *working*!

Why so irritated? Why so cold? Why did she even have children? Why, why, why, *why*?

Stop it, I told myself as I pulled out the cakes. 'They think she's developing a kidney infection,' I clarified. 'So they're keeping her in for a bit. But no major harm done, thank goodness.'

Isabel cocked her head slightly to the side, and frowned. 'Oh, *bless* her. Your lovely mum. It's all just so *sad*, isn't it? I was saying to my nan earlier. You must have been so worried about her. I know everyone there was. Still, at least she's in the right place,' she added brightly. 'And I'm sure she'll be back to her old self in no time. I'll put the kettle on, shall I?'

Then she stopped, looked at me quizzically, and, presumably reading my expression, placed a hand momentarily on my arm. 'Are you *okay*?' she mouthed silently, giving it a little squeeze. Then, deploying some secret skill she seemed far too young to have mastered, changed her tone completely, grabbed the kettle, and waved it towards Daniel. 'Oh, and by the way,' she trilled, as I gratefully swallowed the lump in my throat. 'By the *flippin' WAY*. Isn't it just the *best* news about Dan getting into the B team?'

'*What*?' I said. 'I didn't *know*! Oh, sweetheart, that's amazing!'

He made a 'tsk' sound. 'Mum, I left you a voicemail.'

'We thought you were probably in theatre,' Isabel added quickly. 'And then what with your mum and everything . . .'

By now, I was already rummaging for my mobile. Where, right there, amid the slew of Mum-related calls and texts and WhatsApps, was a lonely missed call from my son.

'Are you *crying*?' Daniel asked, looking bemused now. Then he grinned. 'Chill out, Mum. It's only the B team.'

'Of course your mum's crying,' Isabel told him. 'Mums *always* cry when they're happy. D'oh, Dan. *Everyone* knows that.'

I could only blow my nose and nod gratefully.

It was getting on for ten by the time Matt was finally home, by which time we had eaten what felt like half our body weights in pizza, and I'd recovered at least some of my misplaced emotional equilibrium.

But my mother, currently lying in her hospital bed, oblivious, was still dominating my thoughts. I was still dumbstruck by what I'd found, and had by now created an inverse correlation; the more I was able to slot the correspondence into an orderly timetable, the less ordered were my increasingly racing thoughts. What the *hell* had she thought she was doing?

I poured Matt a beer, got out some cheese and crackers for him to eat in lieu of dinner, and once he was sitting down at the kitchen island, and he'd inspected my eye, I finally presented him with the evidence of Mum's betrayal.

'That's a strong word to use,' he said mildly. 'Even for your mother.'

'It's still the right word. The only word.' I pointed to the cards and letters now before him. 'She was doing all of this, right under my nose, for, as far as I can work out, at least five or six *years*.'

He picked up one of the cards. 'So Mary is definitely Norma, by the looks of things.'

'Of *course*. That was obviously the way they'd decided to play things. They couldn't introduce her as Norma, could they? The boys might say something to one of us, mightn't they? So I imagine they decided to tell the boys she was her friend.'

'Logical. But wouldn't Dillon have recognised her anyway?'

'I did wonder about that. But from what I can work out here, she didn't actually meet up with them till at least two years after we cut off all contact. How likely would it be? He wasn't even two the last time he saw her. No, they were obviously speaking on the phone at first, and Mum was sending her photos. And you know what's worse? That I've even worked out how they did it. And, seriously, it beggars belief.'

I passed him one of the letters. 'This was when we both went to Edinburgh for that awards dinner, remember? When she said she'd have the boys and we drove down and dropped them off with her, and then flew up to Scotland from Gatwick?' I grabbed another. 'And this was when you were away on that big road project in Cumbria, and I needed a couple of days to revise for my MRCS exam. Remember how she offered to have them, and how astonished I was? And this one—' I picked up the letter I'd first opened – the angry, threatening, '*don't make me come round*' one. 'This was when she was supposed to have them while they fitted the new kitchen in our old house. I'd arranged everything but there was that last-minute delay with the cabinets, remember? And I ended up deciding to stay down there as well?' I handed Matt the letter. 'Remember when I told her I'd decided to stay as well? Save driving up to London and back twice when I didn't need to? Especially with the kitchen in such a state. Remember me telling you how she'd huffed about having to make me up a bed? I was just working on the principle that she wanted to spend time with them without me there, but she was obviously agitated because her plan to meet up with Norma had been scuppered. I double-checked the dates. The letter's postmarked that Friday. Which means we were still actually *at* Mum's when it arrived. And you know what? I even remember her being a bit strange and distracted. D'you remember me telling you? How we'd wanted to go to that lifeboat charity event on the front, and she'd insisted on dragging us off to that bloody falconry centre near Hailsham instead? It all makes sense now. She must have arranged to meet Norma there, mustn't she? And was worried about the risk of us bumping into her with the boys there. And *God*, that's another thing. Her phone! Yes, I remember now – it kept on ringing and ringing, and when I asked her who it was, she was all odd and cagey – I think I even mentioned that to you as well, come to think of it. *Yes. Yes*, I *did*. And we'd laughed, thinking she might have a secret boyfriend. God, can you believe she was doing all this right under our noses?'

Matt drained his beer. Put the glass down. Shook his head.

Said, 'Honest answer? Yes. Absolutely.'

I started gathering the letters and cards into a pile. I still couldn't quite get my head round the extent of her treachery. Which had clearly troubled her too – it was presumably the reason she hadn't passed the cards on; to do so might have led to me asking questions. 'And do you know what else I've been thinking? That her haring off up to Hope's grave today didn't happen out of the blue. It was obviously triggered by something or someone – and, seriously, you should have seen the state of her flat – so what if that someone was Norma?'

But Matt was off on another trajectory. 'But *why*?' he said. 'Why would your mother befriend Norma Kennedy in the first place? What's her motivation? Why would she befriend Aidan's *mother*, given what her son had done to Hope? Why would she want anything to do with her? That bit doesn't make any sense.'

'But it *does*. Think about what we were saying last night. Suppose Mum had already gone through the same thought process as we have? And don't forget, Hope kept a hell of a lot about Aidan from her. So perhaps she felt guilty—'

'Guilty? About what?'

'About *Norma*. Well, maybe not so much guilty as, I don't know, sorry for her. That it wouldn't hurt to send her pictures of Dillon from time to time. Stay in touch.' I raised the wodge of cards in my hand. 'I'll *bet* that's how all this started. In fact, I'd put money on it. After all, she made no secret of the fact that she felt bad for Norma, did she?'

'Which was pretty rich, coming from her. Like she was ever granny of the century. Or mum of the century, for that matter. To either of you. Jesus. What a Judas.'

Which made me think then. About Judas. And his remorse at his treachery. Was that what Mum had been babbling about earlier? Was *this* what had got out of hand?

Chapter 16

I fell asleep that night in seconds, but at two I was wide awake again, agitated and restless. I could hear a tawny owl calling ('our' owl, as Daniel called it now; perhaps that was what had woken me) but, apart from that, the silence pressed in on all sides, only emphasising the clamouring of anxious thoughts inside my head. I knew there was no chance I'd fall asleep again.

The light in the bedroom felt strange, too. Not quite dark enough, faintly pink, distinctly milky. And once I'd slipped out from under the duvet – grateful for Matt's earplug habit, as I didn't want to disturb him – I could see why: the garden was blanketed in snow.

I knew I would never get back to sleep now, so grabbed my dressing gown and went downstairs to make myself a mug of tea, then headed across the hall and living room into the conservatory.

Though, technically, it wasn't actually a conservatory. It had low walls on three sides, as opposed to being fully glass, which apparently made it an orangery. It had come up during one of only two conversations I had had with our nearest neighbours, a child-less retired couple who'd known the previous owners well – and, I suspect, liked them better, too. (The only other time we'd spoken to them had been a slightly frostier encounter involving Daniel's football.) Whatever it was called, there were no oranges growing in it. Just a couple of beanbags, a coffee table, and the low L-shaped sofa that had been in our living room in London. We'd replaced it, for this house, with a substantially scaled-up model, which I hardly ever sat on, because I didn't do much sitting. And when I did, usually to read, I liked this one much better. Twelve years old now, it was sagging and on its last legs, but it had so many memories woven into its tired, threadbare fabric that it was like an old friend. Matt and I, newly married, curled up on it together, falling asleep on it, in the small hours, after a night at a party, and during all those barely awake 5 a.m. sessions breastfeeding Daniel before work, knowing, even *then*, that they were moments of precious babyhood I must burn into my soul, because they were ones that I would never have with him again.

I lowered myself into it now, in the same spot I always did, and recalled the day when Matt and I had sat on it with Daniel, and explained that his cousin was coming to stay.

'Which cousin?' he'd asked.

It said it all.

After Hope's death, I knew relationships were bound to get messy, and not just the complexities of assimilating a toddler we barely knew into our little family. Losing a loved one, especially so unexpectedly and tragically, is like dropping a rock into a pond; it's not just about the ripples that inevitably spread out, it's the violent displacement of previously calm water. Most will flow back, but some inevitably seeps away.

I had no idea what my mother was going through. I could guess – it's not like humans aren't wired to try, after all – but it was such a huge thing to imagine what it must be like to lose your child that I was no different from anyone else in that respect. I could sympathise but – with luck – I'd never be able to truly know, not on a visceral level.

Visceral it was. Mum was, for a while, lost to us. Wholly, worryingly absent. Had joined a club, one with a very small, exclusive membership. One nobody wanted to join.

We took Dillon straight back to London, of course, the day after Hope's death, and tried hard to persuade Mum to come and stay too, at least for a couple of weeks, so we could all be together. She wouldn't. She sat tight, with us visiting in the week before the funeral, and refused to leave Brighton after it as well. It was out of the question, even for a night, she insisted, since she had to visit Hope's grave every day. Sometimes, I knew, she spent hours there. Hours she'd rarely spent with Hope when she was well. But perhaps that *was* the reason, right there.

We never spoke about it. We'd rarely ever spoken about anything meaningful, and this was no different; in fact, I think it suited her. She'd taken full ownership of the family grief from day one. Had ring-fenced it so completely that I sometimes found myself wondering if she'd had some Damascene moment of shocking maternal clarity, wishing that perhaps I'd died instead. Because mourning me would have been so much more straightforward a business, so much less cluttered by guilt and remorse and regret.

And perhaps the knowledge that I *knew* that, as well?

Somehow, however, she got back to work, and sooner than anyone expected. She had taken barely half a term off, and was back in her classroom immediately after Easter, finding a way through the forest of the pain she was thrashing around in by leading the kids who'd always seemed a much more natural fit for her than her own daughters out of thickets of mathematical incomprehension. She retired the following year, at sixty-five, very reluctantly, by which time our relationship had shape-shifted so dramatically that what had once been a random musing on the complexity of grief now felt like a personal truth. Whether it was because I didn't share her loss, quite (not in her strict hierarchical system), or because she genuinely couldn't stop herself from feeling the way she did, she seemed to resent me every bit of my life: my work, my marriage, and our boys – particularly our boys.

And as I sat looking out over the garden, another brutal truth settled on my by-now chilly shoulders. There was no getting away from it. She hated me being happy.

I recalled one conversation all too vividly.

'They're throwing me a party,' she'd told me, once she'd set the date for her retirement. 'On the fifth, at the school. A special assembly. The mayor's coming. Can you bring the boys?'

The fifth. Which was a Thursday a scant nine days hence. 'I can try,' I'd said, my heart sinking. 'Though it might be a bit tricky.'

'Tricky why?'

'Because it's rather short notice, Mum. And I'm on call. Which would mean trying to swap it, which means—'

'But you *have* to bring the boys down. It's my *retirement*.'

'I know, and if I can I obviously will. But if I can't—'

'Well, where's Matthew?'

'In Glasgow, remember?' He was working on a road-building project at the time, necessitating frequent days-long trips away. The boys were still in nursery, the one at the hospital, and my weekdays were not so much a nine-to-five routine as a five-to-nine, mile-a-minute blur.

'Well, can't you take a day's holiday?'

'I can try. It might be difficult.' It would, in fact, almost certainly be impossible.

'But it's important. It's my *retirement*.'

I remembered wanting to scream then. *And I work for the NHS! And I am on sodding call!* 'Mum, I'll try, okay? I'll call you tomorrow.'

And I'd done so, the following evening, just as I'd promised, Matt's advice not to let her bully me ringing in my ears.

'Mum, I'm sorry, but I really can't do this. So, we were thinking, how about we bring the boys down to Brighton that weekend? Take you out for dinner. Somewhere nice. Have a family celebration.'

The silence was short. Short and sour. No hint of sweetness. And, in a flight of steps we both climbed up like medal-hungry Olympians, we went from regret (I did my best) and polite acceptance (thanks for trying) to a place we had probably both visited in our thoughts many times, but never, up till that point, together. Thus I was selfish and work-obsessed (*I'm* selfish? *I'm* work-obsessed?), she was unreasonable and demanding (oh, pots, kettles, young lady!), and, dig by dig, we arrived at the inevitable stalemate of disagreeing about whose needs mattered most here. Which inevitably veered away to whose *rights* mattered most here. Mine, not to move heaven and earth for her party. Or hers, bottom line, to have '*her* boys' there.

There's a point in chess, called the endgame, when the strategy changes. When the king, previously passive, becomes aggressive. 'Mum, they're *my* boys.'

The words escaped before I could catch them and kill them. They'd spent far too long confined to risk missing their moment.

A heartbeat of silence ensued. And despite knowing she'd been the one to press the button, I shouldn't have reacted, so I deserved what was coming. I'd been petulant and childish, and should instead have taken a breath and had the guts to air the more important truth. That these days my status as her 'rock' or her 'good girl' were contingent only on need, or as a conduit to *her* boys. And only then so she could display them, like trophies.

'You know,' she said, 'there's something you'd do well to keep in mind, Grace. That these are *my grandsons* we're talking about.'

'And your point is?'

'You know full well what my point is.'

'No, I really don't. Look, I really don't want to argue with you, Mum, but if there's something you want to say to me, then say it.'

'You *know* what my point is. If you weren't in *London*—'

'London, which *is my home*.'

'Exactly!'

It was my turn to press now. To make her come out and say what I knew she really thought; that no matter what the law said, she had the greater claim on Dillon. Without a word ever being said, it had come down to that. It was sickening. I said again, 'And your point is?'

'That *both* my grandsons are in London. Which I don't need to spell out would *not* be the case had you not—'

Fearing opening up a chasm that would never be bridgeable, I put the phone down so I wouldn't have to hear the rest.

We made up, as was traditional in our family, by pretending. That there was nothing to see here. That there was nothing to say here. Least said – everything *un*said – soonest mended.

In short, we reverted to family type. In ours, we didn't have such conversations. We liked to nurse all our grievances, not air them.

I considered that now, as I watched the snow continue to float down. It was getting heavier, the flakes the size of fifty-pence pieces. The boys were going to be so excited when they saw it, and the beauty of it almost made my mother's betrayal worse. I had come down here to care for her, given up so much that was dear to me. A home I loved, friendships. A support network. Trusted colleagues. Dragged Matt and the boys away from all they knew and cherished too. Would I have done that if I'd known what I knew now?

And had that ugly conversation been the line in the sand? The catalyst? Was that the point when my mother took full-throated ownership of the notion that, in taking Dillon to London, as opposed to moving to Brighton, I had cruelly and thoughtlessly compounded her loss by, in effect, taking her grandson away as well?

It was already so familiar, this grinding mutual resentment. But was it also the furnace in which she and Norma forged their unlikely bond? Had it helped them set aside their differences and find common ground? Had it united them against a bigger enemy? Me?

Because, to some extent, there was an element of truth to be found there. We'd been at loggerheads from the start about Dillon – there was no getting away from it. Over the difference between me honouring my sister's memory and making sure Dillon knew how much she'd loved him, and, as my mother seemed determined to, having the circumstances of his birth constantly rammed down his throat.

I'd tried to be accepting of Mum's obsession with making sure Dillon knew who his *real* mother was, understanding that it was almost certainly an unintended consequence of her own maternal guilt. But for Dillon, who had never asked for this complication in his life, it only created a chronic anxiety about his place in the only family he *did* know.

We had never resolved it. So the shocking truth was that I could *see it*. See Mum doing it wilfully. Self-righteously. For *years*.

I drained the last of my tea and unfolded my legs from beneath me. It was almost three now, but I was still as sleepless as when I'd come downstairs. Why would Norma go to Mum's? To collude with her further? To threaten her? Because it was unlikely that she'd have known about Mum's dementia.

Or would she? If she'd been in touch with her right after Aidan's accident, might she know now? And with the police having been to caution Norma – assuming they had – would that mean she wanted to cover her tracks? Or might there be other things Mum might have knowingly kept from me?

Even more agitated by now than I'd been when I first came downstairs, I went out into the garage, retrieved Hope's holdall from the boot of my car and brought it back into the conservatory to investigate further.

It would be eerie, I knew, to be reacquainted with its contents, and I had a powerful sense of Hope watching over my shoulder. The last time I'd looked inside it had been a few weeks after her death, when Mum and I had gone to her house to perform that most bleak of jobs: sorting through, and getting rid of, her possessions.

Perhaps because of that stark reminder that the story had so abruptly ended, we'd tackled it in similar fashion – spit-spot, like a military operation. We'd booked a collection from the British Heart Foundation and had them take most of the furniture, and bar what was left of Dillon's toys, and the few things of Hope's we'd decided to hang on to, everything else, pretty much, we had methodically bagged up or boxed, bound for the local Cancer Research charity shop.

All that was left, then, was the paperwork, the files and bills and knick-knacks, which Mum, who was beginning to fray at the edges by this time, had gathered up indiscriminately, for sifting through later. Everything that looked private, or official, or might warrant further investigation, she simply decanted (in some cases by upending entire drawers) into the enormous holdall we had found beneath Hope's bed. I let her get on with it, busying myself by running the vacuum over the carpets. I knew she was desperate to be gone before her grief so overcame her that she'd collapse and never leave the place again.

I knelt down on the rug and unzipped the holdall. Hope had bought it to go travelling around Europe with Aidan – one of many such grand plans that had never materialised. So, though many years old, and liberally scuffed from its time covered in shoes in Mum's wardrobe, on the inside it looked almost new.

Once open, it had an odd, sweetish scent to it. Perhaps a long-discarded hand cream, or a leaky bottle of perfume, part of the creepy smorgasbord of personal detritus. It was almost too personal; I felt as if I were an archaeologist, picking over remains. The half-used ChapSticks, the tampons, the expired store cards, the lidless ballpoints, the scribbled shopping lists, the random coins, the lone mitten, the tweezers, the single condom in its black crinkly wrapper.

I found another cache of photographs, in an envelope from one of those mail-order photo services that everyone used to use. All of Dillon. *Only* Dillon. All taken down here, in Brighton. And all of them – I didn't recognise a single one – taken by Mum. Must have been. And some had duplicates, others didn't, so were these part of a collection expressly curated for Norma? How could she have done all of this and still looked me in the eye?

But then I found something I recognised: a long-forgotten journal. It was in a pink hessian bag that I remembered from Hope's childhood, among what looked like the contents of her bedside-table drawers, and within that, as if the prize in a long-ago game of pass the parcel, it had also been wrapped up inside a polka-dotted scarf. It wasn't a diary, as such. There were no pre-dated pages. Just an exercise book, bounded by a soft metallic fabric jacket, and held together by a wraparound raw-edged leather fastener, as if the property of a medieval monk. On the front the words 'Sparkle Every Day' were embroidered. I'd definitely seen it before. I didn't know where, but I remembered it.

Though now I'd discovered it, a part of me didn't want to open it. This was too personal a thing for me to feel comfortable delving into. But this wasn't a secret teenage diary, complete with padlock and tiny key. Just a journal. And hadn't I already had the evidence, in the form of all those voice recordings she'd sent before she'd died, of just how keen Hope had been to bare her soul to me?

But it was private. Why else would she have buried it inside a scarf, inside a bag, and tucked it away in her bedside drawer? Because she harboured secrets that, at the time, she very much *needed* to keep secret?

I untied the leather strap. The first pages I flipped through told me little. They seemed mostly to consist of long lists of flower names, both common and their Latin counterparts, some grouped together – perhaps a wish list for an arrangement she'd been tasked with making? – others with question marks, underlines, numbers, presumably quantities and costings. And I realised why I'd recognised it. She had it with her often because she'd used it for work.

But it wasn't so much what was written on the pages as what was hidden among them, in the form of an envelope, a white A4 one, which had been folded in half, and half again, and which slipped from between the pages and fell into my lap.

I opened it out. It had been addressed to a Mr D A Prentice, at a firm of solicitors whose name I immediately recognised, because they'd been the ones to execute Hope's by then miniscule 'estate' and carry out the wishes in her will. There was a piece of paper too. Not inside it, but folded with it, on which Hope had started writing a letter.

The deterioration in my sister's handwriting shocked me. I knew fine motor skills could be affected by brain tumours; that forming letters might prove challenging once the cancer progressed. But seeing Hope's tremor – so obvious in all the tailed letters, the way the words meandered across the paper, swelled and shrank, misbehaved – was a powerful reminder that all had not been as it had seemed, at least from my long-distance perspective.

Dear Mr Prentice, it read. *Further to our phone conversation earlier, please find enclosed the ~~testimony~~ statement intended for my sister. It's _really_ important that this gets into no one's hands other than Grace's, and, as I mentioned, _ONLY_ in the circumstances we discussed. And only then, if Grace specifically*

At which point she must have been interrupted.

And had never gone back and finished it.

It was undated. So when had she written it?

I looked inside the envelope, in which there was another, smaller envelope, which had been stuck down, both with its own glue and Sellotape.

On the front, in Hope's handwriting again, it read, *For Grace's eyes only.* (So very Hope, I thought. So very Miss Marple.) And I guessed what it might be straight away.

I picked it up. Felt the bulge. Knew there was something solid in there. Something rectangular – about the size of one of those matchboxes you used to get in high-end hotels. But this wasn't a matchbox. It was covered in rows of tiny knobbles.

I unstuck the envelope. The knobbles were diamanté crystals. Which, again, I remembered, because Hope had shown this very thing to me – it was the diamanté-encrusted memory stick her friend Daisy had bought her for her last birthday.

I scanned the unfinished letter again. Ran a finger over the crystals. What could be on here that must get into no one else's hands but mine? And in what circumstances?

I felt a rush of adrenaline. Light-headed, as if I'd stood up too quickly.

What the hell was I holding in my hand?

Chapter 17

I went back into the kitchen, where my laptop was charging overnight, to find Mr Weasley thundering round and round on his wheel. So, partly to stop the noise, but also so I could hold him, I went over to the cage, lifted the latch and got him out.

It was a novel thing for me, having a pet. Because my father suffered from asthma, we'd never had one as children, and though Matt and I had discussed getting a dog on several occasions, there were too many obstacles – the hours we worked, the amount we travelled, our tiny London garden – so the right moment had never been found. So although Mr Weasley was technically the boys' pet, it was me who most often sought him out. It was probably this – just the fact that I handled him so much – that meant he never bit me, or, whenever I picked him up, showed any desire to wriggle free.

Shoving the laptop under my arm, I took him back with me, spooling him hand over hand the way he liked, grateful for his warm, undemanding presence. I had no idea what I'd found – wasn't sure I understood enough yet to even make a guess – but whatever it was, Hope had taken great care to keep it hidden. So what might it be? A stumbled-upon manifestation of some kind of brain-tumour-induced mania, after all? Or something real?

Something serious? Something so explosive that it could not be voiced, to me or anyone, before her death?

And about what? Dillon's future, surely. It had to be about Dillon. *For Grace's eyes only. To get into no one else's hands.*

Back in the conservatory, having transferred Mr Weasley to his tiny Zorb ball so he could ping around the room a bit, I opened my laptop and immediately realised I'd fallen at the first hurdle. Time had moved on a long way, and technology with it. Diamonds are forever. Diamanté memory sticks, less so. I realised I was stymied without a USB port. But then I remembered Matt digging an adapter out of a box a few weeks back, so he could attach his old wireless mouse to his new Mac. I padded back into the study, pulled out the drawer, and was in luck. It was still there.

It took a while then – a few verses of round and round the hard drive – but eventually, up it popped, and I was in. It was date-marked November 2010, so she'd recorded it less than three months before her death, and, unlike the recordings she did for Dillon, it seemed to have just one enormous file on it. A massive audio data dump, even by her verbose standards.

I pressed play.

And there was my dead sister's voice again, clear as day.

◆ ◆ ◆

18-11-2010. 14:47.

Okay. We're go.

Aidan's left, G. He's gone. Gone for good. And let me tell you, weirded out doesn't even begin to cover it.

Funny, isn't it? This should *so* have been a crying kind of day (*obviously*) but go me – I completely styled it out. You'd have been really proud of me – your feckless, reckless, *dying* little sister. I managed to stay dry-eyed like a pro, even when he was giving it both barrels.

I'm crying now though. Not sobbing – not even seeing him disappear round the corner. Not even with the knowledge that I'm never going to see him again. These are quiet tears. Not even tears, really. More leakage. That's the word for it. Like I'm full to the brim and they have nowhere left to go. You should see me, G, standing in my finery, dripping tears on to the laminate – like I'm a modern-day Miss Havisham, with my clock about to stop.

And by this time tomorrow, I'll have called you, and you'll be round here. And by the end of it, you'll be having to pick up all those pieces. And I'm going to *be* in pieces, you can be bloody sure of that. I have no choice. I really don't. And I know you'll understand.

Anyway, to the point. Which is to tell you the truth. Only please remember this, sis. Whatever happens when I'm gone – no, whatever happens *now* I'm gone (*shit*, that's a hell of a thing to say, isn't it?) – I just wanted to die having done the right thing.

That'll be a first, eh?

But no time for rambling. I have *such* a lot I need to tell you. But where to start? The beginning or the end? No, you know what? I think I need to start with Dilly. Oh, my precious, precious boy. Can you imagine how much my heart hurts right now? How much it aches? How much it's bleeding? Of course you can. You're a mother. I'd say a better one than me, too, because of course you probably are. Though I wouldn't exactly know, would I? *Shit*, Grace – isn't that *awful*? And now I never will. But I trust that you are. I *have* to. And you're bound to be. You're just better at everything than I am. Always were. Except, actually, again, how would I know, *really*? How do I know I'm not a fabulous mother? Or at least might have become one. I have nothing to measure myself against, do I? Well, apart from you. And between you and me, I'm not sure either of us really has this thing nailed yet. You know, I've watched you with Daniel and it tickles me, it really does. Fumbling around. Not quite on top of things. Your veneer of calm cracking. It's been good – and I honestly don't mean this in a bad way – to see you realising there are some things in life that you can't ace, can't control.

But you *are* a mother. So I don't need to waste time telling you any more about that, do I? You'll be *fine*. Hark at me, telling *you* that!

I will tell you this, though. There's this itch I keep scratching at and scratching at. It's frightening. Because it's *that* strong. It's *that* fierce, it's *that* compelling. I lie in bed with him sometimes and watch him sleep. Literally, just lie there and look at him, and look at him – I know you'll get that – and up it pops. I think: *why don't I just take him with me? Fuck the afterlife.* This is not about the afterlife because there *is* no afterlife. When you're dead, you're dead, you're *dead*. I just think (and, boy, would you have something to say about *that*) that he needs me *that much*. That he'll miss me *that much*. That there's no one who'll love him the way that *I* love him. How can they? So isn't the simplest thing, the best thing, the right thing, the *only thing*, to take my baby with me? Have him *die* with me?

Won't lie. It's *incredibly* scary. It's such a hum in my head, such a constant angry hum. Like a wasp's nest you poked a stick in, you know? It's so bad that I nearly said something to Kayleigh about it yesterday. You know – that nurse I was telling you about last week, at the centre? I came *that* close to telling her about the thoughts I was having. But then I thought – *shit*. If I tell her what I'm thinking they'll take him away, won't they? As in right now. Because they would, wouldn't they? Because they have a duty of care. And I have a sodding great brain tumour.

So this is where we are now. This is just how high the stakes are. There's only one person standing between me and these terrible urges. And, though you don't know it, and won't know it, that person is you, Grace.

Come good for me. *Please.* Just come good for me.

God, though. Aidan. Aidan, Aidan. How to make you understand? Because you never did, did you? Not as in now, as in you listening to this, obviously – I'll get to that, I promise – but as in how I felt about him. Why I loved him. What I *saw* in him. Ha – I can hear your brain working, sis – 'What on earth *do* you see in him?' Because you couldn't understand. Not really. Because to do that you'd need to be me, wouldn't you? Have lived *my* life. Not yours. Remember that first time you met him? When you came home from uni that weekend? God, your face was a *picture.*

I say home. It wasn't any kind of home for you by then, was it? You were *soooo* outta there. God, I was *so* bloody *wretched* about you leaving me there. Sorry. I know I'm going off topic, but did I ever tell you about the day you left for uni? Do you remember it? Our sainted father turning up, smelling of Gauloises and that *fucking* bitch's perfume, and Mum refusing to come out of the kitchen while the three of us loaded his van up with all your stuff, and then me standing on the doorstep, all on my own, waving you off? Once you'd gone I went straight up to your bedroom and slammed the door shut. And just lay on your bed, crying and crying for, like, an *hour.* And Mum never came to check on me. Not even *once.* And I was *twelve,* for God's sake. Can you imagine that?

Oh, I know what she'd say. She'd say she was leaving me to cry it out. Or giving me some space, or some other of her usual bullshit. Heaven forbid that she should actually have to *comfort* me. But you know what? I've been thinking about stuff like this a lot lately – sorry, I know, *major* digression – and I think I know why now. I think it was because she finally understood. That the *reason* I was crying was because you'd left me with *her*.

Sorry. Seriously, I need to stop rambling on, don't I? Because I need to get this done before Daisy gets back with Dill. Which will be in . . . *shit*. Okay, okay, so the first thing you need to know, sis, is that the thing I hope for above *anything* – and I really *mean* anything, despite what he's put me through – is that what he's done will never need to come to light. If it has to it has to, then fair enough, no choice. Absolutely no contest. And if it *does* come to it, then I hope – no, I *know* – that you'll forgive me when you realise just how many lies I've had to tell you. First of which – might as well be honest with you up front here – is that Aidan hasn't ever laid a hand on me. *Ever.* And he hasn't just upped and walked out on me, either, despite what I'm going to tell you when I speak to you tomorrow. He's gone because I gave him no choice. Because I made it clear to him that if he didn't go – and go for good, I mean, as in having no further part in Dill's life whatsoever – that I would have no choice but to tell you.

He's promised. He gets it. He hates it but he gets it. God, apart from anything else, he *knows* he couldn't give Dill half the life you can. He's not stupid. Well, he's stupid in lots of ways, but not when it comes to this. It's going to be tough on him – for starters, his mother is going to *freak*. But he's promised, and, at least for now, I do genuinely believe him. Because much as he cares for Dill – and he genuinely does, in his way, Grace, I promise you – he knows he's not up to the job of raising him, not without me. He can barely organise his own life, let alone anyone else's. He can barely change a nappy, let alone dress him or anything. Yeah, he says he loves him, and I honestly think he does, but fatherhood is a *whole* other headache. Bless him – I think he genuinely thinks his time will only come when Dill's old enough to kick a football. Till then . . . well, *you* know. He is *never* there for bedtimes, *or* mealtimes, *or* night feeds, or – well, need I go on? No. Ha – there you go. A bit of truth you *will* be able to get your head around!

And you won't be remotely surprised to know I don't entirely trust him. The womanising, the cheating, all sadly true. Her name's Candii, by the way – spelt with two bloody 'ii's – I mean, says it all, really, doesn't it? Ha – she's got a shock coming when he buggers off up north, that's for sure. A small but significant consolation! Bitch.

Shit. Where's the day gone? I have to pause this for a bit in a minute and get some stuff done before

Daisy gets here. But, look, the point is that I have to do this for insurance. You've got to know that Dill finding out about any of this, *ever*, is the last thing I want for him, the last thing he should *ever* have to know about. So I'm counting on you, if you do end up listening to this – which I hope you don't – to know what to do with it. To work out how to play things. To use it in the least damaging way. But I'm hoping the threat of your knowing will be enough. Confession time, by the way. I have laid it on *thick*. Laid *you* on thick. Laid Matt on thick too. Because he *has* to believe you'd go after him. I've had to, and I'm sorry, because you really don't deserve it. But I've *had* to. Because when I die Dillon *has* to go to you.

But not for the reasons I think you suppose. Not for the reasons I've spent the last couple of months *making damned bloody sure* you supposed.

Because you know Conor? Aidan's half-brother?

Aidan killed him.

Chapter 18

I paused the recording, and looked out over the white world outside, stunned. It was almost too much to take in. All those tears and recriminations. All those texts from him she'd forwarded. All those phone calls; those endless bitter sob-strewn accounts of his crimes and misdemeanours. His sudden unprovoked violence. His controlling behaviour. He'd done this, he'd done that. He'd smashed her heart into pieces. It was textbook. No wonder I'd lapped it up so readily. Most astounding was that, the very day after recording what I'd just listened to, she had asked me to come down, her voice so desperate and desolate, and almost every single word she'd said to me had been a lie; a piece of acting of Oscar-worthy proportions.

Bless him, she'd said. *Bless him*. About *Aidan*.

I thought again about the gap that had so effectively separated our respective childhoods. That apparently unbridgeable gulf. Hope just *was*; in my life, but not *of* it. A presence often only seen from the corner of my eye. A flame that flickered and occasionally flared.

And what I'd just heard now confirmed it. Which somehow made it feel even worse. In the year before her terminal diagnosis, I had developed – or so I'd thought – a much stronger, surer sense of her. A hint towards a future, more equitable relationship, that we could, and hopefully would, gently coax into being – a new dawn. Mums, together. A genuine friendship.

But as I continued to listen to the story she was telling, it hit me hard that I was labouring under a misapprehension. Because the seventeen-year-old Hope – the Hope who perhaps had burned then at her brightest – I had known, I now realised, hardly at all. That girl was not someone I recognised. She was another Hope entirely.

She was Aidan's.

And remained so to her death.

Fearful of what I'd find now, I pressed play again.

I had his back from the beginning. Said I'd have his back always. And from the moment I made the promise to him, I had meant it, too. *Always.* Despite everything. Despite being tested to the limit. Because he loved me.

And more than that, Grace. Because I loved *him*.

I was smart. So much smarter than anyone ever gave me credit for. One of the things I most loved about Aidan from the get-go was the way he kept telling me how smart I was. How clever. How he'd lucked out, how he absolutely didn't deserve someone like me. How sometimes he had to pinch himself that I wanted to be with him, which, of course, made me love him all the more.

You have no *idea* how much I loved him. How my life changed because of him. I was seventeen and it was like I hadn't lived before. Or that I'd lived in black and white and had suddenly discovered colour. Or lived in the shadows and been thrust into the light. Or had lived without purpose, and had finally found one. I was *seventeen*. And it really had been that big a deal: I'd found a place of peace. A place of sanctuary. A *home*.

We both had. And it turned out he'd needed one even more than I had. And not just an escape from the suffocating attentions of his mother, either. To keep him from drowning beneath the maelstrom that raged inside his own head.

Up till Aidan, I'd had the usual preconceptions about child abuse. Doesn't everyone? At least, my thoughts on the term, which felt ridiculously inadequate. Like neglect, another word so beloved of the authorities, eh? – as if parents who'd starved a child to near emaciation were guilty of nothing more than carelessness. Like Mum would so often neglect to clear the ironing pile, or neglect to remember to pay the milkman or the paper boy.

Or to love me the way she'd loved *you*.

Abuse is the same. I have thought about this a *lot*. It says everything, yet nothing – don't you think? Like abuser. That's another one – a word pretty much guaranteed to make you recoil automatically. But it's such a bland word. Such a nothing word, such a *beige* word, when you think about it. When you consider all the horrible ways in which a child can be defiled.

It gave me clarity, to think that. To get a sense of perspective. To meet Aidan, and, as a consequence, be able to relocate myself a little lower on the league table of horrible childhoods.

Why me in particular? I used to wonder that often. Why choose me as the recipient of his darkest, saddest secret? Sometimes, looking back, I can see it for what it might have been: a simple case of time and place. The stars aligning at the zenith of our early, rabid passion. The right place, the right time, the right post-coital moment.

Other times, I see it differently. As a function of being *me*. Of him knowing, having kept it to himself for so long, that the time had arrived, because *I* had arrived.

But perhaps it didn't matter either way.

You know Conor, babe.

Your brother.

No, no, no, babe. My *half*-brother. Well, when I was little, he—

When I was little, he . . .

I'm not going to spell it out for you. You don't need the details. But trust, me, Grace. Abuse is *such* an insufficient word.

It sometimes seems, looking back, as if time slowed in that moment when he told me. We'd smoked a joint (I'd be a fool if I didn't imagine that had played a part) but as soon as he started telling me, it had warped and weaved around us; become fluid, loose, elastic. Metamorphosed.

It delivered me a gift. A gift I didn't know what to do with. All I could do, in the moment, was hold him – hold him tight – and tick off all the boxes. The way he'd square up to people. The way he'd cry for no reason. The way he'd work out and work out and work out and work out, as if preparing for a role in a post-apocalyptic world, where there'd be trees to fell, shacks to build, outlaws to vanquish, and any number of damsels and maidens to deflower. The way his appetite for *me* – all soft skin and curves then, all feminine faux-coy acquiescence – was so urgent, so insatiable, so voracious.

He called me Babe. I called him Aid. Which felt right and appropriate. Because I knew one thing for definite: I had been given something broken, and only I, with my magical powers, could fix him.

Daisy – you know Daisy? Who I never told, obviously – she thought he was no more than a common or garden tool.

Not worth the grief, she'd said. Not worth the effort.

Hope, she'd said, you are *way* too much the nurturer, you know that? (As if being a nurturer was a failing, was a dangerous thing.) Which is actually, she'd gone on to say, statistically unusual. As the youngest, you're more likely to be the demanding one, the diva.

Ha! I didn't know if any of that was true or not. I supposed it might be. (I'd asked Aidan about the diva thing. His response had been 'hell, yes!') But what I *did* know was that I'd never *ever* seen myself in that way. I'd seen myself as the child neither of my parents had wanted. As superfluous, but at the same time, an inescapable duty. Which, after you, Grace – *perfect* you, Grace – they had both discharged with particularly *bad* grace.

It's a mug's game, Daisy said to me, trying to fix guys. Trying to change them. Everyone knows that, she said. Keep your guard up, she said. Remember, he has form (by the time I met him, by the way, he'd already notched up a suspended sentence for aggravated assault) and, even more important, he has *form*. We were all doing catering then, in our spick and span chefs' whites (did you ever even see me in my chef's whites? I don't think you did, did you? Whiter than your ivory tower, that's for sure), and Daisy knew he had form because they'd come from the same school, where he was, variously, a bad lad, a 'proper ledg', and a player. And every 'popular girl' ('popular girls' having been a thing then – ugh, ugh, ugh) had been determined to be the one to claim and tame him. I mean, *look* at him, Daisy said. Total babe magnet, that one. So be *careful*. As if he were a sleeping volcano. (Which, as it turned out, wasn't really that wide of the mark.)

I wasn't 'popular' ever. (Point of order – I hadn't *actually* at any time *aspired* to be 'popular'.) Too emo. Too kooky. Too spiky. Too intense. But where like poles repelled (see? I did know a few clever things, G, even then), unlike poles attracted.

We just couldn't help it.

He just couldn't help it.

He had blood underneath his nails. That was the first thing I noticed. From where he'd lifted his brother's head up from the ground. He'd already guessed he'd smashed his skull because he'd heard it hit the pavement. From all that way up, despite the rain, despite the wind, he had actually *heard it hit the pavement*. Then, from an instinct born out of his many previous brushes with the law, he'd had the presence of mind to tug down the sleeve of his parka so he left no trace of himself on the cool metal handrail of the outside stairwell, as he descended to see what he had done.

But he'd made himself check. And got blood under his fingernails. Then ran all the way home to me, through the 2 a.m. silence, and in the twenty-four minutes the journey had taken, gone from fight through to flight through to fight again – he deserved it – to flight again – wasn't there a night ferry to Cherbourg? – back to fight – he *deserved* it – through to terror. Intent to kill or not, he would surely go to prison now. Where, if he knew one thing, it was that he would be fresh meat. He would be prey.

I'd been so deeply asleep when he'd come stumbling into the bedroom that for a moment I thought he was part of a dream. Wild-eyed, wild-haired, a flailing, keening apparition. Wake up! Wake up, babe! Oh fuck, babe! Oh shit!

So I did try to wake up, but there he still was, his cheeks smeared and wet and his hands in his hair. As if he were literally trying to pull his own head off.

What's happened, I asked him. Aid, just *tell* me, what's happened?

He'd made the biggest fucking mistake of his entire life, that was what. He should never have agreed to meet Conor in the first place.

Conor had been years in the army, and only came home infrequently. And when he did it was like there was evil in the house. With his number-one buzz cut, his vein-rippled biceps, his habit of holding his arms up like Popeye, of mussing his little brother's hair if he passed him on the stairwell – bloody girl's hair, he'd taunt. Get it cut, you vain wanker, as if the past were a place he didn't want reminding of. As if the beautiful little boy in whom he'd taken his pleasure had no business still being around to taunt him.

He'd kept the hair, built the biceps, built a fearsome reputation. When he was still an inch shy of Conor's five foot eleven, he laid a guy out, in school, and got a four-week suspension. He carried it around proudly, like the prize he knew it was.

And then he grew. Another inch, another inch, another two. He had never known his father, but he was grateful to him for that. (He'd never known Conor's either, but he knew what he was. The father, the *mentor*, to the son.)

I need to go to the police.

You mustn't go to the police.

I have to. Babe, I *have* to.

But you can't.

Seriously, babe, I have to. What the fuck else can I do?

But they'll charge you with murder.

I didn't murder him! It was an accident!

I know, I said, soothing, and patting, and smoothing. The hair on his forehead, the hairs on his forearms. The slick of sweat that had beaded at his temples. But they're not going to see it like that, are they?

But the truth is the truth.

That you pushed him down the stairwell.

Accidentally!

But how are you going to prove that, without witnesses?

How are they going to prove otherwise?

And so it went on.

And all the while I was fashioning two parallel futures for us. The one in which Aidan – *my* Aidan – was dragged off to prison. And another, in which, if I was smart now, he was not.

Explain to me again, I said. From the beginning. Let's think it through again.

And because he knew I was smart, he put himself in my hands.

They'd gone to the pub as planned, he'd said, Conor antsy, already flying.

Bro, he'd said, more than once, we're okay, you and me, right?

They drank. Drank prodigiously. Drank with tedious machismo. As if the strength of a man's character could be measured in units. As if being male, on its own, could never quite be enough.

Bro, he'd said, more than once, we're okay, you and me, yeah? And it hit him that Conor wanted to see him because he needed some kind of 'closure'

– a term the therapists from Youth Offenders often bandied about. As if the wounds he'd inflicted could be stitched up and mended. He was back now. Demobbed. Had a flat, with a mate. Had a job, in security. Had a new civilian life, to pick up. He needed closure so he could go about his business. Bro, he'd slurred, more than once, we *are* okay, aren't we?

Then, later, much later: the pub shut, turfed out. And after they'd ambled aimlessly round Brighton in search of a club, after taking more coke and talking shit about nothing, he said, come back to Craig's, yeah? We'll get a Domino's. Have a smoke.

And he realised. He got it. He had just the one job.

To say yeah, bro, we're fine.

But he couldn't say that, ever. Because they were not. Because he burned with the shame, and the memories, and the *shame*. He'd been so weak. So afraid. So scared to tell his mother. It was like in stories, where you had to do things that *took every ounce of courage*. But he didn't have an ounce. He didn't even have a *quarter*. At least till one middle of the night, when he saw his mother *see* them. See Conor. See how they *were*. What was going on in *his* bed.

He remembered the shadow from the landing light. How her perfume came in with it. How it lingered in his nostrils long after she'd slipped away. How it gave him the ounce of courage he needed to tell her.

So he told her.

But she didn't believe him.

Don't be silly, she'd said. *You're imagining things*, she'd said. *It's just playing*, she'd said. *Don't be silly.*

Because she had to, he realised. She couldn't *not*, he realised. And once he was older, and cleverer – once he was eight, and it had ended – he thought he even sort of understood. It couldn't be true. Not of her boys – not her lovely boys, her precious 'booful twosome'. It couldn't *be*. It couldn't happen. So it mustn't have happened.

So in her story it *didn't* happen.

The End.

It would never end. Not for him. It was part of his DNA now.

He'd said nah, bro, you're alright. Got to head home to Hope.

Home to *me*.

(Conor had met me just the once. And acknowl-edged me. And dismissed me. And described me as his 'bit of skirt', which had riled Aid no end. And called him 'skirt chaser Aid'. Which had riled him as well.)

'Fuck*sake*!' he'd said. 'Does that bint fucking *own* you?'

As if the strength of a man's character could be measured not just in units, but in adherence to the credo of not being *owned*.

So he walked all the way back to Craig's with him. Pissed, wired, coked-up still. Along the front. Up the hill. On out towards Whitehawk. Down a lane, across a car park, round the side of Craig's block, to the evil-smelling cold outside stairwell. Then up the stairs. Why, in God's name, *up the stairs*? Why, the fuck?

'Come in, bro! The night is young! Got some good gear. Come *on*.'

He'd stood his ground then, the altitude giving him perspective. No. You're alright, bro. It's late. Hope'll worry.

Fuck Hope. Fuck your *girl*friend.

Mate, *please*, just leave it.

Then the zinger, the shocker. The sideways look.
The sneer. The visible thought process. The clearing of the throat. Before delivering the killer line
that would make a killer of him. Ah, methinks the
lady doth *protest too much.*

Come again?

Well, we both know what you *really* like, don't we?

Then the arm, snaking out. The hand grabbing his
hair.

The memories.

The *shame.*

The disbelief – was he *joking*?

It was in the last moments of his half-brother's
short life that it hit him. Conor didn't want closure.
Didn't even want *him*. He was chancing his arm on
a hunch – a basic instinct. That he could keep him
where he wanted him. Complicit.

I said it again. Calmly now: You cannot go to the
police, Aid. (*I couldn't let them take him. I couldn't
let him leave me.*)

Jesus, Hope, I fucking *have* to!

No, you *don't*. You were here. You got back just after midnight. You left your brother in town and you came home, to *me*. No one saw you. You said that. You saw no one. No one saw you. (*I couldn't let them arrest him. I couldn't live without him.*)

You can't know that. They might have.

They wouldn't have.

They might have.

No, Aid, they *wouldn't* have. (*I couldn't let them have him. I couldn't let him leave me.*)

So I thought. I was smart. It was a Tuesday – well, Wednesday. A stay in and early night kind of day. It was cold. It was raining. It was – I checked – moonless. The odds were better than evens.

So it wasn't just a risk. It was a calculated risk.

And I was willing to take it.

And I knew I could persuade him. He was so scared. *So* scared.

Aid, I said, you *should* be scared.

We took it.

Chapter 19

Okay. And breathe . . . So we got away with it, sis. Can you *believe* that? I'm not sure I can, even now. But you know what really blows me away the most? That every single bit of it passed you by. Did I even see you when it was all going on? I don't think I did. Me down here. You up there. I'm not even sure we spoke about it, did we? Why would we have? How often did we speak at all back then? Almost never. You were busy living your life and I was busy – ha! – trying to keep some kind of a grip on mine. We were just worlds apart back then, weren't we? And who was Conor to you anyway? Just the random half-brother of your little sister's still relatively new, *definitely* unsuitable boyfriend – and how many times had you even met Aidan by then? What – three or four times? Maybe fewer.

Which was perhaps for the best. *God*, you would have sniffed my criminal manoeuvrings out a *mile* away. But it doesn't matter. The point is that we never, not in a million years, thought it would all be so easy. I mean, it was horrible, obviously.

Bloody terrifying. They interviewed Aidan, being the last person known to have seen him, but it was obvious from the start – he was in such a state, as you can imagine – that they didn't even *suspect* any foul play. Conor had tested positive for drugs, of course (and how), and it was literally only a matter of a couple of weeks before the whole thing died down because they really did think he'd just fallen down the stairwell. So then there was an inquest and, I don't know, around four or so months later, they recorded a verdict of accidental death. Isn't it incredible that you can just get *away* with something like that? Then, of course, all we had to do was somehow learn to live with it. And, of course, Norma.

Here's the irony. It was the thought of Norma finding out what really happened that finally persuaded him I was right. We'd kept on going back and forth, back and forth, weighing the options, weighing the risk. If some evidence had shown up then it would have been even more serious, of course. Hard to pass it off as an accident during an altercation if you've already said you weren't even there.

But just the thought of it. The thought of Norma knowing Aidan had done it. Even knowing it had been an accident, she'd still have had to know that they'd fought, that he pushed him. It was bad enough, but can you imagine? As a *mother*? Knowing one of your sons has killed the other one?

Stuff of nightmares. She'd have *completely* lost her marbles. And if she ever found out *why* . . . No *way* could we go there.

Okay. Focus. It's late. Oh, but, Grace – I can't tell you how sorry I am to have dumped all this on you. I don't mean Dill – I can't regret that, because I know you won't either. He's *such* a good boy. And he'll *love* you to bits. I know he will. And he will feel me with him *through* you. He'll be so happy you're his new mummy. And you'll love him too, I promise you. I genuinely believe that. I *promise* you.

Jesus. Must. Stop. *Crying.* But I really do mean it. I'm *sorry.* Because if you're listening to this, it means they must have made contact. And it really, *really* matters that you keep them away from him. *And* her. *Especially* her. No ifs. No buts. They must *not* be in his life. And that's not because I think Aidan's going to suddenly turn into his brother and do something despicable to him. I genuinely don't think he would ever do that. But I can't take the risk that he won't damage him anyway. He's too messed up. And don't forget he has a *massive* substance addiction. And his mother – whatever you might think, and trust me on this, because you really don't know her – is *evil.* And I mean that. You don't know her.

She had a cat when I met Aid. I don't think I ever told you. And it wasn't neutered. And a while after we moved into our flat, she had kittens. I was round there when she had them. Six of them, all different colours. I went on and on at him about us having one when they were old enough, and in the end he caved in. But when we went round a week later to see Norma, they'd gone – she said she'd have kept one if she'd known, and she was sorry and everything, but we were too late because she'd already given them all to the local pet shop. But she hadn't. And it was only when I'd gone on about it to Aid – I mean, you don't take week-old kittens from their mother and give them to a pet shop, do you? They'd never take them – that he told me the real truth. That she'd drowned them in the toilet.

One by one. Held them under till they drowned. And I know people *do* do things like that. I'm not stupid. But it was the thought that *she* could do it. And then lie about it the way she did. I mean, you can imagine, can't you? The whole thing went right through me. I didn't even understand *why* she did it. Aidan said I was being all middle-class and wet, that I needed to get real. But I never forgot it. And I keep thinking about it now. How she killed those tiny kittens with *her bare hands*. Her *own cat's* babies. How could anyone be so cruel? So inhuman?

How can a mother see what she saw and pretend she hadn't seen it? Because she couldn't bear it, gotta be. Couldn't bear what it would mean if it was true. Could have done the right thing for Aidan, but couldn't bear the consequences. Knew he'd suffered what he'd suffered but still *let* him suffer.

Turned a blind eye, so she wouldn't have to suffer *herself*.

I sometimes wonder what she *did* do. I mean you'd have to do *something*. Did she say something to Conor? Did she threaten him? I mean, what would *you* do? I mean – the *consequences*. It *doesn't* bear thinking about, does it? They'd probably take one or other of them into care, wouldn't they? So I did have *some* sympathy.

But it didn't *stop*. Didn't stop till he was old enough to *make* it stop.

You've got to wonder, haven't you? What kind of person would be able to *live* with something like that? But then I keep coming back to those kittens.

Did I ever tell you, by the way? She's helped Aidan out a *lot* with money. Probably even more than I know, because I've always been *so* not okay with it. Her father had a car showroom and I think he was pretty minted when he died. I don't think she's ever worked much, except for something to do. And I think she did stuff like that for Aidan – sorted him out all the time, got him out of scrapes – not just because he was all she had left, but because it was guilt money.

Anyway, look, you must believe me when I tell you this is not about revenge. I'm sick, but I'm not *sick*, whatever anyone might tell you. This is not about getting back at Aidan for cheating on me, either. You won't believe it – I can see your face – but that was just another of his addictions. I genuinely think he had to keep proving to himself, over and over and over, that he wasn't gay. No, that's wrong – being gay was never the issue. Being told he'd enjoyed the things his *brother had done to him* was the issue. Because if you're told something often enough, and you're still just a child, and you're confused because it's your *brother* – who you love – who is doing those things to you, there's always going to be a part of you that wonders if it *was* true, isn't there? Even if it's only at an unconscious level. Bloody hell, it breaks my heart just to *say* that.

So it's not about getting even with him – I want Aidan to be *happy*. It's one hundred per cent about doing the right thing. And you know the saddest thing? When I found out I was pregnant, I really thought – *we* really thought – that it was meant to be. That after all the shit, it was something good happening for us, finally. That once he was a dad, he would finally be able to break the cycle. The self-loathing. The depression. The whole self-destruct thing. Put the whole thing behind him. Learn to love himself. Move on.

Ha ha – you know me, sis – hyperbole and all the clichés! But I genuinely did think that might happen. And perhaps it would have, if I hadn't got this bastard cancer. Perhaps he *would* have come into his own once Dill was old enough to kick a football. But perhaps he wouldn't. And hoping's not enough.

But, look, I genuinely do not know if Aidan meant to kill Conor. I suspected – still do – that he did. And, believe me, if you knew what I knew, you wouldn't blame him either. That bastard deserved it, no question.

But I persuaded him he didn't. That it was an accident. And if he had gone to the police, who knows? They might have believed him. They could so easily have believed him – what evidence did they have otherwise? But I was so terrified that they wouldn't. That I'd lose him.

That really, really haunts me. The knowledge that if things had panned out differently – if he'd not had the chance to come home to me and tell me – that it maybe would have been better. Not for Norma – Jesus Christ, no. It would have finished her. But maybe better for Aidan. Because all I achieved was to burden him with another massive secret. Another lump of guilt. Another reason to hate himself.

God. I was so young. So headstrong. So *stupid.* Because I believed my own hype – I really did think I could fix him. But I couldn't. He wasn't fixable. And I think you probably already knew that. I imagine you listening to this, nodding sagely – thinking how you could have told me that, like, a *million* times already. You know what gets me most? Just how sad it's been to watch you, to listen to you, since I decided what to do. To see that big-sister, told-you-so thing of yours in overdrive. To see how easy it's been to make you swallow all my lies. Because you didn't need convincing, did you? Because you already knew he was trouble.

You just didn't know why.

Chapter 20

You know me, sis. Hyperbole and all the clichés.

It's almost five now, and after listening to Hope's voice for so long, that's the thing that keeps going round and round in my head, like a line from a song you just heard. It's like she's here with me. *You know me, sis.* But I didn't really, did I? I sit back, click away, pull out the stick and adapter, and lower the lid of my laptop back into place. Then I sit, staring out into the night, seeing nothing, turning the sparkling stick in my hand, over and over.

Hyperbole and all the clichés. I suppose I'm still in shock – it's quite a thing listening to a voice from so long beyond the grave. An even bigger thing, listening to a voice that's both so familiar and yet, at the same time, so strangely *un*familiar. But the biggest thing of all is that she'd used the word hyperbole. Just tossed it out there, in jest, as if an everyday utterance. A word she was familiar with, a word in her vocabulary. And I find – no hyperbole – that I am disgusted with myself.

What was it she said to me that time? After one of our tetchy not-quite arguments? Please don't patronise me, Grace. Don't think you're always so bloody clever. Yeah, yeah, you've got all your As and distinctions and whatever. But they aren't *everything*, you know. I'm not *stupid*.

And I never thought she was. But did I ever really listen to her? Did I ever, far above, in my 'ivory tower', as she put it, really give her proper credit? Ever really attach value to her opinions?

No. Because of Aidan. I could never get past Aidan. Could never get past that one inalienable truth. That sticking with Aidan (I could see it, Matt could see it, everyone could bloody see it) was surely the very *definition* of stupid.

I have no word for what it was that made her act the way she did. None quite fit. Just like me, she was the sum total of her genes and her childhood. A tangle of insecurities, resentments, contradictions.

But whatever else she was, my little sister *wasn't* stupid, and it sickens me to realise how much I've failed her. To know I barely scratched the surface of her hopes and dreams and heartaches. To know not only that I wasn't there, but that she knew it all too well. To know it's me, and not Hope, who's been the stupid one here.

Too tired to think straight, I put Mr Weasley back in his cage. Then creep upstairs and climb silently into bed.

I wake the next morning, feeling groggy and disorientated, to find Matt's half of the bed empty, and a mug of tea on my bedside table, which has long since grown cold. The clock informs me that it's almost eleven thirty. Sounds float up from the garden, so, remembering the snow, I throw the duvet off and go over to the window.

The boys are placing a head on a misshapen snowman and just seeing them together makes my heart ache. It's this, I think. This is what Hope visualised for Dillon, what drove her. A happy home life. A loving family. A *brother*. A part of me wishes I believed in an afterlife. One with a rear-view mirror, so she could see this and know she made the right call. But the greater part, as what I listened to in the night comes flooding in again, says yes, all well and good. *But at what cost?*

I hear Matt but don't see him. Watch Daniel nod, then hold out his gloved hands and catch a carrot. Then I grab my dressing gown from its hook and feed my arms into the sleeves. I need to tell Matt what I've found.

The kitchen's wreathed in a familiar and comforting scent. Onions and garlic. Vegetables. Stock. I go to the stove, lift the lid of our biggest cast-iron pot. Matt's been cooking – he loves to cook. Made a huge pan of soup. He comes in through the back door as I lower it, and stamps snow off his boots. He has his favourite beanie hat on, and his ancient Puffa jacket. He hardly looks different to how he did a decade earlier. I can't wait for him to be here properly. For things to be normal. For him to be here, making soup. To be here to eat it, and not on call. For all of this to go far, far away.

'That really is some shiner,' he remarks with a frown when he sees me. 'I forgot to ask. Did you get around to calling the police?'

I shake my head. 'Didn't have a chance.'

He takes the mug from me and empties it down the sink. 'We should chase them today,' he says. 'Keep the pressure on. Check they've actually been to see her. And what time did you come back to bed last night?'

'Around five?'

'*Five?* What the hell were you doing down here till five?'

I reach into my dressing-gown pocket. 'Listening to this.'

He takes it from me. Turns it over in his hand. 'Was this in your mother's stuff? I saw you'd had the bag out.'

I nod. 'I recognised it straight away. It's the one Hope's friend Daisy gave her for her last birthday.'

He puts the memory stick down and picks up the kettle. 'So what's on it?'

'Another of her voice recordings. A very long one. I'm still try-ing to get my head round it. There was a letter with it, only partly written. She'd planned to send it to a solicitor's. You probably need to listen to it. It explains a lot.'

'As in?'

I clamber on to one of the bar stools under the kitchen island. 'God, I hardly know where to start. She lied, basically. About every-thing. Well, almost. I was on the right track – he never hit her, or abused her.'

'Seriously? She actually said that?' He looks unconvinced.

'Seriously. The whole lot. All lies. He didn't do any of it. And his wife was telling the truth. He didn't walk out on Hope either. Not willingly, anyway. She *made* him.'

'*Seriously?*' Matt says again. 'She admitted that?'

I nod. 'And much more, believe me. You know what you were saying the other night about him disappearing without a backwards glance and how you didn't buy into the whole idea of him being a martyr and doing it for Dillon? Well, it turns out you were right.' I nod towards the memory stick. 'Well, half right, at least. He didn't want to abandon Dillon, but it wasn't just altruism on his part that made him go. It was because Hope had something on him and she threatened him with it.'

He frowns, looks confused. 'You mean the drugs? Didn't we already know that?'

I shake my head. 'Not the drugs. This goes way back. I mean *years* back. Back to when they were seventeen, not long after they moved in together. You're not going to believe this, but Aidan killed his brother.'

'*What?*' He looks down at the stick again as if he's only just see-ing it. 'What, as in murdered him?' I nod. 'Good God. You mean he actually *murdered* him?'

'So she says.'

'*Why?*'

'Because apparently he abused him when he was little. And for a long time, it sounds like.'

'His *brother?*'

'There were about nine years between them, don't forget. He would have been in his teens then.'

'As in sexually?'

I nod again.

Matt frowns. 'Okay,' he says. 'That *does* explain a lot. So how did he do it?'

'During a fight. He pushed him down a stairwell.'

'On purpose?'

'She thinks so. But she gave him an alibi, and he got away with it.'

'*Wow*,' he says, tugging the beanie off, giving his head a scratch. 'You couldn't make it up, could you?' Then he laughs. A short humourless bark. 'Actually, knowing Aidan bloody Kennedy, that's exactly what you *would* make up. God, what must she have been thinking to go *along* with something like that? If the police had found out, she could have ended up in prison herself. No wonder he was only too happy to bloody scarper. But what on earth possessed her to agree to cover up for him in the first place? Was she *mad?*'

'That's just it. She didn't agree to it. It was her who *suggested* it. He was all for going to the police. He *wanted* to. She managed to talk him out of it. She thought she was doing the right thing.'

'The *right* thing?'

'Yes. Because she didn't want to lose him. But also because she didn't think he deserved to go to prison. Thought he'd suffered enough. She really loved him, Matt.'

'She'd have *had* to.'

'She did. It was only later that she realised she'd probably done the wrong thing. God, I can't believe we knew absolutely *nothing* about it. Can you?'

Matt shakes his head. 'And she's confessed all that on there?' He nods towards the stick again.

'All of it. She recorded it just after he'd gone. She'd planned to send it to the solicitors and have them keep it in case we needed it.'

'*We* needed it?'

'In case Aidan changed his mind after she'd died and tried to go for custody. Or his mother did. Which she *did*. It was exactly as you hypothesised. Not revenge. She was just being pragmatic.'

'Hmm. That's certainly one word for it.'

'No, she really was. She knew exactly what she was doing. She needed to convince us, beyond doubt, that we had to adopt Dillon, and she knew exactly which strings to pull, didn't she?'

Matt's silent for a moment and I think I know why. Because we're both thinking the same thing and then assiduously un-thinking it. She had us adopt Dillon by deceiving us, grotesquely. Yet to feel duped, to think 'what if?', feels even more grotesque.

'Right,' he says eventually. 'Soup. We need soup.' He then strides to the window, pulls the handle up and opens it. 'Neeps and tatties soup in ten minutes, boys!' he shouts. Then comes back and envelopes me in a hard, lengthy bear hug.

'Fuck 'em all,' he says. 'Just for the record.'

After lunch, dogged by duty, I take the boys to visit their grandma, so they can take her the paintings they've made for her. I warn them both on the way that she might be incoherent – to not worry if she babbles or talks nonsense at them. 'It's just the dementia,' I remind them. 'So don't take it personally, okay? Whatever Nanna says.'

Daniel, in the front with me, is only half listening, because he's busy typing away on his mobile phone. 'Is Alzheimer's spelt h-e-i or h-i-e?' he wants to know. 'Ah, h-e-i,' he adds, the spellchecker already having answered his question.

Dillon's listening, though. 'Is Nanna going to die now?' he asks me.

I glance at him in the mirror. He is gazing out of the window. 'I can't answer that, sweetie. But no, I don't think so. She just needs to stay in hospital till they can clear her infection.'

'Can they fix her dementia too?'

'No, bubs, they can't.' And I'm just about to add that he mustn't fret about it, that, some time soon, she won't even remember she has dementia, when he emits a little huff. 'Aww,' he says, my mother apparently forgotten, 'Dan, look. All the snow's already melting down here.'

And by the time we're on the main road to the hospital, it has.

My heart, however, hasn't. Not where Mum's concerned. Will it ever? So when we arrive up on the ward to find her asleep, I'm only too happy to accept the nurse's whispered suggestion that perhaps it's best if we don't wake her. 'She's had a trying morning,' she confides. 'Got herself in a bit of a state about wanting to go home. You know how it is.' I assure her I do. 'I'll let her know you've been,' she adds, even though we both know it's information she'll retain for all of a couple of seconds. 'And she'll be *so* thrilled with these,' she says, picking up the paintings, which the boys have placed at the foot of the bed. 'Especially knowing her grandsons have done them for her. What a talented pair you are!'

We don't stay long. Just sufficient for me to top up her water jug and check her stats, while the boys, at something of a loss (neither, thankfully, has ever spent time in a hospital), hover at her bedside, whispering to each other and pointing, as if examining a zoological specimen. Which I understand. Because she doesn't look quite like their Nanna. It's only in the nuances – her hollow cheeks, her general pallor, the paraphernalia around her – but they have never seen her in this inert and diminished way before. And till just a few days ago, neither had I. Though in my case it's what's on the inside that matters more.

It transpires that I'm not the only one who's been visiting the hospital. An hour after we're home, the boys and Matt working on the Lego Land Rover while I catch up on emails, my mobile rings. I pick it up. It's Siddhant.

Siddhant, who, like me, is not on call this weekend. But who, unlike me, is still at the sharp end of his training. Who is anxious about the fiendishly hard exams in his immediate future. Who is too driven and conscientious for anyone's good – his most of all. I have told him, more than once, not to haunt the hospital when he's off. To relax. Get some rest. Have a social life. Have a *life*. Burning out is a very real threat.

I go out into the hall to answer. 'Sid,' I say. 'Please tell me you're not at the hospital.'

'I'm sorry, Mrs Hamilton,' he says. 'Literally, it's just for an hour only.'

'I don't believe you. We've spoken about this, we will speak about it again. Anyway, apart from tearing you off a strip, which I will do on Monday, what can I do for you?'

Which is when he says something that stops me in my tracks.

'It's just something Mr Porter thought you might want to know about. About that patient, Aidan Kennedy? He was brought in again this morning. By ambulance. Another overdose.'

Aidan. Back in hospital. Was in hospital while *we* were there. 'Serious?'

'Fatal. He's just been pronounced brain-dead. They're keeping him on the ventilator while they search for potential matches. We just saw his wife arrive.'

'And his mother?'

'She's up there too. I think she is the one who found him. I think they plan to harvest the organs on Monday.'

I thank Siddhant. Remind him to go home. As in *now*.

Brain-dead. So Aidan's dead. So he's gone. So he's done it. And the wildest thought occurs to me. But perhaps it's not so wild. Has he always assumed I might already know about his brother? Has that particular sword of Damocles been hanging over him all his adult life? Has encountering me again made that life – that fear of exposure – unbearable? I don't doubt his wife leaving him will have had the greater impact, but I almost wish now that I hadn't found what I found.

No, I profoundly wish I hadn't. Because seeing him in this new light, as the victim of such horrific circumstance, has thrown everything I trusted as being truth into chaos. I'm not naive enough to glibly mark people down as essentially good or bad – behind almost every bully is a damaged soul. I *know* that. But now everything is coloured by the tragedy of his youth. By the knowledge that he was not the man Hope persuaded me to think he was. By the real man behind the avatar I have hauled around for two decades, and whose ghost will now haunt me forever.

Matt's looking at me quizzically, a part-constructed piece of Lego in his hand. '*What?*' he mouths.

'Aidan,' I mouth back at him. 'He's killed himself.'

'Back in a tick,' he tells the boys, and follows me into the kitchen. 'Did I read that right?' he asks. 'Is he *dead?*'

'Technically. They'll keep him on life support till they have as many matches as they can find for his usable organs. Oh, Christ, Matt. I don't know what to think. This is *awful*.'

He looks shocked at this. But then he hasn't listened to Hope's confession, has he? I mentally check myself. Is *confession* even the right word? 'It is what it is,' he says firmly. 'Look, I know it sounds harsh, but the guy was a train wreck. By rights he should have died when he smashed into that lorry, and perhaps he knew that too. Perhaps he was always living on borrowed time. Look, the bottom line is that at least this means we can put it all behind us. Move on with our own lives without it all hanging over us. We know the truth now. And given some of the things his wife told you, perhaps it was always going to end up like this.'

'God, his poor wife. She's going to blame herself. She—'

He shakes his head. 'Not our problem. It's not even our business. This is nothing to do with us. Don't even *start* going down that road. No, just be grateful—'

I gape at him. '*Grateful?* Matt, he's *dead*.'

'Let me *finish*. Grateful that nothing *else* has happened. Grateful that this will hopefully be the end of it. Of course it's a tragedy. But it's not of our making. And perhaps now we can lay these ghosts to rest.'

Ghosts again. The ghost of Hope. The ghost of Aidan. The ghost of Aidan's dead brother. I think again of Norma – about how I'd feel if I lost one of *my* children. Beside myself. Enraged. *Apoplectic.*

'She's lost both her sons now.' It's a thought, but it comes out as a statement. 'And her grandson. And almost certainly her granddaughters too now – well, as good as. How much loss can a person take before they lose it altogether?' I touch my hand to my cheek, the action unthinking. Automatic. 'Matt, it won't be the end of it. What about Norma?'

Chapter 21

Both the sun and the rising temperature have gone about their business. The snow has completely gone by the time I wake up on Sunday morning. Every last vestige of it, even up here on the downs, bar a small, grubby ice ball in the middle of the lawn, with two bark chips and a carrot sticking lopsidedly out of it, and wearing Matt's Glasgow Rangers scarf as a necklace.

In the far distance, our wedge of sea view is a uniform grey, the colour I still associate most with my childhood. Like many kids raised at the seaside, I spent a great deal of time with it. Sometimes reading, sometimes not, sometimes walking, sometimes sitting. On a groyne, on the shingle, or, out of season, cross-legged on a favourite bench.

It's those times I remember most vividly and clearly. Not the high-summer days of endless blue and crowded pavements. The grey days, the chilly days, the angsty, need-to-get-out-of-the-house days, when I'd escape the oppressive confines of our dark, unhappy home and walk, sometimes for miles, along the seafront. And always accompanied by the waves' comforting babble, as they slurped up the shingle and hissed and gurgled back again, leaving lace bubbling down into the pebbles.

It was one of my constants, that sea. A much-needed antithesis to the tumult of my home life; an undemanding, comforting, largely unchanging vista. A fitting gunmetal backdrop to so many winters of discontent.

A few years back I went to the Gower coast, in South Wales. A girls' minibreak, with Julia, my old friend from med school, who by that time had a holiday cottage there. I didn't think I'd ever seen a sea, a beach, a stretch of coast so lovely. So wild and exuberant and untamed. So seductive. A technicolour dreamcoat to this comfortable grey old cardigan.

Which I thought I'd feel happy to slip back over my shoulders. But I don't. Because what's been happening, what has *just* happened, has coloured almost everything. I want so desperately, suddenly, to be back in my real home. To just bundle all of us into the car and drive north.

I'm first up – no surprise after my disrupted Friday night – and as I pad around, feed Mr Weasley, put the kettle on, empty the dishwasher, I'm overcome by the strongest sense of not being where I should be. Realise that what I feel is homesick, right to my very bones.

An hour later, breakfast made and eaten, Sunday morning marches on, and the feeling – the compulsion to run away – persists. It isn't helped by the fact that, at some point, I will have to go back down to the hospital and see my mother. Because however much I wish it, I cannot visualise a scenario where avoiding this onerous duty won't make me feel worse than if I do go. Because it will. That's the nature of my personal beast.

Also persistent – distressingly – is the image of Aidan Kennedy, currently lying in an ICU bed, dead but not dead, while his fate as a donor awaits. I wonder who signed the consent form. Jessica Kennedy, almost certainly. Not Norma. Because his wife will still surely be his next of kin. That dotted line – *Just here, my love . . .* That pen so gently proffered. Those closely packed paragraphs, each explained, with due solemnity. *So that others can live on after his death.*

Matt's scrolling through his iPad. The world keeps on turning. 'D'you wish we'd never moved here?' I ask him. 'Tell me honestly.'

He rolls his eyes. 'Seriously? Hen, can we please just not go there?'

'Seriously. Because I do.'

It's a while before he speaks. 'We don't have to stay here forever.'

'But the boys . . .'

'Will be fine. As long as we're fine. As long as *you're* fine. Look, let's not talk about this just now, eh? It's a pointless conversation.'

'So you do, then. Look, it's *fine*,' I add, seeing his frown. 'Genuinely. I should never have asked you to. It wasn't fair. It was selfish.'

'Will you just stop it with the "I made you do it" line? *Please?*'

'But—'

'You made me do nothing. And you're responsible for none of what's happened either. So how about we just—'

He's interrupted by an ear-splitting shout from the living room. A bellow, almost – which sounds like Daniel – and another then, from Dillon. We both rush in, to find the precious Lego Land Rover, constructed so painstakingly and carefully, over so many weeks now, now *de*constructed – and fatally, too. At least half of the 2,500 pieces (or so the box said) are strewn in clumps of various sizes around the floor. I have sons. I know Lego. There is no remedial-work option. It will have to be completely broken up and rebuilt from scratch.

Daniel knows this too. From painful experience. And is lunging at Dillon – and for a second time, I calculate, as Dillon, red-cheeked and flinching, already has his hands clenched across his stomach.

'Whoa!' Matt barks, as he grabs Daniel's wrist. 'Enough,' he says. 'Enough, now. *Enough*. What just happened?'

Daniel, clearly in no mood to furnish him with an account, yells again at his brother. 'You dickhead! You *idiot*! I'm going to get you for this!'

Presumably hoping for sanctuary, Dillon rushes at me, flings his arms round my middle. 'I didn't mean it! I didn't mean it! *You're* the dickhead. I didn't *mean it*!'

'He *did*!' Daniel is railing mostly at his father now, gesticulating with his free hand. 'I *saw* him! He did it on purpose. I saw him! Don't lie,' he screams at Dillon. 'You so *did*! Tell the truth!'

'I didn't!'

'*God!*' Daniel is growling now. 'He's a liar! You are *such* a *liar*!'

'But, sweetheart,' I say to him. 'Why on earth would Dillon do that?'

'Are you sure, son?' Matt adds.

Daniel has tears in his eyes too now. 'I saw him *do it*!' he barks. 'God! Why won't you *believe* me? I saw him! He deliberately pushed it off the table! He did it because I wouldn't let him play FIFA!'

'You *never* let me play!' Dillon is properly sobbing now.

'No! Because you always ruin it! Because you're *stupid*! You're a *retard*!'

'Daniel!' Matt snaps. 'Enough of that language!'

And it *is* enough. At least for me to think I know the truth of it. I remember one of my mother's mantras. A staple from my childhood. That the only thing you need to know when catching boys making mischief is that, when interrogated, their initial default is to lie.

Every time, she said. *Worth remembering.* Which I thought was outrageous. I said so. She'd shrugged. *It's true nevertheless*, she said. *You'll see.*

I prise Dillon's arms from around my middle and force him to look at me. 'Truth now,' I say to him. '*Did* you do it on purpose?'

He shakes his head. 'But I wish I had! *He's* the retard!'

We both swing into weary action with our usual four-D system. Defuse. Do a debrief. Work on damage limitation. Deliver homily – which we do and which we hope will, at some later point, stick. Daniel and Dillon don't fight a lot, but when they do, they go big; both are still-simmering balls of regret and resentment and are likely to remain so for the rest of the day.

But, being boys, they will shrug it off. Quickly and completely. Nothing tucked away to stew over. Because that is their special boyish gift. More likely, at some point in the future (I am absolutely sure of this), they will bring it out, dust it down, shake it out, re-examine it. And they will laugh. *Do you remember the time*, one will say – it could be either, it doesn't matter – *when you*, or *when I*, or *when that bloody Lego Land Rover* . . . And they will laugh because the memory will be a part of what bonds them. A family heirloom of the best kind; a bit of history that connects them. That binds them together, as such anecdotes do. Which makes them brothers in a way that Hope and I were never sisters. I envy them that. And am grateful.

For now, though, while Dillon goes to his room to sulk and lick his wounds, Daniel and Matt set about gathering up all the pieces, so the Land Rover can rise, phoenix-like, from the multicoloured plastic ashes. And I contemplate the rest of the day with a profound feeling of gloom. Visit mother. Return home. Miserable early-evening dinner (detente will, by then, probably still be a while away), boys to bed, Matt to London. And then I'll be alone again, with a head full of horrors.

Matt thinks I'm insane. 'Why?' he says, when I go into the living room to tell him I'm going to nip down to the hospital. 'You only just went to see her yesterday.'

'And she was asleep.'

'What difference does that make? She probably wouldn't remember even if she hadn't been.'

I head back out into the hall, pull my coat from the newel post. 'She's sick, Matt.'

He follows me. 'She'll still be sick whether you go and see her or not. Or are you thinking she's really sick? As in dying?'

I shake my head. 'No, but I just need to check on her. She'll be disorientated, frightened. I can't leave her there all day without seeing a familiar face.'

He shakes his head. 'After everything you've just found out? She's lucky you haven't totally disowned her.'

'I'm trying to see past that. I'm not sure it's going to be helpful. Anyway, I'm not just going for her, I'm going because I'll feel bad if I don't go.'

'Because you're worried people will think badly of you if you don't show your face.'

'Partly.'

'Which is not a valid reason. And you can see her tomorrow morning.'

'Noted and noted.' I pull my car keys from my bag. 'I shouldn't be gone more than an hour.'

I drive to the hospital feeling cross and guilty. Feeling cross *for* feeling guilty. And anxious now, as well, because I know there's a very good chance Norma will be there. But at least that practical problem, to an extent, can be ameliorated. As I drive, I plan a route through the hospital that will keep me away from ICU and, for good measure, don't head to the hospital car park but instead down to the front, where I park on the promenade, as if part of a SWAT team secretly crossing enemy lines. I arrive on the geriatric ward on reluctant, heavy legs.

In contrast to yesterday, Mum is wide, wide awake. But her expression is blank when she sees me approaching, and at first I think she's perhaps moved on to the next stage of her dementia, and, as I know will be coming one day (but perhaps not as soon as this day), has absolutely no idea who I am. I wonder, guiltily, if that will be better.

I'm wrong. 'Oh, you're here then,' she snaps once I reach her. 'About time. Leaving me to rot in this place with all these *idiots*. They think I'm doolally,' she adds, lowering her voice a little. 'But I'm *not*! They're the doolally ones, all those *nurses*.'

The first thing I notice is that her bedside cabinet is covered in cards now. So has Holly been to see her? Almost certainly. So I needn't have come after all. I try and fail not to mind. There is no sign of the pictures the boys brought for her yesterday.

I perch on the visitor chair, and the action of my sitting down creates enough of a gust of air that half the cards flutter to the floor, like so many pale, dying moths.

All those friends. Who all care for her. Who do not share our history. Whose relationships with her are in the landscape of the present. Which are simple and mutual, untroubled by malevolent ghosts.

They have it licked, I think. Their cloudy gazes hold a clarity that seems to constantly escape me. Say that whatever she is, whatever she's done in the past, it's all done with. The slate needs to be wiped. After all, she's a little old lady who will *be dead soon*. They wouldn't say it, but they would think it. They'd think get *over* yourself.

214

I wish I could work out a route to that acceptance. I've been struggling, in any case, but now I know how systematically she betrayed me – for just how long she lied – it's like someone has felled a tree and dumped it in the road in front of me. How could she have done what she did to me? It breaks my heart. Not a big, noisy break. Nothing showy or dramatic. But she's chipped away a piece of my heart nonetheless. 'I haven't left you here, Mum,' I say, grateful to be occupied in gathering all the cards up again, since once again I am finding it difficult to look at her.

So many cards. The Beeches is a bit like a school in that respect; a primary school, swinging, as if a battalion, into action. Let's do what we can to make the poorly child feel better. There must be twenty or more of them, of all types and sizes. Plucked from boxes-for-the-purpose, kept by better people than I am. I sit up again. Place the cards back on the cabinet, in a disorderly pile. Then, conscious of her glare, I pick them up again and square them off. She can stand them all up again when I'm gone. 'Mum, they're keeping you in because you have a kidney infection, and they need to be sure you're on the mend before they discharge you.'

'On the *mend*. I'm not a child, Grace. And I don't need to be here. I haven't got a kidney infection, I've just got a chill.' She sits forward slightly. 'They all think I'm doolally. I am *NOT doolally*! Now, where are my boys?'

Why do I let that term get to me so much? Why does it still make my hackles rise the way it does? 'At home, Mum. With Matt. They came to see you yesterday.'

'No they didn't.'

'You were asleep. The nurse didn't want us to wake you.' I almost add, *And brought you pictures. Where are the pictures?* But it's pointlessness personified, so I don't.

She scowls. 'When can *I* go home?'

'Soon.'

'*How* soon?'

'I'm sorry, but I don't know, Mum. Just not yet.'

'This is ridiculous,' she huffs, slamming her head back against the pillows. 'I thought you were supposed to be in charge here. Or so *you're* always telling me. So are you or aren't you? And where are my boys? Don't think I don't know what you're up to, young lady.' She waggles an accusatory finger towards my face. 'I'm not an *idiot*. You'd do well to remember that.'

I stay only long enough to prove beyond doubt that there is no benefit in my lingering, as Mum is becoming shriller and more agitated by the moment. A nurse comes over and, after distracting her with a 'Get Well Soon' helium balloon (which I feel sure is meant for someone else, and will presumably find its way to the correct bedside eventually), she motions me aside, a few steps from the bed.

'Try not to let it get to you,' she counsels. 'Sometimes you just have to cut your losses and run. She'll have forgotten all about it the minute you've gone, you'll see. Be right as rain again. And don't forget,' she adds, 'it's always the ones they feel closest to that they tend to be the most unkind to. If you can try to see it that way, it will help.'

It's the sweetest, rightest thing she could say, even though I'm not sure it's true. *In vino veritas*. I suspect *in dementia veritas* too, at least sometimes. 'Thank you,' I say. 'I'll try to keep that in mind.'

I tell Mum I'm off. Say goodbye. She ignores me.

When I leave the hospital, I take the same complicated detour I used to get there, and emerge on to the street with the same sense of having escaped enemy territory. Which, to some extent, I remind myself, I just have. My mother is up there. Aidan Kennedy is up there. His mother will no doubt be up there as well. The only missing person in the mix is its architect.

I head back down to the prom along the side street I came up, clutching my coat lapels together against a stiff onshore breeze, which is barrelling its way between the houses, herding twigs and scraps of litter into miniature tornadoes. And by the time I'm on the front again, I realise it's strangely appropriate that I should have chosen this route, given that my dead sister, and the consequences of what she's done, are both so much on my mind.

Because, down on the prom, I can see myself twenty-eight years earlier, looking up at the hospital I've just emerged from. I'm at almost the exact spot where Hope and I stood all those years back, and, though she didn't know it, my professional future was sealed.

It had been four days after Dad left, home a Hammer House of Horrors, as Mum, way beyond trying to maintain a brave face, lurched from room to room, variously weeping, or shouting, or sobbing down the phone to friends, or – the most frightening – randomly grabbing heavy objects and hurling them against the walls. It was (naturally) the beginning of the school summer holidays, and my escape room – the local library – was no longer available, since it was understood ('Grace, for pity's sake, just do as you are *told*, please!') that my role in the hurricane-tossed boat we were sailing was, at all times, to Look After Hope. Hope, who had not the least interest in going to the library, and once there, would doubtless kick off and make it impossible for us to stay.

So we'd get the bus into town and tramp the length of the seafront, and she'd ask endless questions, like what was going to happen to us? Would we ever see Daddy again? Would Mummy be put in a mental hospital? Would we end up in a children's home?

Would Aurélie be arrested by the gendarmes? Because wasn't there a law about stealing children's daddies?

This day was different. No questions, just tears. Because, rattling down the stairs, having gone back up them to grab her backpack, she had overheard something that she was never going to un-hear. My mother, pressing cash into my palm (I recall the sound of the ten-pound note crunching into my hand as if it were yesterday), saying, '*I* don't know – *anywhere*. Just, for God's *sake*, get her *out of my sight!*'

There was worse. At some point – I don't know when – during those hot, hellish days, Hope had stumbled upon something that had already rocked her. A letter from our father's new – not so new, as it turned out – girlfriend, tucked inside a book on the desk in his study. It had been written just a couple of months previously, right before we had all gone away as a family for a cheap cottage break down in Cornwall. (Why, I've always wondered? What was the deal there? Did he think taking us to the seaside – we already *had* a seaside – would somehow ameliorate the damage of what he was about to do?)

She had not minced her words. *I know the holiday will be tedious* (the stand-out line for Hope, that) *but it will quickly be over, and we will be reunited, mon chéri.*

I'd had to squint to read it against the bright July sunshine. Had to hold the paper tight to stop the wind snatching it from me. I remember reading 'holiday' and hearing Aurélie's voice, saying ''oliday'. Remember thinking *really*? Actually writing *mon chéri*? Did she not realise how utterly *naff* her Frenglish sounded? How utterly unoriginal were her words? Like Hope, I particularly remember the word 'tedious'. Can see the damning string of letters, just as she'd written them, even now. She knew that much about it. *Us.* What on earth had he said to her? And what part, precisely, had he then *found* so tedious? The walks to get ice creams? The

218

sandcastle-building? The day when, at dawn, we'd taken buckets and spades to the rocky end of the shoreline, and dug for razor clams and tiny crabs and cockleshells? I was *sixteen*. It was MY job to declare holidays tedious. His, *surely*, to cherish those final few days with us, when we were still a family, still whole. Yet he'd obviously already decided it would be tedious.

But mostly I remember Hope, on the prom, on that morning in Brighton, looking up at me, her cheeks pink, saying, 'We're orphans now, aren't we? To all intents and purposes?' Then she'd scowled up at the sun. 'Well, at least *I* am,' she'd finished.

And I'd smiled, and I'd hugged her, said, of *course* we're not, stupid. And I'd told her she'd made me giggle, for the first time in ages, with the comical way she'd huffed 'to all intents and purposes', with her fists bunched up so tight against her skinny hips.

But at that very same moment, I had looked up towards the hospital, whose creamy frontage I could just spy above the terraced streets between us. And what had previously been an ambition had in that moment become a yearning. I ran pell-mell towards it, never daring to look behind me, because I knew that if I thought too much about what I was leaving behind, I might never escape.

My little sister *did* know, I realise. I was abandoning her too.

No wonder she couldn't bear to have Aidan taken away from her. He was all she had left. How can I find it in me to blame her?

Chapter 22

When I was in the upper sixth at school, just before the deadline for applying to study medicine, I had the opportunity, along with half a dozen others, to spend a few days at a medical school in the north of England, to get a snapshot of what life as a doctor might be like. We stayed in halls of residence, went to lectures, and toured the hospital they were attached to; and on the last day, via a video link, we watched an operation. Watched in real time, as a surgeon, wearing a head-mounted camera, talked us through as he replaced a patient's hip.

I had never seen anything quite so compelling. Or as unlike anything I'd ever imagined surgeons did. My diet of TV medical dramas had misled me. Yes, I had most of the images correct; how they gowned up, made incisions, probed around cavities. How they prodded and cauterised. How they excised and inserted and stitched. I knew all about babies being hauled out of bloody wombs. About catheters, and ventilators, and ever-bleeping monitors. How the patient's journey was told via multicoloured snail trails.

But I'd never seen an artificial hip being put in. Had no idea about all the tools, the contortions, the sheer brute force they had to use. Hadn't expected the enormous physicality of it all. Had no idea it would all be so thrilling.

It really *was* theatre. A show unlike any other. One girl fainted. Two others switched to biomedical sciences as soon as they were home again. But I was hooked. I'd found the job I was made for.

Nothing has changed. Theatre is still my safe space. My sterile sanctuary. So when I arrive at work on Monday morning, my spirits can't help but lift, despite the constant buzz of anxiety and foreboding. I have a full day of operating, which makes it my favourite kind of work day, and I'm acutely aware that, not a very long way from here, someone else is in theatre, undergoing surgery of a very different kind, at the end of which no anaesthetist will bring him round again.

The day whooshes past in the way days in theatre always do, and when I hear my mobile ring I'm surprised to find it's already past four. I'm scrubbing up with Sid, in the side room, while the last patient of the day is prepped, and as my phone's still in theatre, Terry, one of the ODAs, goes to fetch it. He returns holding it aloft. 'Someone called Isabel?'

I know Isabel wouldn't call me at work unless it was important. She would text me. I think back towards this morning, and the sourness that still lingered after another small skirmish about whose turn it was to clean out Mr Weasley. I wonder if the boys have had a falling-out again.

With my hands out of commission now, Terry holds the phone to my ear. 'Is everything okay?' I ask her.

'Grace, I'm so sorry to bother you, but Dillon's not come home yet. Might he have gone to have tea at a friend's, perhaps? There's nothing on the calendar.'

I check the time again. Four fifteen now. And school ends at three twenty. And we both know there is nothing. We are scrupulous with the calendar. Which is why I can hear the slight anxiety in her voice. 'No,' I say. 'At least, not that I'm aware of. Is Daniel home?'

'Yes, he's just arrived. And he can't think of anything. And Dillon's teacher said he left with his usual friends, so I thought I ought to check with you before getting in a flap. We'll walk up to the park, then. He's probably there and just forgotten the time. Don't worry.'

She promises she'll keep me posted. Says don't worry a second time. And right now I need to concentrate on the hip I'm replacing; my patient's already anaesthetised and ready. I finish scrubbing up. All being well, it should take no more than an hour. But as I put on fresh gloves, worry starts to stalk me anyway. Dillon walks home, with three friends, to the corner of our lane. He does not forget the time, because he does not forget the rules. He is allowed to walk home with his friends *on that condition*. He knows that unless something different has already been arranged, he must meet Isabel at the end of our lane. That is the *rule*.

I try not to worry. Tell myself that, like Isabel, I mustn't start flapping. That perhaps, these days, things are more fluid than I realise. Perhaps, on occasion now, Dillon doesn't hurry home. Perhaps Isabel, who is in loco parentis, is more flexible – allows him a slightly longer leash. After all, managing independence is a continuous process. Perhaps sometimes half an hour in the park is allowed. *How would I know?* I think. When was the last time we had a conversation about coming-home logistics? November? October? September? I am out of this loop now, I remind myself. I mustn't worry.

I go back into theatre to begin dismantling my patient's hip so we can clear the way to insert a glinting metal new one. Sid assists, his natural competence outstripping his confidence, as always. Something I mentally file away to work on. And for most of the next hour I am free of anxiety, as between us we're focused on the familiar choreography of surgery; the dance of scalpels and clamps. Of retractors, bone forceps, and chisels.

We're almost done before Isabel rings again. I ask Terry to tell her I'll call her back in five minutes, and once I'm happy that I can let Sid and the anaesthetist take over, I strip my gloves from my hands and return the call.

'So we went to the park,' Isabel says. 'And everywhere else we could think of, and no joy, so we went back up to the school. Mrs Patterson had already left—' *Mrs Patterson, I think, Mrs Patterson. Who is Mrs Patterson?* 'But the secretary was still there, and said she'd ring around for me. So we headed back – she's going to call me – in case Dill came home. But he hasn't yet, and I was wondering if there was anyone I might have missed. I know he walks with Max and Thomas, but there's that other boy he's recently made friends with, isn't there? The boy he went to tea with a couple of weeks back, remember? You picked him up from there, didn't you? Is it Will?'

Mrs Patterson. It finally comes to me. Dillon's temporary teacher. While Miss Kemp, his usual teacher, is on maternity leave. I should *know* this.

'Yes, yes, it's Will,' I say. What the hell is his surname? But I know where he lives, at least. And perhaps Dillon's there. Perhaps this is nothing. Maybe this is just him choosing today – of *all* days – to bust out of his shackles. Choosing today as the first of what will so surely be many in which my maternal patience, my maternal mettle, will be tested. No. *Is* being tested. 'I'm on my way,' I tell Isabel, already tugging my gown off. 'If you hear anything, let me know, okay? I'll be as quick as I can.'

Siddhant catches the end of this. 'Is everything okay, Mrs Hamilton?'

'I hope so, Sid. One of my boys has gone AWOL.'

He looks confused. 'AWOL?'

'Absent without leave,' I explain. 'He's not come home from school yet.'

'Oh,' he says. 'Troubling. Well, fingers crossed then.'

'Indeed,' I say. 'Anyway, I'd better get going. I'll see you tomorrow. *Don't* stay too late.'

And as he promises he won't, it occurs to me why AWOL wouldn't be in Siddhant's personal vocabulary. It's because – hanging around the hospital when he shouldn't be aside – he doesn't strike me as ever having been the kind of child who'd have been anywhere that wasn't exactly where he was supposed to be.

But then, isn't that also true of Dillon?

I don't bother changing out of my scrubs. Just swap my theatre clogs for my boots, grab my bag and clothes and coat, and head straight down to my car, already cursing every other driver who I know is going to be on the road. It's getting dark. And a hammering in my temple is starting up – a steady, insistent pulse. Please, I think, let this be something and nothing.

It takes me over half an hour to get home, to find Dillon still hasn't. There's just Isabel in the kitchen, on her mobile. 'The school secretary,' she mouths at me, as I put my bag and keys down on the worktop. 'Okay, thank you,' she continues, nodding. 'Yes, we'll obviously let you know if he does. His mum's just come home now, so we'll put our heads together and if we think of anyone else he might have gone home with, we'll let you know . . . Yes, thanks,' she then finishes. 'Thanks again. Yes, this number.'

I slip my bag from my shoulder and pull my arms from my coat sleeves. The digital clock on the cooker says it's ten to six. And getting darker.

'So, as far as she knows,' Isabel says, once she's finished the call, 'he left school with his usual friends, just like normal. Not Thomas. He had the dentist this afternoon, so he left school at lunchtime. And she's not had any luck getting hold of Will or Max's mothers yet, but she's left voicemails and is going to call as soon as one of them gets back to her. She thinks he might well be with one of them. That's most likely, isn't it? D'you want a tea? Coffee? Anything?'

'No, no,' I say. 'I'm fine. And yes, you're right. He probably is. Where's Daniel?'

Isabel tilts her gaze towards the ceiling. 'He's just gone up to have a shower. He was still in his football kit when he got back from school, and of course we went straight back out again.' She frowns. 'He's a bit upset. I think he's worried it might be something to do with him. Because of the tiff they had this morning,' she adds. *And the fight they had yesterday*, I think. 'I keep telling him not to be silly,' she goes on. 'That Dill's probably – ah.' Her phone screen has lit up again. 'Here we are. Any news?' she says, as she accepts the call and puts it to her ear. 'Actually, let me hand you over to Mrs Hamilton . . . It's Mrs Gregg,' she says to me. Another name that barely registers. I take the phone. Put her on loudspeaker. Say hello.

'I've just heard back from Max's mum,' she says. 'He's gone to the Sea Life Centre with William and his mum and sister. He's due to be dropped back any time now so she says she'll let me know once he's home, but she thinks Dillon might have gone with them as well?'

Without asking Isabel? Why would Dillon have done that? No, I correct myself, Dillon *wouldn't* have done that.

'Straight from school?' I ask.

'No, she said Max went home and changed first. Will's mum picked him up around four.'

The pulse in my temple is growing more and more insistent. 'But she didn't know if Dillon was with them?'

'No. She didn't go out and speak to her, so she doesn't know if he was in the car or not. But he might have been, mightn't he? Anyway, if they're on their way home we'll know either way shortly, and as soon as I hear anything I'll be back to you immediately, I promise. And in the meantime—'

'Would you perhaps be able to give me William's mum's number?'

'I'm sorry. I'm not allowed to. But, as I say, the very moment I hear anything, I'll—'

'No, I understand. Of course you can't. Thank you. We'll stay by the phone.'

'But that's *mad*,' Isabel says, as I disconnect the call. 'Dill would *never* do something like that. He would have come home first and asked me, and changed out of his uniform. He wouldn't just go off . . .' She looks exasperated. 'And as if William's mum would even let him, anyway! She'd have checked with me first. Oh God, this is *awful*. Where *is* he?'

I go over to the sink, run the tap, and pour myself a glass of water, my mouth suddenly dry. 'I think you're right,' I say. 'He'd never go off like that without asking. I think I'll drive round to Will's house and see if they're home yet. Because if the boys left together, they might know something, mightn't they?' I grab my car keys. 'Might have an idea where he might have gone.'

The pulse becomes a constant pressure, like the beginning of a migraine.

And who he might have gone *with*.

I've only been to Will's house once before, and I can't recall the number. Just the street and a general impression that it was one of a pair of semis at the far end of an avenue, on the left. But in the dark – it's fully dark now – and with the houses all looking so similar, I'm struggling to remember which pair. I park the car on the road in what I hope is roughly the right spot, and am just climbing out when another car sweeps past, and then turns across the front of me, into a driveway on the left. And I'm in luck. I immediately recognise Will, tumbling out of the big 4x4 with typical ten-year-old insouciance.

'Oh hi,' he says, seeing me. 'Mum, Dillon's mum's here.'

But Dillon clearly isn't. The woman backs out from where she's been unstrapping a toddler from a baby seat, her fair hair haloed by the security light that blazes above their garage door. I note her noting my scrubs. 'I was just going to call you,' she says. 'I have literally, just this second, finished speaking to Mrs Gregg. I'm so sorry. I had my ringer off. I wouldn't have even known she was trying to get hold of me if it hadn't come through on CarPlay. He still hasn't turned up then?'

Which renders my first question redundant. I shake my head. No, I think, no joy. Just fear. 'Not yet. Mrs Gregg thought he might be with you.'

She hefts the toddler – nearing three, I estimate – higher on her hip. Now she shakes her head. Frowns. 'Sorry, no, he isn't.' She turns to Will then. 'Did you walk home from school with Dillon?'

'No,' he says. 'Well, for a little bit. He got a lift.'

His mother is half a second ahead of me. 'A lift from who, Will?'

Magician-like, he then conjures up my fear and lets it fly. 'Just some old lady,' he says, shrugging. 'I think it was his granny.'

Chapter 23

I sit in the car for a few moments, both hands holding the wheel, temporarily overcome by a kind of mental paralysis; held vice-like in the iron grip of terror.

Thankfully, then, adrenaline starts doing its work, and the rational me, long practised in harnessing it, takes over. Though it's unconscious, it's a process that's wholly instinctive, formed over years of having to respond to clinical emergencies. For almost every one of which there is a protocol to turn to. Protocols run my life. And for very good reason. There are few crises that aren't made at least a little less frightening by being broken down into a series of practical steps. There are options I can choose over succumbing to panic. Decisions I can take, plans I can follow, things I can *do*. Because anything is better than being consumed by the monster that is hysterical, impotent fear.

I think hard, as if trying to stare down a bear. Because if I can focus every vestige of my attention on the doing part, I can beat back my imagination, dampen down its frenetic image-making. Then, a strategy decided upon, I start the engine and drive home.

I find Isabel and Daniel in the utility room, busy clearing up after having cleaned out Mr Weasley. The fluorescent strip light is on the blink, and I've not yet found a moment to buy a new one, and both look at me, owl-like, when I appear.

'So,' I say. 'It looks like one of Nanna's friends might have picked Dillon up from school. So that's good, isn't it?' I add immediately, registering their relief at these words. And relieved myself, because my strategy seems the right one. 'She's probably got it into her head that she needed to see him for whatever reason, and asked one of her friends to go and pick him up from school. So at least we know he isn't wandering around in the dark.'

'Which friend?' Daniel asks. And though she doesn't say anything, I can tell Isabel is asking herself the same question; in her case, zipping through a mental file of potential contenders, and no doubt wrestling with multiple questions of her own.

'I think a friend of hers called Mary,' I say, watching Daniel's face carefully. And though I can tell Isabel is trying to recollect if it's familiar, Daniel's expression seems to indicate it's not. At least, not rung any bells for him yet. 'So I'm going to see what I can find out,' I hurry on briskly. 'Which means I'm going to need to make a few phone calls. So I was thinking, while I'm doing that, assuming Isabel doesn't have to be anywhere—' (I glance hopefully at Isabel as I say this.) '—I thought maybe the two of you could drive down to McDonald's, or Domino's, or wherever you fancy, and get us all something to eat? And get something for Dad, too, because I expect he's going to be home soon as well.'

'Dad is?' Daniel asks.

Of course he asks that. It's Monday. Matt's not due back till Friday. 'Yes, he's, er, got to work from home tomorrow, so he's coming home tonight. And he's bound to be starving. Does that sound like a plan?'

'But wouldn't Dillon—' Daniel begins.

'An excellent plan,' Isabel says. 'Come on, DI Dan, let's go and get our coats, yeah?' And while I rummage in my bag for my purse, we lock eyes. She has no idea what's going on, but she knows something is. She waggles her mobile. Raises her eyebrows a touch. 'Keep us posted, yeah?'

I promise I will. And I curse myself for not having told her more earlier. 'I'll text you,' I promise. She understands.

My first call once they've gone isn't to Matt, but to Jessica Kennedy. I spend the time it takes for the kettle to boil agonising over making it, but the protocol devotee in me knows I can't not. She might have information that could be vital to the police, after all. She'll almost certainly know what colour of car Norma drives, and I need to know that more than anything. But as soon as I think that, my imagination shifts gear. Which I can't afford to happen. I grab my phone and make the call.

I don't know where she is, but I can hear a child crying.

'I am *so* sorry to bother you today of all days,' I tell her. 'I know this is the worst time, and this is going to seem so insensitive, but I just wondered if you knew where Aidan's mother is.'

'Norma?' she says. 'No, sorry, I don't. Why?'

'Dillon has gone missing. He didn't return home from school earlier, and his friends say he was picked up by a lady in a white car. Does Norma have a white car?'

She answers immediately. 'Yes. Yes, she does. She drives a white Renault. But – sorry. I mean, you think it might be her? That she's *abducted* him or something?'

I have a new, chilling word in my day-to-day vocabulary. 'Yes,' I say. 'That's exactly what I think.'

'Oh my God,' she says. '*Really?*

'It was an elderly lady with black hair, in a white car. That's what I've been told. So I don't know what else to think. I mean, has she said anything to you? Because under the circumstances . . . with Aidan . . . I'm so sorry, I truly am. I feel terrible bothering you with this, but did she—'

'She won't hurt him,' she cuts in. 'I mean, if it *is* her . . . I mean, I don't know why she would do something like that, but she just *wouldn't*. That at least I *do* know. She wouldn't harm a hair on his head.'

How? I think. How can she possibly know that? But I'm at least comforted by the conviction with which she says it. 'That's reassuring,' I say. 'But, look, if you can think of anything, if you hear anything . . .'

'I can try her mobile. Shall I do that?'

'Or give me the number?'

'Of course. I'll ping it across, and—' The crying is getting louder. 'Look, I have to go, but I'll do that right away, okay?'

'And can I give the police your number, just in case they—'

'Yes, of course. I'll get back to you. Shh, Polly, *no*! Okay, bye now.'

My call to the police – the first time I've dialled 999 ever – feels interminable. The dispatcher, once I've been triaged to the local police switchboard, seems to want to know every last detail about me before she will even countenance discussing the reason for my call. And when she starts going through her list, I have to will myself to keep calm. To just answer all her questions in the order she asks them. This is a system. This is a protocol. There is a reason for it all.

Finally, when she's satisfied she has everything she needs, from a description right through to any reason I can think of – however random – why Dillon might have felt unhappy at home, why he might have run away, she is happy to listen to my hypothesis about who took him. And to reassure me that, being the age he is, he's definitely considered vulnerable and that she'll dispatch someone to come to the house as soon as possible.

'As in now?' I ask. 'Because—'

'As soon as possible,' she says again.

Which makes me feel vulnerable as well. I'm not used to there being nothing I can do. There is always *something* I can do, isn't there? But what?

I have to brace myself again, then, to call Matt and tell him. He's driving home to the flat, which suddenly feels much too far away; I can hear his indicator plink-plonking in the background.

'I think Norma Kennedy has taken Dillon.'

'Jesus. *What?*' He's on loudspeaker, and his voice sounds all echoey. 'Taken where? Taken when?'

I tell him what I know, and what I've found out from Jessica. Black hair. White car. Black and white, I think. Just like Cruella De Vil. *And Dillon got into her car.* Of course he did. Because he thought he had nothing to fear. *Please*, I think. *Please let that be true.* 'I've just called the police. They're going to send someone round as soon as they can. Can you come home?'

Only then, once he's checked his satnav and given me an ETA, do I allow the battle that's been raging in my head to spill out; let the fear grab the victory it was always going to have, and submit to a torrent of tears.

And once that's done with, I lay the kitchen table.

By the time Isabel and Daniel return, some twenty minutes later, I have changed out of my scrubs and into jeans and a sweater, and put my head back together too, at least to some extent. I've had a text from Jessica Kennedy, sharing her mother-in-law's number, which predictably has gone straight to voicemail. I have absolutely no doubt in my mind that Norma has taken Dillon, because he would never get into a stranger's car. Ever. And though I know the pointlessness of speculating what her motives are in doing so, I've fashioned a theory even so – I can't help it. Aidan's life-support machine was switched off today. His life is over. And I can certainly imagine what a maelstrom of emotions must be swirling around inside Norma's head. In my theory, in that maelstrom in which she's currently being tossed, she is desperate, distraught, in an intense mental storm, and has it in her head that she needs one thing above any other – to have her still-beloved grandson to herself. In my theory, all thoughts of me, and of vengeance, are forgotten – all subsumed beneath that one simple primeval need. So in my theory, Jessica's right. She *will not hurt him*.

All theories need testing. But for now, mine feels sound. Because it must. Because I cannot allow any alternative to muscle in and try to take up space in my head.

By now, I have already texted Isabel. I've explained that Nanna's 'friend' Mary isn't a friend, that she's actually Dillon's paternal grandmother. The mother of the man whose arm I had to amputate before Christmas – who died over the weekend, after taking an overdose – and from whom we've been estranged for many years. *It's a mess*, I finish. *The boys know nothing about it. I'm sorry. I should have told you all this earlier. Police on way. Let's try to keep calm for Daniel.*

She's texted back. A thumbs-up emoji and a kiss.

They've been to Nando's, and despite all the knots in my stomach, once we've put Matt's into the oven, I find it easier to eat than I expected. Being required to seem calm and strong and optimistic and reassuring has the benefit of keeping me calm and reassuring for Daniel too, which has helped. He has segued now from fear and anxiety about an 'if' to a more manageable 'when' Dillon gets home. He's with Nanna's friend. It's a muddle, a miscommunication. That's all. So there's little to fear.

All of which will change, I know, once the police are on the doorstep, and a part of me wants to ask Isabel to stay. But I know she is supposed to be seeing her boyfriend this evening – they have flights and accommodation to book for their trip – and, as much as Daniel, I want to reassure her as well.

So I go out to her car with her. It's so dark now, so cold. And run through in more detail what I told her by text.

'Wow,' she says. 'Complicated.'

'Yes, you could say that.'

'And none of this would have happened if he hadn't had that accident, would it?'

'No, probably not. Anyway, you get off home. I'll let you know the minute we hear anything, I promise.'

'I mean it. Even if it's in the middle of the night, I want to know, okay? And I'll be back here first thing—'

'Sweetheart, you don't need to do that.'

'I *do* need to do that.' She is struggling to keep her chin from wobbling. 'I'll never forgive myself if anything happens to Dillon. If only I'd *known*, I could have . . .' She clamps her mouth shut. 'I'm sorry. I didn't mean that.'

I summon Jessica Kennedy's words to mind, and try to force myself to believe them. Try to transmit that belief to Isabel too. 'It won't. Aidan's wife said Norma Kennedy would never, ever hurt him. And I absolutely, one hundred per cent, believe her.'

But as I watch Isabel's car turn the corner, I feel desolate. Because if she's wrong, the fault will be all mine.

When I get back inside, Matt has texted to say he's just stopped for petrol, and should be home, give or take, in half an hour. And Daniel's in the conservatory, on the floor, with Mr Weasley. I get down on the floor as well, and, just as the boys often do, we sit opposite one another, legs spread, and our feet soles to soles, to make a diamond-shaped arena for him to run around in.

'It must be weird being a hamster,' he observes. 'Being on your own all the time.'

'Well, he's not strictly alone,' I say. 'He has us for company, doesn't he?'

'But he wouldn't have in the wild.'

'No, you're right, he wouldn't. They're solitary animals. Which is why they fight if you put them together.'

There's a silence. Which lengthens. And lengthens. 'It was an accident,' Daniel says finally. Whispers it.

'What was?'

'My Lego. It was an accident.' His eyes are glistening with unshed tears. 'I just said he did it on purpose because he threatened to do it . . . he didn't mean for it to *really* fall. That bit was an accident. I don't know why I said that. I just—'

But he can't speak any more. I scoop up Mr Weasley and scramble across so I can hold him.

'I wish we didn't fight yesterday,' he sobs. 'I wish I wasn't horrible to Dillon this morning. What if she doesn't bring him back and the last thing I said to him was—' He can't bring himself to say the word.

'Oh, sweetheart.' I grip him tightly, Mr Weasley clutched between us. 'She *will* bring him back,' I tell him firmly. 'She's Nanna's friend, remember. Mary. It's probably all just a muddle, and—'

He pulls back a little suddenly. 'I remember her now,' he says. 'She's Nanna's friend from before.'

'Before?'

'Before we moved here. She came on a picnic with us once, when we went on a sleepover at Nanna's. And to Drusillas once, too. You know – the farm that's a zoo?'

'I do,' I say. And I never knew a *single thing about it*. They might even have said something about it, and I wouldn't have batted an eyelid. Why would I? 'And there you go,' I add. 'See? It's probably just a big silly muddle, like I said.'

Which reassures him, but only brings my fear crowding in again. This woman has threaded her way through my children's lives like a stripe in a piece of Brighton rock.

Or a tapeworm.

Matt and the police officers arrive almost simultaneously, the police car pulling up just as Matt is getting out of his. One is PCSO Wallace, looking a great deal less sanguine than he had in my office, the other a younger man in plain clothes, who introduces himself as Detective Sergeant Lovelace. I show them into the living room with a sense of strange dislocation, as if this isn't really happening. As if we're all playing roles in a television drama. Because this cannot be happening, can it? I take an armchair, Daniel sitting on the arm, pale and tense. Matt stands by the fireplace. He cannot sit. He's too wired.

'So,' says the DS, once they are both perched on our sofa, 'I know you've already spoken to the dispatcher, Mrs Hamilton, but can you run through what you already know again for us?'

I do so, including the discovery of the memory stick on Friday, acutely conscious of having to choose my words carefully. Acutely conscious that Daniel is listening so intently. He shouldn't be here. But where else can he be? The officers listen in silence, the DS nodding at intervals, while PCSO Wallace makes notes on a pad. Why the *hell* didn't I call the police over the weekend? Explain the connection? Make it clearer the sort of woman Norma is?

Because I didn't *think*. Because I never imagined anything like this would happen. God – why didn't I just *think*?

'So,' says the DS again, once I've finished, 'Norma Kennedy is the person your son knows as Auntie Mary. Which would explain why he would be comfortable getting into her car, wouldn't it?'

'Yes.'

Daniel touches my arm. '*Mum*. Who is Norma?' he whispers.

I place my hand over his. 'I'll explain,' I whisper back.

Matt's looking at PCSO Wallace. Pointedly. 'You did speak to her, right?' His tone is accusatory. And I tense, wondering if he's going to mention the assault in front of Daniel. Thankfully, he doesn't. Doesn't need to.

PCSO Wallace shakes his head. 'Not as yet, I'm afraid. I did try, but—'

'What the *fu*—'

Matt grabs the word back before he finishes it, and shakes his head. Shoots a look at me. Lets PCSO Wallace finish his sentence.

'Mrs Kennedy wasn't at home,' he continues. He doesn't meet my eye. He looks sheepish, but not even remotely as sheepish as I feel I have a right to expect him to be. I swallow down my anger, which I know will get me precisely nowhere. Instead, I squeeze Daniel's hand to reassure him.

'So what happens now?' Matt says.

'We'll need a recent photograph,' the DS says. 'If you have one you can loan us?' He stands up, as does PCSO Wallace, flipping his pad closed. 'We'll get that out, and we'll start making the usual inquiries, starting with the car and a visit to Mrs Kennedy's home. On the face of it—' (the DS looks over at Daniel as he says this) '—it looks as though she's managed to get her wires crossed about something. I'm sure there's nothing to fear. And I'm sure Dillon's *fine*.' And though I know he can't know that, I'm grateful for his tone. For his willingness to go along with that narrative for Daniel. Whose hand I squeeze again. 'And while Dad does that,'

I tell him, 'let's get you up to bed, bubs. Let the policemen get off and find Dillon.'

He doesn't protest. But where to start? All the years we've spent quietly burying the truth have made it flower into impossible proportions. Leaving Matt to see the policemen out, I take him upstairs, and potter around the bedroom while he changes into pyjamas and goes to clean his teeth, determinedly avoiding looking at Dillon's empty bed. Then, once Daniel's back and in his own bed, I cuddle up beside him.

'So,' I say. 'Auntie Mary. She isn't just Nanna's friend. You know my sister, Dillon's Mummy Hope, who died when you were little?' He nods. 'Well, he also had another nanna – as well as Nanna Jean in Scotland, this is – a lady called Norma. And before his Mummy Hope died – this was back when Dillon was still a baby, which is why he doesn't remember it – she would look after him sometimes, to help out when she went to work, and so on. So once Dillon became your brother, and came to live with us in London, we would bring him down here to Brighton to see her from time to time, because she missed him. And then, because that's how it works in life sometimes, we stopped taking him to see her, and—'

'But why did Nanna call her Auntie Mary?'

'Because . . .' I grope for words. For truth. For the right truth. For *now*. 'Because by that time he wasn't seeing his Nanna Norma any more. Wasn't supposed to be, anyway.'

'Why not?'

Another perfectly reasonable, logical question. I grope for words again. 'Because . . . well, because it was getting confusing for Dillon,' I settle for. 'Because lots had changed. Because he had a new mummy and daddy now, didn't he? And a new life, *and* a brother.' I squeeze his shoulder. 'And we knew it was only going to get *more* confusing for him. And, well, we ended up having a bit of an argument about what was best for him. For all of us.

And that was why Nanna told you her name was Auntie Mary. Because perhaps she thought I might be cross about you both seeing her. Because of the argument. You know what it's like with arguments—'

'But why did she go off with him today?'

'Well, I think it's because something sad has happened for her. And she's probably upset, and, well . . . I think, *maybe*, she just wanted to see Dillon for a bit. To cheer her up, perhaps.'

'So she fixed it with Nanna Joy?'

'Kind of, I expect, yes.'

'And she's her friend.' It's not a question. 'So she won't hurt him.' He grabs the thought as if a passing life raft. Then finds another. 'But why didn't she just *ask* you if she could see him?'

I am struggling now. How the hell do you explain stuff like this? You just don't. You just can't. You just shouldn't. You shouldn't *have* to. But he's here, and needs an answer. 'Probably because she knew I'd say no,' I say eventually.

'But why?' His tone's sharper now. 'Why couldn't you just have let her?'

'There are lots of reasons, but mostly because it would just become too difficult. Too upsetting. And she's sick, sweetie. That's the main reason. She's not very well. She's upset and she's sick. So if she *had* asked, we wouldn't have thought it would be a good idea, that's all.'

He seems to accept this. 'And she's going to bring him back again? *Definitely?* You're not just saying that?'

'Definitely. Now, shall I stay here till you fall asleep?'

'I'm not going to fall asleep till Dillon's back. I know I'm not.'

'I know, bubs. I'm not going to either. Not till he's home.'

But after I sing three rounds of 'American Pie' he finally drops off, and once I'm sure he won't wake again, at least for the moment,

I carefully extricate myself, then tuck him in, and tiptoe silently from the room.

I leave the door open so the light from the landing can spill in, and the sight of Dillon's empty bed – that horrible flat expanse of duvet – sends such a stab of fear through me that it makes me catch my breath. And something else. An emotion so powerful that it takes me by surprise. I've never felt anything like it, but I recognise it. It's rage.

If anything happens to him, I decide, I will track her down myself. And when I find her, I will tear her limb from limb.

'What the *fuck* do we do now?' Matt says when I find him in the kitchen.

'I think we try to keep calm, and—'

'Calm?' he snaps. '*Calm?*'

'Yes, *calm*,' I tell him firmly. 'There's food for you in the warmer. Shall I—'

'*No,*' he says. Then he frowns. 'Sorry, hen. I shouldn't have snapped at you. I just – *Jesus.*' He looks despairingly at me. 'What the fuck do we *do?*'

We do nothing. Two hours tick by with unbearable slowness, because there is nothing we *can* do. I try and fail to think of any time I've felt so wretched and helpless. So unable to do a single thing to change my situation. Ever wished quite so hard that I could be in theatre, the only place where I can obliterate every single other thought.

At ten, I go upstairs, undress, run the shower, and get in. Then, once I'm done and dry, I re-dress, in the same jeans and sweater. I need to be dressed because I need to be ready. I have to be in a state of readiness, for whatever happens next.

Where *is* he?

As I start down the stairs again, Matt's talking on the phone. I hurry down them, and when I get into the kitchen he's just disconnected and is ferreting in the pot on the worktop for a pen. He's been on my phone, I realise.

I look hopefully at him. 'News?'

He shakes his head. 'Hang on,' he says, casting his gaze around and settling on the takeaway menu. He writes a name on it. DS Winters. In my current state of gloom, it seems horribly prescient. 'PCSO Wallace,' he says. 'Just checking in as he's about to go off duty. This guy's taking over from him.'

It's a small comfort. 'And? Anything to report?'

'Not yet. They've searched her house, found her phone—'

'Her phone?' I begin. 'So can't they use it to—' I stop, immediately realising the idiocy of my question.

'They think she probably left it there precisely so they *wouldn't* be able to track her. And they found something else too. A photo of Dillon in his school uniform. As in a *school* photo. Which I'm guessing she must have got from your *fucking* mother.'

The missing school photo. So she *has* been round to Mum's. And now we know why. So she could find out where he went to school. Oh God, oh God, oh *God*.

'Christ, I could do with a beer,' he says.

'*Have* one.'

He shakes his head. Opens a cupboard. Starts making coffee.

I clamber up on to a bar stool and start towelling my hair. 'God, I just wish I could work out what she's *thinking*.'

'Well, good luck with that,' he says. 'The woman is a fucking *lunatic*.'

'I just keep thinking about what Hope said on that recording. You know, at the very beginning, about how scared she was of the urges she kept having, to take Dillon with her. Suppose Norma's got something like that into her head too?'

He bangs two mugs down on to the counter and shoots me a warning look. 'Don't even *go* there.'

'*Think* about it, though. What has she got left to live for? She's lost both her children. She's lost her granddaughters – well, as good as, because I don't doubt for a moment that Jessica Kennedy will be going back up north now, and like a shot. And *Dillon* . . .' I can hardly bear to voice what I'm thinking, but equally I have to say it. 'What if she's decided that if she can't have him, then no one else can? What if she plans to kill herself and kill him as well?'

'Stop it,' he says. 'Just *stop* it, hen, okay?'

But how can I stop it? It's too obvious. Too logical.

I'm a mother. Which I realise means I *do* know what she's thinking. And to me, it all makes terrifying sense.

Chapter 24

Matt goes upstairs just after midnight, to lie down for a bit. He doesn't think he'll sleep, even though he's been up since five – he'd had to get out early to inspect a site in the Midlands – but he's physically drained, and needs to be horizontal. I don't go with him, because I cannot even bear to go to bed. Instead, I lie on the sofa in the conservatory, with just the hum of the hamster wheel for company, and, despite trying my best not to, start thinking dark, complicated thoughts.

Just after Dillon was born, Matt and I decided to try for another baby. It wasn't a decision that was in any way related – we'd always planned to have two, and to have them close together, because I wanted them to grow up side by side. To be friends. And now I was done with exams for a bit, it had seemed the perfect time. But then along came Hope's tumour, and then her terminal diagnosis, and we decided to wait for a bit. Which decision was, of course, very much related.

At first, that 'for a bit' felt like a good thing, the right thing. The subconscious mind works to an uncensored agenda, and mine, ever pragmatic, saw the immediate future with clarity. To have a baby in the midst of what would almost certainly be my sister's dying months felt intuitively and profoundly wrong. Whereas to have a baby after her death (my conscious mind would have never entertained such a selfish thought) would be something to cling on to, a reward for our forbearance. A light after the darkness.

But then, in a way we'd have never imagined, Dillon came into our lives. And the light was snuffed out.

The ghost of that baby haunted me for a very long time. That baby – who was never even more than an intention, just a plan for the future subsequently crossed off on a mental calendar – followed me around like a thread clinging to a coat hem.

You could still try. It kept telling me this long after the point at which Matt and I had drawn a line – and drawn it for all the right reasons, as well. It would be logistically complex and emotionally exhausting; didn't we have enough on our plates as it was, caring for Dillon? Wouldn't another baby make everything even *more* difficult?

It was a boy, this non-baby, this baby whose very existence we had rejected. And he haunted me because he was a *different* boy.

There is sudden stillness in the hamster cage. Mr Weasley has done with exercise. And in the quiet I have a small but comforting revelation. The horror that's pulsating in every pore of me has a tiny light shimmering within it too, because I know for sure now that the ghost of that much-wanted baby has gone. Been gone a while. Slipped away without my even noticing. I want my baby back. My Dillon back.

And that's *all* I want.

I had always thought that the years of being on call – not generally known for having any unexpected benefits – had, as well as giving me that sixth sense that my phone's about to ring, also inured me to the existential dread of the 4 a.m. phone call. Or at least shortened, and blunted, that period of raw terror that a ringing phone in the small hours always evokes.

But I'm not on call tonight. And I immediately know this, even though I'm still floundering in that place between sleep and full consciousness. And then I realise where I am – still on the sofa in the conservatory, and it all comes crashing in again. Dillon's missing.

I reach for my phone. Which isn't there. It must have slipped off while I've slept. I have *slept*. How have I slept when Dillon's out there somewhere, missing? It feels like a terrible betrayal. I kick off the blanket that Matt must have thrown over me at some point, and see the phone, still bleating urgently, face down on the floor. It'll be the police, I think. To tell me *what*? It's the middle of the night. If they'd found him, they would have just brought him home, surely? So what then? I pick it up, scared, bleary-eyed, fingers fumbling.

It's not the police. The display says Jessica Kennedy. It's 6.40 a.m.

'Mrs Hamilton?' It's a whisper. 'Have they found Dillon yet?'

'I don't think so,' I say, rubbing my eyes, trying to clear them. 'And it's *Grace*.'

'Okay, look, so I just thought of something, okay? Norma has a caravan – a static, over in a holiday park near Pevensey. And I just had a thought – might she have taken him there?'

I clamber up to consciousness, hearing low mournful sounds. A small child whimpering, I realise, and in my mind's eye I see them – those two little girls, sleeping with mum, in her friend-in-Hove's spare bedroom. 'Shhh,' I hear her cooing. 'Shhhh, now, it's okay. Mummy's here.'

I swing my legs down to the floor. The darkness is absolute, both inside and outside. 'Whereabouts? Do you know?'

'Yes. I've been there. I took the girls there for a couple of days the summer before last. It's on the Pevensey Bay Road. I can't remember the name of it but it's big, so I don't think you could miss it. And her van's one of the ones on the edge, by the shingle, about halfway along – it looks straight out to sea. She's had it for years. She calls it her bolthole. And I know she still has it, because I remember her talking to Aidan about paying this year's ground rent. I don't think the park's officially open yet, but I don't think that would mean she couldn't go there. I don't know if it's any use to you, but I just wanted to tell you. It might help? Look, I'd better go—' The whimpering is escalating to a cry now. Those poor babies. That poor woman. I'm close to tears again and I know it's as much for them as myself.

'Yes, yes,' I say. 'Thank you. Take care of yourself.'

I'm just hanging up when a dark shape approaches. It's Matt. In his jacket. Come in from the cold. Frigid air swirls around him and strokes my bare ankles. 'Where've you been?'

'Just walking around the garden – I needed some air. Who was that on the phone?'

'Jessica Kennedy. She's had an idea.' I tell him about the caravan, my thoughts rabbit-hopping ahead of me. Kangaroo-hopping ahead of me. Olympic long-jumping ahead of me. I'm fully awake now. Fully present. Locked and loaded. 'I'm going to get my boots,' I say, decided. 'I think we should go there.'

'No. We should call the police, hen. Have *them* go.' He's already turning around as he says this.

I follow him. 'But—'

'No.'

'But—'

He turns around. '*No.* No, because we don't know what we're going to find when we get there. What we're *dealing* with.' His tone is pointed. 'Okay?'

Which makes it not at all okay, because fresh images – there is an inexhaustible supply of them, I'm learning – burst immediately into terrifying, technicolour view.

It's an effort of will to banish them, while Matt stabs the numbers on his phone screen. *A bolthole.* For a woman who has *nothing left to live for.* Bolthole. Or bunker. Oh God. *This urge*, I think, *to just take him with me.*

To keep hands and brain busy, I fire up the coffee maker. Get mugs out of the dishwasher. Find pods and fetch milk. Pull out the cutlery drawer. Snatch up a teaspoon.

'Okay,' Matt is saying. 'Right, yes, okay. Okay, we'll do that. Okay, thanks, if you could.'

'So?' I ask, when he's done.

'So they're going to send someone out there.'

'Now?'

'So he says. And they're going to speak to Jessica Kennedy again, see if she can tell them anything else. And in the meantime—' He is clearly reading my expression. 'There is nothing we can do except *wait*.' He puts his arms around me, then. Rests his chin on my head. 'You know what I was thinking? When I was out in the garden? That big oak down at the end would be the perfect place to build that tree house I promised the boys. It has exactly the right arrangement of branches,' he continues. 'And I've already worked out the best place to put the ladder, and if we make it big enough, I think we can put a window in such a position that there'll be a sea view from up there as well. No, *seriously*,' he adds, 'I know what you're thinking, but there will be, at least in the winter months, at any rate. Tell you what, while I deal with the coffee, why don't you go and get your coat as well? Then you can come down the garden and take a look with me?'

'You worked all that out in the dark?'

'*No.* I used my phone torch.'

As I hurry out to grab my coat, I reflect that everyone has their own ways of managing darkness. And right now, in the absence of any other useful strategy, I am happy to cling to his, and hang on for grim death.

And that's what I do.

We're still outside in the garden when Isabel arrives. It's getting on for seven thirty now and the dawn is beginning to break, on what looks like being another cold but clear day.

Isabel doesn't ask if there is any news, because it's obvious there isn't, and when we head back indoors, the walls start closing in again. If the police had dispatched someone to the caravan park straight away, as they promised, then surely we'd have heard something by now?

'So why don't you call them again?' Isabel asks, when Matt poses that question. 'I mean, I know you say they say they'll call you if they have any news, but that doesn't mean they'll call you if they *don't* have any news. Or maybe they have *some* news, but it's still an ongoing situation. And I'm not sure they prioritise keeping people in the loop to that extent. They'll be too busy actually conducting the investigation. And they're bound to be short-staffed and working on multiple cases . . . and there's always a chance they haven't got anyone *to* send there as yet. But at least you'd have an idea, wouldn't you? I'm sure they won't mind updating you if you ask them.'

Matt looks astonished. And then the penny drops, for me at least. I keep forgetting Isabel's father is a policeman.

And as if to prove the point, when Matt calls DS Winters it goes straight to voicemail. 'That's it,' he says, in an about-turn that I think surprises even him. 'I can't sit here doing nothing any longer. I'm going to drive down there.'

'I'm coming with you,' I say.

'Hen, you can't. What about Daniel? If he wakes up and neither of us is here—'

'*I'm* here,' Isabel points out. 'He'll be fine with me.'

And as if to prove another point, Daniel then appears in the kitchen. 'Come here, DI Dan,' she says. 'I think we both need a hug, don't we?' And when she holds out her arms, he immediately runs into them. 'Mum and Dad are going out,' she tells him, 'to try to find Dillon. And find him they *will*,' she adds firmly.

I try to keep that in mind as we drive out of the village, because it's got to be better than endlessly moving worst-case scenario pieces around a mental chessboard. We *will* find him and he *will* be okay. I keep reminding myself of what Jessica Kennedy told me, that Norma wouldn't harm a hair on Dillon's head. But every time I bring it to mind, it comes with an unwelcome companion – one with a louder voice, which keeps reminding me that such absolutes can never truly be absolutes. The dog that never bites who one day turns on its owner, the starry-eyed bride who swears undying love and then leaves, the functioning brain that inexplicably malfunctions, the brilliant mind that starts unravelling before your eyes. *Nothing* about this can be certain.

Matt's phone remains stubbornly silent, as does he, while I use mine to search Google Maps for local caravan parks, of which I'm sure there will be several. But only one fits the description Jessica Kennedy gave me, a big sprawling site on the beach, just as she described, with rows of statics lined up like white dominoes.

It feels almost inexplicable that while we're in the middle of such a nightmare, the day is simply going about its business. We emerge on to the A27 to find it already thick with rush-hour traffic, which is only going to get worse. I glance across at Matt. See the tic that is pulsing in his jaw. And it strikes me that my own murderous rage at Norma Kennedy would be as nothing, if played out, compared to my husband's. 'He's going to be okay,' I say. 'He *is*. She won't hurt him.'

We continue in this vein, shoring one another up, as the traffic stop-starts its way east, down to Pevensey, and then on, past the village, on to the coast road. But once we've driven up the track that leads to the park's reception building, I see something that dashes every last hopeful thought. I see a police patrol car, and three men, one of which I recognise as DS Lovelace, and, in his hand, a flash of something purple.

A purple I recognise.

It's the colour of Dillon's school sweatshirt.

Chapter 25

The reality hits me then, not so much as a punch in the gut as a tsunami, and as I get out of the car, I think my legs are going to give way beneath me. I have to grip the door and take several deep breaths to try and steady myself before I dare let go.

All three men have turned around and, as they watch us approaching, I see there's a supermarket carrier bag hanging from DS Lovelace's arm as well.

'Dillon's parents,' DS Lovelace tells the other two. 'Mr and Mrs Hamilton, this is Detective Sergeant Winters. Mr Carter here is the owner of the park.'

Matt nods in acknowledgement. 'What's happening?' he asks. I cannot take my eyes off Dillon's sweatshirt.

'They're not here,' DS Winters says. 'But they've been here. Overnight, by the looks of things. We've found these . . .' He lifts the sweatshirt, and then unhooks the bag from his arm. Opens it out for Matt to look in. 'Your son's school uniform, yes? It was sitting by the door.'

I take the sweatshirt from him and put it to my face. Stifle a sob. *Mum, my clothes smell of flowers. Pleeeease. Can't you wash them in something that doesn't smell of flowers?*

'Anything else?' I hear Matt saying. 'Any other clues?'

'Not a lot,' DS Lovelace says. 'Only that they've slept here, and eaten. And they've not been gone long. Mr Carter here is fairly certain he saw Mrs Kennedy's car leave the site around twenty, thirty minutes back, and the kettle in the caravan was still warm.'

Mrs Kennedy, I think. How can they dignify such a monster with the name Mrs Kennedy? And why the hell didn't we just go there as soon as we knew? We were *nearer*. We would have *got there before they left*. Guilt and terror make my gut roil, my legs even shakier. I try to slow my breathing. In – pause – and out – pause – Dillon is *still alive* – pause. But a car. He saw a *car*. He *didn't actually see Dillon*.

'So what now?' Matt asks. 'What happens next?'

'We continue our investigations,' DS Lovelace says. 'Now we've traced them to here—' *No*, I think, *Jessica Kennedy did*, then correct my wayward thoughts. This is how policing works. Obtain evidence. Act on it. Detect. *Get a grip, Grace.*

'Do you need this?' I ask, holding out Dillon's sweatshirt.

He nods. 'If you wouldn't mind.' He holds the bag open, so I gently fold it and place it on the nest already in there, made from Dillon's grey school trousers and white Aertex polo shirt. This, I realise, is what they must mean by a living hell.

'So you're confident she's left *with* him?' Matt asks, gesturing towards the bag. He is voicing my own unspoken terror.

'We can't be confident of anything, Mr Hamilton,' DS Lovelace says. 'We've alerted the Officer In Charge, and we'll step up the appeal on social media, and as soon as we've taken a full statement from Mr Carter, we'll be better placed to decide on next steps.' He gestures to the bag himself now, then looks at both of us in turn. 'This counts as *positive* news. There's no evidence, as far as we can see, of any mistreatment or violence. No evidence that anything untoward has taken place.' *Yet*, I want to scream at him. The word you need is *yet*. 'And wherever they've gone now, we will *find* him.

It's just a matter of time. Traffic have her number plate on their watch list, and they are actively looking out for her. And now she's mobile—'

'And what can *we* do?' Matt asks. 'There must be *something* we can do to help.'

'Just *think*,' the policeman says, 'of anywhere else you suspect she might have taken him.'

I have a memory, one of a select few that I try never, ever, to pull out for inspection if I can help it. Of a trauma case that came in a couple of weeks after I took up my post here. Five a.m., Caucasian male, twenty-seven, barely alive, brain-stem injury, multiple compound fractures, query attempted suicide. He died in A and E half an hour later. It was me who declared him dead.

So I can immediately think of two: Birling Gap and Beachy Head.

I keep my mouth shut. I cannot, will not, say them.

With little choice but to leave the police to go about their business, we climb back into the car, and into our own personal chambers of imagined horrors. They would not let us go down to the caravan (preservation of potentially vital evidence) and not let us have Norma's car registration number, either (preservation of Matt's liberty, or so goes my reading of the situation, in the event of him finding Norma Kennedy before they do).

The silence is broken by Matt thumping the steering wheel. 'What the fuck do we do now?' he says.

'Go home and wait.' Now Matt's beginning to lose it, we automatically change places. I also fervently wish to be gone from *this* place. If I don't, it won't be long before I jump out of the car again and wrestle Dillon's clothing out of the officer's hands. If I don't, I will scream. I fear I might scream anyway. Instead, I chant in my head to make the noise go away. *She wouldn't harm a hair . . . she wouldn't harm a hair . . .* Because I do not dare to let my terror take further root. 'Go home to Daniel,' I say. 'What else *can* we do?'

He starts the car. Bangs the gear lever into first. Skids away. 'Well, we could drive around ourselves, for one thing. Back to near where she lives. What's to say she isn't heading back there? Where does she live now anyway?'

'I don't know. Somewhere near Patcham. But I don't know the exact address. And no one's going to tell me that, are they?'

'What about Jessica Kennedy? Why don't you just ring Jessica Kennedy and get it from her instead?'

'Matt, let's drive to Beachy Head.'

'*What?* Oh, fuck, hen. You—'

'Because the police won't do that, will they? Not specifically. Not as in sending a car to sit there on the off-chance.'

He's driving but I can feel him staring, as if I've just unleashed a monster. 'You don't really think—' he begins. But he doesn't get any further. His car display flashes up Isabel's name.

It goes straight to loudspeaker. 'Matt?'

'Yes, we're here,' he says.

'I have amazing news – Dillon's come home!'

The traffic is even heavier on the return leg of the journey. The same journey Norma Kennedy took to bring Dillon home? Almost certainly. Odd to think that we may well have passed her on the road. Dillon's fine, Isabel has told us. A bit tired and teary ('But you're absolutely fine, aren't you, DS Dill?') having been dropped, or so he's told her, at the same place she picked him up from. And looking forward to us getting home, so he can tell us all about his 'little adventure'.

I make calls while Matt drives. First to the police, to let them know. Then to Jessica, who bursts into tears when I tell her. 'I knew,' she said. 'I *knew* she wouldn't hurt him.' I then text Siddhant, and post a message on our consultants' WhatsApp group, to let them know too. And that I'll be back in tomorrow. Panic over.

And is that what this was? A lot of overblown panic?

Possibly. Because when we get home, Dillon – perhaps through shock, or perhaps not – does indeed seem barely any worse for wear.

They are all sitting at the kitchen island, eating toast, when we appear, Daniel still in his pyjamas and Dillon in unfamiliar and expensive-looking clothes. A Fortnite hoodie, a New York Yankees beanie, and a pair of dark, artfully distressed skinny jeans. An ombré Puffa jacket hangs off the back of his bar stool.

I've already dried the tears of relief that spent most of the journey falling out of me. And before they threaten to start spilling again, just looking at the expression on Isabel's face, I allow myself to give Dillon just a small, crushing hug – for my benefit more than his, it seems – before moving immediately into 'sleeves up and get on with it' mode. I know the police will be here soon, because they've already told us they will, and also that they'll need to interview Dillon, probably at some length, and though I have a creeping fear now that they will make less of this than instinct still tells me they should, I decide to park it and run with the story. Whatever is going on here, it seems important that I stick with it. At least for the moment. 'I'll make some more toast,' I announce to the kitchen in general. 'I'm starving. Are you starving too?' I ask Matt.

'As a horse,' he says. 'A big horse.' He looks similarly bemused. 'Nice threads, mate,' he says to Dillon. Then he goes across and plucks the beanie off so he can ruffle his hair. 'Where did these all come from?'

Dillon doesn't miss a beat. 'Auntie Mary bought them for me.'

Daniel catches my eye then. There's definitely something going on here. Something Matt and I aren't yet privy to. He looks down again, then over at Isabel.

'And spent a bit on them, by the looks of things,' Matt's saying, touching the sleeve of the Puffa jacket. 'Where's this from, then?'

'That's from River Island. We went shopping after school. Because I didn't have anything to change into – I didn't have a key or anything, did I?' He looks at me then. 'Mum, is Nanna really going to be okay?' And for the first time since we got back, I see fear and anxiety cloud his face.

'Nanna's going to be absolutely fine,' I reassure him. Because, as far as I'm aware, that's the truth. Though I realise I haven't so much as given her welfare a single thought in the last twenty-four hours. But now I do. What the *hell* is going on here?

But I'm saved from having to think further, because the door-bell then rings. Presumably the police. Whose presence is going to muddy the waters further.

'I'll go,' Isabel and I both say in synchrony. So we both go, not least so she can fill me in better.

'I don't know *what* is going on,' she says, once we are safely out of earshot. 'He seems to think he had to go on a sleepover with this Auntie Mary character because your mum was very sick and you had to stay over at the hospital. And when I asked him why he didn't just come home and speak to me first, he said it was because she said I'd gone on holiday! I didn't want to interrogate him about it, because he doesn't even seem that traumatised, so I told Dan we'd better just go along with it till you and Matt came home. I hope I did the right thing. I didn't want to frighten him unnecessarily.'

We're at the front door now. 'You did *absolutely* the right thing,' I reassure her. 'Anyway, we'd better let them in. Do you want to head off now?'

She shakes her head. 'I thought you might want me to take Dan to the park or something? I don't have anything else on. It's no bother.'

I tell her she's a star, and open the door to DS Lovelace and DS Winters. And it's then, when the two of them are standing in our kitchen, that Dillon's expression changes. Now he *is* scared.

And also confused. After Isabel and Daniel leave for the park, we take the police officers into the living room, where they explain to Dillon that they just need to have a chat with him, because, despite what he'd thought, none of us knew where he was.

Now he looks truly terrified. 'But she said I had to go with her because *Mum* said,' he tells them. 'She said Nanna Joy was ill.' He looks at me. 'She said *you* said.' His chin begins to wobble. 'Am I in trouble now? But I *had* to go with her. She *said*!'

'No, no, son, not at *all*,' DS Lovelace reassures him. 'And your Nanna Joy—' (he glances at me now) '—is just *fine*. We just want to hear all about it, that's all. So. What did you get up to? Did you do anything nice? How about you start from the beginning and we'll go from there?'

At least partly reassured – he's still flicking his gaze back and forth to DS Winters, who is making notes – Dillon begins recounting his story. Says she drove up when he was walking home with his friends and called him over, and explained that I'd sent her to pick him up from school because his Nanna Joy was very poorly and that he had to go and stay with her.

'And what about Isabel?' DS Lovelace asks. 'Didn't you wonder why it wasn't Isabel picking you up?'

'I *did*. I asked her why I wasn't supposed to just go and meet Isabel, and she told me it was because she'd already gone on holiday. That's why I had to go with her instead. She said it had all been fixed up.'

'And what about your brother? Did you wonder what he might be doing?'

'She said he was on a sleepover with his friend.'

'And she explained who she was?'

'She didn't need to. She's Nanna's friend, Auntie Mary. I *told* you. Was I not supposed to go with her?' He's looking anxious again.

'No, no, don't worry about any of that,' the officer says. 'So, where did she take you?'

'To the shops first, so we could get some clothes, because I only had my uniform. Then we went for tea at Nando's' (Christ, I think, they might have missed Isabel and Daniel by minutes) 'and then we went to her caravan, and we went for a walk on the beach in the dark. And then we watched telly for a bit – she has this *huge* telly in her caravan – and then I went to bed, and when I got scared in the night, because I didn't remember where I was, she sat on the bed with me and read me lots of stories. And this morning she made me breakfast, and then she brought me back. I was supposed to stay longer but I wanted to go home. I was missing Mum, and I was worried about Nanna Joy being okay.'

'So she was nice to you.'

'She's always nice.'

He nods. 'And she didn't say anything, or do anything, that made you feel uncomfortable or frightened?'

'No.' Dillon seems to have a sudden thought then. 'Is *she* going to be in trouble now?'

'Don't you worry about any of that,' DS Lovelace says firmly. 'We just want to be sure you had a nice time while you were with her. We're just a little bit concerned because we think *she* might be poorly, what with forgetting to tell your mum and dad about you going to stay with her. They were obviously very worried.'

Dillon looks from me to the officer and back again. 'Does *she* have dementia?'

'Possibly,' he says. 'Or something similar, anyway, and we'll be looking into that, so you don't need to worry. But tell me, when did you last see Auntie Mary? I mean before this.'

'I don't remember,' he says, shrugging. 'Not for ages and ages. We used to see her with Nanna sometimes, but not for a long time. She's nice. She likes to play. She made me pancakes for breakfast,' he adds, 'with chocolate spread.'

I touch my hand to my cheek, feel the tender spot. Remember. The same woman who made pancakes for breakfast, with chocolate spread. Who was *nice*. And now I know for sure what will most likely come next.

It does.

Because once they've finished asking questions, and Dillon goes upstairs to change his clothes (at Matt's suggestion, so that they too can go to the park), both officers, for all that they accept the seriousness of the situation, have expressions that are very different now. Benign ones.

'Well,' says DS Winters. 'This is a rum one, is it not?' To which I object. To both the words and the unspoken suggestion – that we're dealing with nothing more frightening than a poor abandoned grandmother, who, yes, has snatched our son from the street in broad daylight, but who, well, can perhaps be cut a little bit of slack? But before I can open my mouth to actually say this, DS Lovelace quickly adds, 'Not that we're not taking this *extremely* seriously, Mrs Hamilton, especially in light of her assault on you last week. But the main thing is that your son seems none the worse for his adventure, and—'

'This was not an "adventure",' I interrupt. 'He was kidnapped. And he is *ten*.'

And she's almost eighty. He doesn't say it, but his eyes do. 'And when we apprehend Mrs Kennedy, which I'm confident we will, we will take the appropriate action.'

'As in arresting her for kidnapping?' Matt says.

'Child abduction,' he corrects. 'Because she clearly didn't take him against his will, did she? But let's see what she says. I suspect there's a possibility that the balance of her mind was disturbed, after the untimely death of her own son. But let's just see what we see when we interview her. Rest assured that we'll be in touch as soon as we have anything more to tell you. And in the meantime, let's just be grateful that no harm's come to Dillon.' And in his face, once again, I see exactly what he's thinking. That, in his time, he has seen a *lot* worse.

And, infuriatingly, I know he probably has.

They apprehend Norma Kennedy later that afternoon. Matt and the boys are out in the garden – he's on a mission now, has become a zealot, a tree-house evangelist – when DS Lovelace calls to tell me they have found her.

'It was a call from a member of the public,' he explains, 'concerned that she was ahead of them, driving erratically, out towards Shoreham, before driving her car – they say intentionally – as some speed, into a wall. She was lucky – the airbag saved her. Car is written off, obviously. A bad business.'

'Was she badly hurt?' I force myself to ask.

'Not physically. As I say, the airbag—'

'So what's happening now? Has she been taken to hospital?'

'To the psychiatric hospital. Her physical injuries were fairly minor, but I believe she's been sectioned. They decided to call the duty psychiatrist, and to detain her under the Mental Health Act for her own protection.' He leaves a pause. 'Perhaps the enormity of what she'd done had sunk in by then and overwhelmed her mentally.'

'In what way? Can you be more specific?'

'I'm afraid not, Mrs Hamilton. I'm not a medic.'

Yes, but *I* am, I want to say. I don't.

'So what will happen now?' I ask instead.

'Well, to be honest, Mrs Hamilton, not a lot. She's in the care of the NHS now, so it's difficult to predict. And, to be equally honest with you, we'll be setting this aside for the time being; there's no action we can take until we know she has capacity. And who knows when – or if – that's likely to happen? At the very least, they have a twenty-eight-day order. It's also debatable whether there is anything likely to be achieved by mounting a prosecution if and when it does. She's a very elderly lady, and very frail, by all accounts, and given the circumstances around her actions . . . Well,' he puts into the space where I assume he was expecting me to agree with him, 'let's just see what happens, shall we? We'll obviously keep you informed going forward.'

'I'd be grateful if you would,' I say. 'Because I'm not going to be able to relax knowing she might be back out there somewhere, am I? I know PCSO Wallace doesn't think she represents much of a threat to anyone, but I know the history. I know what she's capable of.'

'I understand. Though to be frank, I think the person she most represents a threat to is herself. Which is easy to say, I know, and I do know how distressing this has been for you and your family. And the hospital will let us know if they decide to lift the section. And if that does happen, I will of *course* let you know. In the meantime, you have nothing to fear from her. Anyway, how's your little boy doing? Is he okay?'

I look out into the garden. See three heads together, Matt drawing on a pad. 'He seems to be,' I say.

'Good,' says DS Lovelace. 'Well, anyway.' I'm expecting him to add 'all's well that ends well', but thankfully he doesn't. Instead, he surprises me by adding, 'As I say, we'll keep in touch, but let's hope this really is the end of it.' He sighs. 'Ah, life's many vicissitudes, eh?'

To which rhetorical question there really is no answer.

And perhaps he's right. Perhaps this *is* the end of it. Perhaps she's done what she set out to, and it's over. And perhaps I should draw the proverbial line beneath it now as well. Because, actually, I find I *don't* care about taking Norma Kennedy to court. I can imagine the process, and I have absolutely no appetite for it. No, more than that, it feels wrong, because it's not as if I have a *need* for her to suffer more. To keep this going now just feels too much like vengeance. No, I can't find it in me to feel compassion for her. I'm not sure I ever will. I just don't want all the hate to infect me. Most of all, though, I just want my family to be left alone; for the archaeological site of our past, and all the horrors that have been excavated, to be filled in, stamped back down again, grassed over.

And I have another gentle reminder that it's the right way to think later that evening. When I'm tucking Dillon into bed – happily, because he's anxious to go to school tomorrow and be the centre of attention – he has something on his mind.

'Mum, you know Auntie Mary?'

'Yesss . . .'

'I think she does have dementia. You know when I was in her caravan?' I nod. 'Well, she said something really strange. She said I was to never forget that she loved me more than all the tea in china. That was a weird thing to say, wasn't it? What does it even *mean*?'

262

'Well, there is a *lot* of tea in China. As in the country, that is – not as in cups and bowls and plates. So it means the same as when I tell you I love you more than all the stars in the sky.'

'Oh,' he says. 'Like, a *lot*, then.'

'Yes, a *lot*,' I agree. 'And who wouldn't?' I place a kiss on his forehead. 'And I love you even *more*.'

He looks anxiously at me now. 'She's not going to be in trouble, is she?'

I think of all I know. All I could tell. All the evidence I could produce. And, for the first time, I realise that power *does* rest with me.

'No, sweetie,' I tell him firmly, 'she's not.'

Chapter 26

One of the last promises Hope extracted from me before she died was that I would not waste time getting mad with the man who had so wronged her, and not try to get even with him either.

It was a couple of weeks before Christmas and we'd gone down with presents, and it was probably the time when I had felt the most fury. Felt it as such an elemental, intensely physical force that I was struggling to contain it. We'd just finished stringing up the outside fairy lights so she could see them from the window. I remember standing looking out through the steamed-up French windows into her barren little garden, in the centre of which were the rusting remains of Aidan's old part-cannibalised motorbike, stripped to provide parts for the latest one, which he had, of course, taken with him when he left. It felt like the cruellest kind of metaphor. I remember standing there and thinking how much I'd love to smash something. Anything to do with him. Had there been an axe to hand, I would have taken it to it.

Weak as Hope was, I could still sense the strength coming off her, just as she could feel the anger coming off me. I wonder now, of course, if there was a part of her that was by now weak with relief; she had done what she'd set out to, after all. But instead she was calm and pragmatic and philosophical, in a way perhaps only the dying can be.

'He's not worth it, Grace,' she told my back, from the sofa she was slumped on. 'Dillon's all that matters, now, okay? Let go of your anger. Just forget him.'

It took a long time for me to be able to do either of those things. And it's ironic that, having done so, the events of the last couple of months have ensured that the one thing I'm never going to be able to do now is forget Aidan Kennedy. Even when I reach a point where I can consign his mother back into my mental strong-box, the sheer tragedy of his life, and its horrible consequences, are going to haunt me in a way they never would have before.

The anger I do still have to deal with is much more pressing and important. And a call on Friday morning brings it sharply into focus, when the question of my own mother – the reason I came back here, and demanded so much of my family – can no longer be anything other than addressed: she's due to be discharged on Monday, her consultant tells me, with a new, 'enhanced care package', and if I'm to be any use to her, 'going forward', as DS Lovelace might have it, I'm going to need to get over myself. And not just for me. For the boys. What kind of example would I be setting them if I don't? Of all the qualities I hope to inspire in them as adults, compassion is surely one of the most important.

Matt's back in London, but with one major change to his schedule. He has around four weeks left to work on the project he's finishing but, under the circumstances, has been in conversation with his bosses about doing most of what he can from home instead. Which means tonight, for the first time, home will *be* home. In the meantime we've been having endless Skype conversations about it all, and whether rightly or wrongly – logic says the former, gut instinct the latter – trying to help the dust settle by sprinkling it with rose-coloured water. Because it's actually entirely reasonable to see this as the end point for Norma. Driven to extreme behaviour by Aidan's death, and with little left to live for, she snatched Dillon for the simple reason that she was desperate to spend time with him, before – and Matt has pointed out that this was always my theory – taking her own life, putting an end to the pain.

And has failed. Dillon's words come back to me. *Never forget I love you more than all the tea in China.* She did. She *does*. I must remember that as well.

I spend most of the morning in trauma clinic with Siddhant, who is in an uncharacteristic state of excited agitation because he's been invited to present a research paper at a big surgical conference; another feather in a professional cap that will soon be bristling with them. I feel rather emotional about it myself. As a consultant, part of my job is now to train junior doctors. Siddhant will be the first of many, but he will always be my first. When he observes that he's going to need a new suit, and needs advice – 'grey or blue? And do you think pinstripe will be too "surgeon-y"?' – it's all I can do not to hug him for joy.

And once we're finished, I head to the geriatric ward.

Mum's out of bed, sitting in the chair in her dressing gown and slippers, and riffling through a shoebox-sized box on her lap. Holly has obviously been in again at some point, because the box is full of photos from her flat. She glances up from them when I appear, but only briefly.

I perch on the bed. 'How are you doing, Mum?' I ask her. 'Home on Monday, I hear.'

'So *they* say,' she answers, still not looking up. Still sorting through the photographs, most of which are old, some of them torn, many fluffy round the edges. Our childhood, her childhood, her parents' and grandparents' childhoods. She's going through them – front to back, front to back, front to back – like a game-show host trying to memorise her cue cards.

'So they do,' I say. Then point to the photos. 'Has Holly been in to see you?'

Now she does look up. 'Holly who?' Then she scrutinises my face, where the last vestige of the bruise is now a smear of chartreuse. 'What's happened there, then?' she asks, a look of concern on hers suddenly. 'Have you taken a bit of a tumble?'

The exact thing she'd say when I was five or six or seven, and had run in, snivelling, from the garden or the park or the street, having grazed a hand, or an elbow, or a knee.

I nod. 'I have indeed.'

She shakes her head and makes a 'tsk' sound. 'Well, let me see then,' she says, waving a bony hand to coax me closer. I lean towards her, and feel the long-forgotten sensation of her fingers fluttering gently against my cheek. 'Nothing to worry about,' she decides finally. 'Dab of witch hazel on that and you'll be tickety-boo in no time.'

Satisfied, she sits back again. Looks down, back at the photographs. Then, abruptly, back up at me again, quizzically. 'What are *you* doing here?' she asks. 'Have you come to take me home, then? And where's your sister? They told me your sister was coming. When's she getting here?'

I'm not sure how to answer that. Whether to even try. What the point is.

'Soon,' I say. 'Soon.'

She leans forward again, whispers. 'They think I'm doolally. *They're* the ones who are doolally. I want my Grace. Where's my Grace?' She flaps a hand again, irritably. 'Well, don't just sit there. Go and *ask* them. And what are you doing *now*, child?'

'I'm crying, Mum. That's all.'

'Oh, for heaven's *sake*. Why? What on earth have *you* got to cry about?'

I pull a floral-patterned tissue from the packet on the cabinet by her bed, open it out, and blow my nose.

Then lower it and reach out, take her hand, squeeze it. *I am never going to know*, I think. And does it even matter?

I smile to reassure her. 'I'm just letting it go. That's all I'm doing, Mum. Just letting it go.'

And as I make my way back up to my office, I feel such a weight lifted from me that it's almost as if I'm floating up the stair-well. Because it really does feel done now; that I've finally drawn the last of several lines under what's happened. That the consequences of what my sister did are over.

Yet, despite that, I'm dogged by a wisp of thought.

It follows me up the stairs, whispering *you hope so*.

Chapter 27

If there's a colour I most associate with Hope, it's yellow. Not because it was her favourite – I don't think I could even name her favourite – but because she died in February, and was buried at the cusp of spring's awakening, when everywhere you looked, there were daffodils. As we travelled to the burial ground, it seemed as though they'd come out just for her; great swathes of them, suddenly, as if conjured from nowhere, in that impossible, almost neon, shade of yellow.

And here they are again, to see Aidan off as well. He was cremated two weeks back – Jessica texted me to tell me – and a part of me wishes I did have some kind of faith, to allow me to believe that he and Hope are back together. That they are soul mates in an afterlife as well.

I don't. Though it feels comforting to imagine it, even so.

And now it's almost half-term, and spring is springing up all over. On either side of the front path to our house, new growth is pushing up through the dark loamy soil. Crocuses and snowdrops, as well as all the daffodils, and the multiple knife points of what look like bearded irises. They are pea-green. Straight and strong. Determined. Almost defiant, as if our new-old house senses I've yet to befriend it, and is trying its level best to make me change my mind. To remind me that life must keep moving forward.

Which it is. And which we are, as a family, by increments. The horrors of the past are finally receding. It's an important day too, this unremarkable Wednesday, because Daniel, to his delight, has been promoted. This afternoon he is going to play his first-ever away match for the A team. So when Isabel calls me during fracture clinic mid-afternoon, it's that that's on my mind, not life's vicissitudes.

But it seems they are on my tail, even so. 'I'm so sorry to bother you at work,' she says. 'But I thought I'd better call you because I've just arrived at yours and there is a teddy bear, of all things, been left on the front doorstep. And I was, like, maybe it's one of the boys' and they lost it and someone's dropped it back or something, but then I was, like, *really*? Do they even *play* with teddy bears any more? And then I thought about Dillon, and, I don't know, perhaps I'm being super anxious over nothing, but it's just so *weird* – I mean, who'd leave a manky old teddy bear on a doorstep?'

I'm in the middle of reviewing a patient's post-op X-ray when the call comes, so it takes a moment for me to focus on what she's saying.

And then I do. And my mind does a little hop, skip and jump. *A teddy bear.* Still, I'm a rational being, so I rationalise. Find a rational-sounding explanation. 'Could the postman have delivered it?'

'I don't think so. There's no packaging. No note with it or anything. It was just literally propped up against the front door.'

I feel a sharp stab of fear. Then immediately rein it in again. I mustn't run away with myself. After all, it's *just a teddy bear.* But—

'Is it a Steiff one?'

'A what?'

'Does it have a little metal button in its ear?'

'Hang on. Yes, it does. Exactly that. Why? Does that mean something?'

It does. *Shit*. But what? I check the time. It's three twenty. 'It might do,' I say. 'Where is Matt?'

'Gone to pick Dillon up. His conference call finished early, so he called me when I was on my way here to say he'd go up and get him, save me going. He's going to take him to the party straight from there. He's taken Dillon's swimming stuff with him. But I said I'd stick around for Dan—'

The party. Of course. Dillon's going to a friend's swimming party this afternoon. 'And it was definitely just the bear, on the front doorstep, nothing else? Nothing put through the door?'

'No, like I say, it was just sitting there. Nothing else.'

And Matt, having gone by car, would have left to meet Dillon via the garage. So it could have been put there at any time since this morning. And it has to be. *Has* to be Norma. So does this mean she's out of hospital?

'So is it something to do with this Norma woman then, you think?' Isabel's saying.

'I think it might be. If it's the same bear. It used to be Aidan's.'

'So you think she might have left it there for Dillon?'

'I don't know . . . Look, I'd better call Matt.'

'Of course,' she says. 'I'll be here.'

I ring Matt next.

'I'm in the car,' he says. 'Hang on, let me put you on loudspeaker.'

'Where are you?'

'Picking Dillon up. I'm just parking. Everything okay?'

'Isabel just called me. She's found a teddy bear on the front doorstep.'

'A what?'

'A teddy bear. A Steiff teddy bear. *Aidan's* teddy bear. It must be. You remember that time when—'

'Yes, of course I do. So does that mean they've let her out of hospital?'

'They must have. Because she's obviously been to our house and put it there, hasn't she? How else would it have got there?'

'But they were supposed to let us know if she was discharged from hospital, weren't they?'

'Well, they haven't. But she must have been, mustn't she?'

'Assuming she put it there. And hang on – wasn't her car written off? Hold on.' I hear the door clunk.

'It has to be her. And she could equally have gone there in a taxi. God, you don't think she's planning to try and snatch him again, do you?'

'Well, if she was, she'd hardly be stupid enough to leave a clue on our front doorstep, would she?'

'Maybe it's not a clue, maybe it's, I don't know, some kind of parting shot, meant as some sort of message. Like that awful plant she sent me that time. Maybe she plans to take him and leave us that in his place. Don't forget, that teddy bear has *major* significance for her. And—'

'Well, if she *is* hanging around here, she'll have me to deal with, won't she? Anyway, no panic, I can see him. He's coming over now. I tell you what, though, we should probably call the police in any case. If she has been let out, it would have been nice of them to let us fucking know.'

'They wouldn't necessarily know themselves yet, not if it's only just happened. *God.* I don't *believe* this. Okay, I'll call them now. You take Dillon to his party. I'll keep you posted.'

I disconnect, feeling calmer. Dillon's with Matt. I mustn't panic. Instead I must think. And my first thought is to verify one simple fact. If Norma's out of hospital. And since it's true that they might not be aware of that fact yet, I don't call the police. I call Jessica Kennedy.

272

Who turns out to be in the hospital today too, just finishing the last of her bank shifts before leaving Brighton. She's heading back to Hull to be closer to her family. As far away as she can get from here, I suspect.

But she hasn't seen Norma. 'Well, not to speak to,' she tells me. 'I saw her briefly at Aidan's funeral, but she came nowhere near us. She had someone from the hospital with her. One of the psychiatric nurses, I think. I did message her last week – I have a lot of stuff to sort out at the house, and some of it's hers – but I've heard nothing back, so I assumed she must still be in hospital. What's happened?'

I explain about the bear.

'Oh God,' she says. 'So they must have let her out then.' And I note she doesn't even question whether we're discussing the same bear. 'D'you want me to see if I can find anything out? I have the number of her next-door neighbour. I could try her, perhaps? And I finish my shift in twenty minutes, so perhaps I could drive round there?'

I'm almost overwhelmed – almost undone – by her kindness. 'Thank you,' I tell her. 'Thank you *so* much. It might be nothing – well, nothing to worry about, anyway. Perhaps she just wanted him to have it. Nothing more malevolent than that.'

Then she *really* scares me.

'I wouldn't bank on it,' she says.

But that is as nothing to my terror fifteen minutes later. I've seen a further patient, and tried to put it out of my mind. Or at least tried to process it differently. It's just a bear on a doorstep, I keep telling myself. Just a gesture. Despite what Jessica has said, my interpretation could so easily be correct. Perhaps she's planning to take her life and, grim though the thought is, perhaps she genuinely wants to leave the bear for Dillon. And he's with Matt. I mustn't panic. No one's in any danger. It's just a teddy bear on a doorstep. That's *all*.

But then my mobile rings. It's Jessica. And I am wrong.

'Grace? Listen, you won't believe this, but my car has been stolen.'

'*What?*'

'I'm in the staff car park right now, and my car isn't where I left it. I think she must have taken it. No *way* is this coincidence.'

There isn't a single shred of doubt in her voice. Not a thread of hope to cling to.

Think, I think. 'Okay,' I say. 'What car is it?'

'It's an old Mini Cooper. Dark red. The utter *bitch*. She must have planned this . . .'

'But how could she have stolen it without a key?'

'Oh, she *will* have a key. The other set's at home still. Or at least was. *Shit*. Why the hell didn't I *think*?'

'So she could get into your house?'

'Of course she could. She had a key for that as well. She used to childmind the girls for me, didn't she? Look, I'm going to call the police and report it, but I thought I ought to tell you first. Because I'm seriously worried now. Grace, your son might be in danger.'

'It's okay. Dillon's fine. He's with his dad.'

There is a heartbeat of space between my words and her next.

'I don't mean Dillon,' she says. 'I mean your *other* son. *Daniel!*'

Chapter 28

Once again I have to make my excuses to Neil Porter, then try to think on my feet as they pound back down the corridor. Down the stairs – there is too big a queue for the lifts – along the main corridor, and out into the sunshine. Which dances gaily off the cars – all bar one – in the staff car park. Of Jessica, now, there is no sign. I call Daniel as I run, but he's not answering, so I text, realising that, given the time, he will still be on the pitch.

I can't remember where the school is. Can't even remember what the name is. All I remember is that they were going up and back on the school minibus and that he was going for food with his friend after they were dropped back at school, and that after tea, his friend's mum was going to drop him home.

I clamber into the car. Find the number of his high school. Call the office. They're playing at a school up near Falmer, and due back around ten minutes after school ends. 'Traffic depending,' the receptionist says brightly. 'You know what it's like.'

I thank her. Start the car. Pull out of the car park, pyrotechnics exploding in my head. Of *course*, I think. I've been so utterly brainless. So *stupid*. All my mitigating nonsense; yes, she might love Dillon more than all the tea in China, but she hates me even *more*. If she's obsessed with anyone, it isn't Dillon – it's *me*. It's me *because* of Dillon. *I'm* her nemesis.

You've stolen my grandson. You've ruined my son's life. Now you've chopped off his arm. Disfigured him. Destroyed him. Do you want to fetch one of your scalpels and rip my heart out as well?

Because she *knows,* doesn't she? Knows the pain that transcends any other. The pain of a mother who has buried their child. I could never rip her heart out because it's already been ripped out. And now she wants to rip mine out as well.

She knows exactly how to do it, too – how to get the ultimate revenge.

But how could she possibly know that Daniel is at a football match near Falmer? Which is a comfort, but only momentarily. She knows where we live. And how do we know she wasn't discharged days ago, and has been waiting for her moment? And she has been in Mum's flat, so she will have seen his school photo – didn't take it, but will have seen it, so she'd *know.* What's to say she hasn't even been on the school website? As my father used to say back when he was still delivering sermons, if you *really* want something, you never give up.

What an idiot I've been. She will *never* give up.

Daniel calls just as I'm joining the traffic on the coast road. 'Winnerrrrrssss!' he sings. I hear a cheer go up around him. 'Two nil and I assisted. Soooo pumped!'

'That's brilliant,' I tell him, all the while scanning cars for Jessica's red Mini Cooper. 'Listen, sweetie, I'm on my way to school to pick you up.'

'But I'm going with Josh. We're going for food, remember? His mum's going to drop me home after. Remember?'

'Change of plan. I've finished early so I'm going to come and meet you. Where are you now?'

'I'm not sure. But you don't need to. I'm going with Josh.'

And wants to, I know. It's important. A precious friendship. 'I'm sorry, sweetie. I really am, but I have to come and get you.'

276

'But Mum, I'm supposed to be going for food *with Josh*.'

'Well, perhaps Josh can come to us.'

'*Mum.* Why are you being weird? It's all arranged. I'm going to *his*.'

'Something's come up. Where are you now?'

'I don't know. I told you. Somewhere on the Falmer Road, I think. *What*, Mum? What's come up?'

'Just something. Something that means I need to come and fetch you. I'll explain when I get there.'

'Why aren't you at work still? You never finish early.'

'Because I'm not and I have. Look, I'm on my way now. If you get there before me, just stay there. Okay? I'll probably beat you, but if I'm not there, just wait for me, okay? With the teacher. In the car park. By the bus.'

'Mu-*um*! *Tell* me!' he barks. 'What's going *on*?'

'Just wait for me till I get there, okay? With the teacher. By the bus.'

'Ok-*ay*,' he huffs. From twelve going on ten to twelve going on fifteen, in what feels like the blink of an eye. My baby.

'I love you,' I tell him. But he's already rung off.

It takes a good fifteen minutes to drive to the high school, during which time I call DS Lovelace's mobile, which goes straight to voicemail, so I have no choice but to leave a message. Then Matt, whose phone doesn't even connect, which I already half expected, because he's probably at the swimming pool, out of signal. So, till I can stop and send a text, I'm on my own.

And I cannot stop and send a text.

Daniel's high school is a sprawling comprehensive, just off a big suburban thoroughfare. It's just past turning-out time and, despite it being on at least two bus routes, all the surrounding streets are rammed with cars, and on my first circuit – all the while scanning for red Mini Coopers – I can't find a place to pull in anywhere.

It has the same knocked-about look that all schools seem to have as they empty for the day. Children streaming out in all directions, a few stragglers loitering aimlessly in pockets, teachers milling around to supervise, looking jaded and round-shouldered, probably weighed down by thoughts of the evening's homework ahead. And the detritus of the day scattered like so much giant confetti: crisp packets, chocolate wrappers, paper bags, plastic bottles, all of which – because this is a school that prides itself on standards – is already being collected, by a man I imagine is a caretaker, with a small detail of morose-looking, bin-bag-wielding pupils.

There are cars parked all over the place, a few with engines idling, some on the road, some listing drunkenly, half on half off the pavements. I scan for red again, on my second pass, as I search for a space. And I wonder what I'm thinking, what I'm doing here, exactly. What on earth can Norma really do to Daniel, after all? She might have plans to snatch him and take him off and— I can't bear to think it . . . But there is no way in the world he would get into a car with her now, is there? Or would he? I've been so anxious to protect him from the darker truths about her – about *everything* – that will he too see her as essentially benign?

No, I tell myself. *No*. He's planning to go with Josh. He is desperate to go with Josh. And perhaps I should dial down my paranoia. After all, Jessica might be wrong. *I* might be wrong. She might not have designs on Daniel. Having delivered the bear, she might already be on her way up to Beachy Head. So perhaps I should let him go. Just see him, be sure he's safe, and let him go with his friend. Leave the police to track down Norma – which, since Jessica will have called them, they might already be doing anyway.

I find a space eventually, up a side street, and park, and try to calm myself. Daniel is safe. He's on the school bus. He's among people. He is *safe*. There is nothing Norma Kennedy can do to hurt him.

I get out of the car and start walking up to the school gates, fifty metres away, feeling like a minnow swimming against a shoal of salmon, being buffeted by backpacks and glanced at incuriously, as waves and waves of pupils make their liquid escape. The very epitome of a fish out of water.

And what *could* happen? In this place? With all these people still around? No, I think, when the bus comes I'll just say hello. Just as long as I see him, that will do for the moment. See him off, with his friend, then head home. And when I see the bus approaching, I'm decided. I'm being ridiculous. I'll see Daniel, get back in the car, speak to Matt, speak to DS Lovelace. Go home. Go from there.

So when the minibus turns into the entrance, I wait. Only when it disgorges its occupants, all jostling and laughing, do I go over.

'Mum, *please*,' is the first thing Daniel says, his new friend hovering beside him. '*Why* can't I go with Josh? *What's* come up? We won't be late or anything. I'll do my homework after. *Please?*'

'Yes, you can,' I say, decided. 'It's okay now. All sorted. Why don't you let me have your muddy kit, though? I'll take it home for you.'

He gives me a sideways look. Which is understandable, given that, as far as he's concerned, I could just as easily have texted him and said I'd see him later. Not turn up to show him up. But he hands the bag over.

'Where's your mum, Josh?' I ask him, because twelve is still twelve. And I need to actually see her to feel completely at ease.

'Just down a bit, over the road, where she normally parks,' he tells me. And Daniel looks at me with an expression I can read all too easily. Waiting in her *car* for them. Like any other *normal* mother would.

279

So I hang back a bit as I follow them out. Out of the gates. On to the pavement. Up the road a short distance, to where Josh is now leading and pointing. To the pedestrian crossing, where they stand and wait, chatting, for the lights to turn red. For the two cars coming up the hill, on our side, to stop. They look both ways anyway, because it's instinct, because they're sensible. Then Josh starts to cross. Because it's safe to. Because there is nothing coming down the hill.

Daniel doesn't, though. He stops and waves, to let me know I'm forgiven. A matter of seconds. A matter of steps. And there is *nothing coming down the hill.*

Until there is.

A red Mini Cooper.

In my life, up to this point, I have never been in a position to test the theory that I would die for my children. Like any other parent, I've just automatically assumed – and on scant empirical evidence, frankly – that if it came to a straight choice, there would be no choice to make: since I'd kill for them, if it came to it I would of course die for my children.

But would I? We all think it, we hope, we trust it would happen, but when it comes to it, we can't ever actually *know*.

As it is, I just see and react. To the fact that where, before, there was no car, there now *is*. A red Mini Cooper, which has been hidden in plain sight, and has now peeled away from the row of parked cars in front of it, and is accelerating towards the crossing, on the far side of the road.

At no point do I think I might sacrifice my life. Which is not because I'm not thinking; I am thinking at warp speed. I've already processed the first part of the equation by the time I've seen her.

Of *course*. Seventy-eight, and with the keys to a car. Was master-minding this very moment how she spent her incarceration? Now I take in the speed. The trajectory. The intent. The lethal power of a weapon that is several tons of metal. See my child, on the crossing. See the car, heading towards him. Make the mental leap, from *no, it can't be*, to *she is driving straight at him*, to *he has already looked left, right, and left – he doesn't realise*. And am already thundering across the crossing behind him, not thinking about dying – not thinking even *tangentially* about dying – just on the matter, the *only* matter that in this moment matters: that I must reach him before the car does and shove him to safety. That I must find it inside me to be Super-bloody-woman, because if I fail to, the sky will fall in.

I *must*. And I can. And I do. A rigid-armed, two-handed, violent maternal thump, which connects with both his shoulder blades – my baby's still-growing shoulder blades – which, with an almighty whump, sends him cannoning on to his friend.

And then I'm spun, like a top that's been whacked by a toddler.

And that's the first time the fragility of my existence hits me. The *only* time.

That, and a kind of righteous validation.

I was bloody right, is what I think, as I slam face-first against the kerb. Then, *RTC, Caucasian female, mid-40s, glancing blow, query hairline hip fracture, compound ankle fracture, possible concussion, high GCS score.*

Still conscious. Eyes open, ears back, every nociceptor firing. I hear the car travel on, even faster, tyres squealing, engine scream-ing. I hear the impact, against the sturdy, red-brick front wall of the school. And as I lie there, heart thumping, I see a sudden flash of white, as Norma's head punches the airbag through the windscreen.

Chapter 29

'Bought you a cup of coffee, Mrs Hamilton. A proper one, from the Costa. I'll leave it here, shall I? How are you feeling?'

Siddhant looks tired – same old, same old – but there is a certain liveliness about him; a spring in his step as he sashays into the side room in his pale shirt and brushed tan suede brogues. I suppose it's not every day in the life of a surgical registrar when you are called upon to assist in emergency surgery on your own consultant.

It's the first time I've seen him since I was wheeled into theatre, because he's been off to his conference, presenting his paper. Was it two days ago, now? Three? I've lost track of time. Being a patient in a hospital tends to do that, I realise.

I smile at him. 'How was it?'

'Textbook. Straightforward.'

'Not the op. Your presentation!'

'Oh, sorry. Yes, okay, I think. Nerve-wracking.' He beams then. 'But I got asked *seven* questions.'

I've told Siddhant that questions are unquestionably a good thing. I clap my hands together. 'Excellent. See, I *told* you. Go on, then,' I add. 'Tell me, how was it?'

He grins at me. 'Textbook. Completely straightforward. Mr Porter barely looked up from his *Top Gear* magazine.' He grins again. 'Only *joking*. Well, okay, so maybe he did do a bit of it. But not all of it. He didn't need to. I was taught by the best.'

I move my leg, to test the pain level, which is just about manageable. Unlike the emotion level, which is borderline not. 'Don't you dare set me off,' I tell him. 'And that's an order.'

'No, don't,' Matt says. He's busy tapping away on my laptop in the corner. Busy filling in an online application form for a new job near Brighton, in the scant amount of time left available between taking Dillon to school, dealing with the washing and the food shop, picking up a prescription for Mum, picking Dillon up from school again, and making the boys' tea, before taking them to the climbing centre, then bringing them back here again, and hopefully smuggling in an unauthorised pizza for me too, as the hospital food turns out to be every bit as unappetising as it's always looked. I cannot *wait* to be home again with them tomorrow. 'In fact, if I were you,' he says, 'I would discharge her right now. Bloody malingerer.'

Safe to say, he no longer feels like a visitor in his own home.

It's been an up-and-down couple of days. I was – I thought – fine till about five the following morning. I knew I'd broken my ankle (my hip was only bruised, thank goodness) and pretty creatively, because it wasn't exactly rocket science, after all: I was on the ground, literally, and with an unobstructed view of it. And could clearly see the spike of bone – jagged, white, and blood-smeared. But it was easy to disassociate because I needed to disassociate. Because Daniel was in bits, and he needed me not to be. I needed to be a super-bloody-woman, so I didn't have a choice.

Matt had quipped that to the boys, while I was being prepped for surgery. And I felt like a fraud. Not just because I was such a

283

low-level casualty. But also because it turns out that when your child's life is in danger, there is not an iota of bravery involved.

And when I came round, my first feelings were of peace. Of relief. It was over. She was gone. Everything was going to be alright now. And I realised that alright was all things would ever again need to be.

But then I woke in the night, sweating, disorientated, panicky. And, when I struggled to sit up, to see a navy-blue night; a full moon, slightly hazy, and a sky full of stars. And I thought about Hope. How much I missed my little sister. And in the near dark, with only the faint hum of air con, I cried.

The loss of someone young creates a singular species of grief; we mourn the past, yes, but perhaps even more the future. All the tomorrows that are now going to be such different tomorrows to the ones we so blithely and confidently set in place for ourselves. I no longer had Hope, so I mourned the stolen friendship we were never going to know now. And because I'd never really known her, I mourned that as well – perhaps more.

I resolved to read every Thomas Hardy novel I hadn't yet read. To accept what I couldn't change and what I was never going to know now. To put the past back in its box, and this time throw the key away. And, I resolved, as soon as I was home and could retrieve it, that I would take Hope's spangled memory stick and, at the first opportunity, hurl it off the end of the Palace Pier.

Then, on the Friday, Jessica Kennedy came to see me. Looking every bit as pale and exhausted as I'd have expected, given that she wasn't only moving to Hull, she was also travelling on that long road from death to acceptance, where you have to hold on, white-knuckled, to the reins of your composure, in case it gallops away without warning and throws you.

She came because she was there anyway, she said, bringing gifts to the ICU staff, and wanted a chance to speak to me before she left.

She told me how it helped that she'd agreed to all the organ donations, because Aidan had, as a result of it, saved seven lives – three from death, and four others from lifelong disability. She was particularly glad, she told me, that those beautiful eyes of his would see again. Even if just the corneas, she said. And I told her I understood. It felt good, she said. And right. That she would sleep better for it. And also, without question, for knowing Norma had gone too. 'I know I shouldn't say it,' she said, 'but I'm going to say it anyway. Between us, Norma dying is the best thing that could have happened. I can leave here and know that I'm genuinely free of her. That the *girls* are . . . I know that sounds awful, but I mean it. I can't help it.'

Then she pulled something from her handbag. An envelope.

'I have been agonising,' she said, 'about whether to give you this. My first instinct was to just rip it up and throw it in the bin, because I'm worried there might be stuff in there that nobody needs to know. And Dillon's got his own life – a completely different life. I mean, does he even know who his father is?'

The letter was still in her hand as she spoke, and I wondered if her giving it to me was contingent on how I answered her. But then she smiled. Corrected herself. 'Sorry. I'll rephrase that. Of *course* he knows who his father is – your husband. But does he know who Aidan is? And does he even need to?' She passed the envelope to me then, on which Dillon's name was written. Just 'DILLON', in capital letters, underlined. 'Anyway, I didn't throw it in the bin, as you can see. Because it's not for me to keep it from you, is it? And he obviously wanted me to find it. But what you do with it is up to you – I obviously haven't seen what's in there. I don't even know when he wrote it, to be honest. Could have been just before . . .' She shrugged. 'I don't know. He could have written it ages ago. Look, just – well, all I'm saying is that you might want to look at it before you decide what to do with it.'

I studied her face. Met her quiet, unblinking gaze. And then it hit me. 'You know, don't you? About his half-brother. He told you.'

She nodded. 'I've *always* known. It was one of the first things I ever knew about him.' She began to choke up a bit then, little lines forming between her eyebrows. 'And I had this really, *really* bright idea. That I could save him from himself.' She put the words in finger quote marks. 'That I could succeed where every bloody woman in the entire history of the *planet* had already failed. Including your sister.' There was a half-smile on her lips then, even as her eyes brimmed with tears. 'But I was wrong. Because you never *can*, can you?'

After she left, I sat for a long time with the letter in my lap. How many conversations had I had with myself, and Matt, over the years, about what to do when the question of Aidan arose? How many hours had I spent scrolling through conversations on forums, where other people agonised about what to do when that issue surfaced? How many times had I wrangled with philosophy and ethics? Fretted about the correct balance between rights and responsibilities; tied myself in knots about Dillon's right to know versus our responsibility to minimise the emotional fallout?

Did Dillon need to know the truth or would it be better if he was spared it? I picked the letter up. Should I open it? See what Aidan had to say about Aidan? Or put it away, for consideration at another, later date?

Or should I dispatch it to the deep with Hope's confession? Because what did a child *really* want to know most of all about where they came from, after all? That they were loved, unconditionally, by everyone who should have loved them. And he was. That was always true. I know that now. He *was*.

He always would be. And if he ever asked, well, then, couldn't I just tell him that myself?

In the meantime, there is a tree house to be built.

I'm still wrestling with my conscience when I'm home the following morning, to find a building site where the end of the garden should be.

I'm supposed to avoid putting weight on my ankle and to sit around in a queenly state for much of the day, at least for the next three weeks or so. Which won't be happening – I'm already working out a strategy to get myself back to work sooner. And I cannot sit now either. I cannot cope with the FOMO.

So I hobble across the grass, flanked by the boys, who are fizzing with excitement. In the three days I've been in hospital, it's as if a whirlwind has blown in. Without telling me a thing about it, Matt has clearly been flat out. Without telling me a *thing* about it, he has made – and executed – plans. As in downloaded them, and collated them, and put them in a binder, and already ordered – and taken delivery of – a truckload of timber. Decking boards, and panelling, and balustrades, and posts. Fascia boards, and ladder rungs, and cleats and bolts and screws. He is going to make something. Something solid. Something substantial. Something permanent.

Something that says we are going to stay here. Make a life here. And thrive here. Make this place – this new-old house – our home.

Daniel has the ring binder because he is master of the plans. 'So this is where the house will be, and this is the observation tower. And there's going to be *actual bunk beds*, so we can sleep out in the summer. And do *owl*-watching.'

'And a light,' Dillon adds. 'It's going to have electricity and *everything*. And this is where the pulley will go, so we can winch up supplies and stuff.'

'Sounds good,' I say. 'Will it be strong enough to winch me up there too?'

'Mum, there's going to be a *ladder*,' Daniel points out.

'I'm not sure I'm going to be climbing up any ladders for a while yet.'

'*Course* you will,' Dillon says. 'Mum, you're Superwoman, remember?'

So supremely confident. So untroubled by doubt. Not a single scintilla of it. Which is exactly as it should be.

I look at Matt, who has a length of wood in one hand, a bolt in the other, his beanie on his head, and the bit between his teeth.

And then up, squinting a little against the watery February sunshine. It's fine. It will *be* fine. The sky hasn't fallen in.

And, before we know it, the wisteria will be in bloom.

ACKNOWLEDGMENTS

As ever, I cannot sign off without saying some thank yous. To my wonderful agent, Andrew Lownie, with whom I've sailed away on so many and so diverse a bunch of writing adventures. Here's to the next, wherever it may take us!

To Jack Butler and Jane Snelgrove, such fabulous editors, and the whole team at Thomas & Mercer. You're the best. Professional, indefatigable, and unfailingly helpful . . . are just three of the adjectives that you deserve to be adorned with, were the crime of peppering prose with strings of three adjectives not one of the creative 'don'ts' I hold most dear. Seriously, though, it's been a joy.

To my one-in-a-million husband, Pete, and to the National Health Service (which, as a consequence of hooking up with a punky medical student some forty-three years back, I've been pretty much married to all this time as well).

To my lovely son Joe, who, like Grace, is an orthopaedic surgeon, and has patiently sat through endless technical questions. If I got something wrong, the fault is 100 per cent mine.

And, at the risk of repeating myself, to my family. Writing about such tragically dysfunctional ones for a living cannot help but remind me how lucky Pete and I are. You are all AMAZING, and I love you a googolplex. Which Google tells me (in case you're wondering, which I know you all are) is a one followed by a googol of zeros. Which makes it larger than the number of atoms in the entire universe. Which makes it just about the right amount.

Well, almost.

ABOUT THE AUTHOR

Lynne Lee was born in London and began her writing career as a teenager. She has been a full-time author since the mid-1990s, writing romantic novels, short stories and ghostwriting bestselling books. *False Hope* is her second psychological thriller and is written under a pseudonym. Find her online at www.lynnebarrett-lee.com, on Facebook at www.facebook.com/LynneLeeAuthor/ and on Instagram @lynnebl.